JORDAN'S ARROW

JORDAN'S ARROW

ALLEN STEADHAM

Ambassador International
GREENVILLE, SOUTH CAROLINA & BELFAST, NORTHERN IRELAND

www.ambassador-international.com

Jordan's Arrow
The Jordan of Algoran Series, Book Two

ISBN: 978-1-62020-755-0
eISBN: 978-1-62020-758-1

Cover Illustration by Christopher Jackson
Cover Design & Typesetting by Hannah Nichols
Edited by Daphne Self

AMBASSADOR INTERNATIONAL
Emerald House
411 University Ridge, Suite B14
Greenville, SC 29601, USA
www.ambassador-international.com

AMBASSADOR BOOKS
The Mount
2 Woodstock Link
Belfast, BT6 8DD, Northern Ireland, UK
www.ambassadormedia.co.uk

The colophon is a trademark of Ambassador, a Christian publishing company.

"The supreme art of war is to subdue the enemy without fighting."

- Sun Tzu

ACT ONE

CAUSE AND EFFECT

PROLOGUE

ERICA MELENDEZ HAD BEEN LIVING among the Ullvarr for nearly a year already. She had grasped their language enough to have moderate conversations and start learning people's names, occupations, and family relations. Kalami, the woman who had helped and guided Erica since her arrival, had made her welcome among her household. Her husband, Village Leader Daraz, and most of the village showed a mixture of pleasantness and wariness with certain degrees of insincerity. Even so, they had allowed her to become a member of their community and they were trying to get to know her.

High quality, vibrant clothing was handmade for her which looked and felt like fine silk. A new hut was built for her as well. It was beautified by a lush flower bed near its entrance. She did not know all the types of these remarkable blooms, but their petals radiated lively shades of red, orange, white, and lavender. Inside the hut, Ullvarr artists had made bright and cheerful paintings directly on the walls and laid a plush bird feather mattress on the wooden floor. The shelves against the opposite wall were stocked with separate bowls of fruit and water. A stone chest was filled with more of the beautiful clothing which had been made for or given to her. The wide oval window allowed both day and moons' light inside. Two wooden chairs and a table lent themselves for conversation or a meal. Each day, someone would bring

Erica fresh supplies of fruits, vegetables, and dried meats to snack on between the community meals in the morning and evening.

Yet, without the presence of friends or regular visitors, the hut usually made Erica feel lonely.

Sometimes Erica's main problems were with herself. She didn't entirely trust her own perceptions. It wasn't just the physical changes she'd experienced, gaining blue hair, icy-colored eyes, and the strange gemstones fused to her neck. Ever since the first day she'd appeared near this village, it felt like she was a second or two out of phase with everything and everyone else. This sensation didn't feel like an illness. Sometimes she could filter it out or ignore it, but it was always there.

Having so much time to herself gave Erica opportunity to reflect upon her life and how she'd come to be here. She thought about her parents, how their marital strife had led to a prison sentence for her mother and suicide for her father. She relived the regrets of not fully committing to her fiancé and how it had ended that relationship prematurely. The culmination of these events had been sufficient reason for her to forsake the world of her birth, leaping through a spatial portal which led to Algoran.

After being separated from Jordan Lewis on arrival, Erica wondered why she hadn't located her yet. Jordan told Erica she'd traveled across nearly all of Algoran just to find a *possible* way back to Earth. And she'd succeeded in that. Didn't Jordan already have knowledge about this world's tribes? Wasn't locating a lost friend just as important as finding a way home? Erica instinctively felt like Jordan was alive and well. And yet, where was she?

Erica wanted to be fair towards Jordan. It seemed like a big planet and she didn't know how far away Jordan was. Did Jordan return to the tribe she knew? Did she get sent to another part of the world, the way Erica had? There were plenty of things to consider but no ways to confirm any answers yet. Despite her efforts, she found herself resenting her childhood companion more often than not. Someday she would find Jordan herself. And when she succeeded, she would demand answers.

One evening at twilight, Kalami introduced Erica to Vakar, the head of the Ullvarr warriors. Kalami explained to them that Vakar would essentially become Erica's bodyguard. He had just finished training some new recruits from the village. The meeting was only semi-formal and Vakar was still drenched in perspiration from his exertions and breathing deeply. At almost a foot taller than her, he was very muscular and handsome, sporting long green hair, shaved on the right side like the rest of these rose-pink-colored people. This man was somewhat reserved, not shy but deliberately quiet. She could tell that he was trying to assess her in some way.

She was certain that Kalami was encouraging the two of them to become mates. Erica wasn't ready for such a commitment. However, she had to admit to herself that, looking at this glistening and robust male, the idea was both flattering and tempting.

Whenever Vakar did speak, it was brief and with sincerity. Erica had sensed a certain reluctance from him towards her but since she felt the same, she didn't think much of it. She imagined that the expanse that loomed between them, being from two different worlds' cultures, could lessen over time. As things stood now, they were barely more than polite acquaintances. And that suited her just fine.

During one of their early chats, Kalami had asked if there was any-one else who looked like Erica. She had even used the word "SnowFire" and gestured towards Erica's blue hair and the gemstones fused to her neck. It had felt like Kalami was probing Erica for knowledge about the mythical figure.

Erica happily talked about Jordan and how she had similar features. But she still had a poor grasp of Ullvarr words. Erica realized afterwards that she must have sounded to Kalami like she didn't understand the question and was rambling on about her close friend. Kalami tried to be polite but was clearly disappointed in the outcome. The topic was never brought up again.

Erica desperately wanted to know what her physical changes meant. Who was SnowFire really? SnowFire had saved Jordan's life by transferring her own blood and it had changed her. Had SnowFire done the same to Erica?

Once Erica was more fluent in the language, Kalami brought her to meet with Daraz. As Village Leader, he had offered to answer any questions she might have. Like others she had seen, she slightly lowered her head and did not look directly in his eyes. She kept her arms relaxed and her feet together. Her phrases were short and to the point. She knew he was a busy man and did not have time for lengthy dialogues.

"I am thankful for your time, Great Leader," Erica humbly offered.

"This meeting is long overdue, Ere-Kah. Relax!" Daraz replied with a magnanimous smile. "Ask me anything."

Inside the Leader's Chamber, a large hut with a wooden floor and decorative weapons displays on the walls, Daraz was sitting on a grand wooden chair that resembled a throne. He wore his leader robe, which was made from animal furs and embedded with valuable-looking gemstones. Kalami stood proudly at his side.

"Why am I important to the Ullvarr?"

"A fine question! Good! Good!" He clapped his hands joyfully. "Ere-Kah, did you know that you fell from the sky to us?"

"No, Great Leader," she responded, her eyes widening and her stance stiffening.

"You told Kalami you are from another world, yes?"

"Yes . . . Great Leader."

Daraz stood up then and began to almost strut around the room. Under any other circumstances, Erica might have allowed herself to be entertained. On Earth, this behavior would be ridiculous.

"I—we—feel that you were *sent* to the Ullvarr, like a gift from the twin stars themselves!" Daraz continued, stopping and swinging around towards Erica, lifting his hands and his eyes toward the ceiling. "And it is our duty to protect, treasure, and honor you."

He turned away from Erica and toward his throne.

"I do not understand, Great Leader. I may be from another world and maybe I fell from the skies," Erica interjected. "But would you tell me—does this 'special honor' have anything to do with SnowFire?"

Daraz froze like a statue but Kalami could not prevent her mask of calm from being briefly shattered by Erica's inquiry. Erica was not sure why it alarmed her so much, but it didn't take a genius to understand that they were hiding something.

Daraz slowly faced Erica, his facade returning. He attempted to regain the upper hand.

"It is true that you resemble that figure of another people's legend," he declared confidently. "But that holds no special meaning for us. We are simply glad to have you with us. You are unique and we only want you to feel welcome among the Ullvarr."

"I do, Great Leader," Erica added quickly. "And I would like a more active role in the village. My time passes slowly and I am sometimes lonely."

Daraz's smile returned. He took Kalami's hand in his and looked at her.

"Teach her our written language. And see if perhaps she might make a good teacher for the children," Daraz commanded. "I feel they might enjoy learning from our Ere-Kah, yes?"

Kalami eyes broadcast that she did not approve of either idea but she complied nonetheless.

"Of course, Great Leader," she acquiesced. "I will make arrangements to give her the necessary instruction."

"Excellent, My Heartpath!"

Then Daraz returned his attention to Erica. She was surprised by his solution but not disappointed.

"Will these things please Ere-Kah?" he asked, looking sincere.

"Yes, Great Leader," she responded, giving the traditional bow with a circular hand gesture as she rose back up. "Thank you for your time."

Daraz smiled and nodded. Then Kalami quietly led Erica out of the chamber.

———

That night, Erica quietly exited her hut and tiptoed stealthily into the nearby woods. It was made more difficult by the intoxication-like symptoms she constantly felt. Even so, she pushed past it. She was fed up with the facade from everyone; it had to end.

I have spent too much time here already, she thought, ironically, in Ullvarr. *I do not know what they want with me, but it does not feel right. And I've got to find Jordan!*

She was frightened at the prospect of leaving the village but excited and determined to make a life for herself away from them.

Her vision quickly adjusted to the moonslight and she tried to listen out for any predators. Then she just stopped. She could not move any parts of her body except her eyes and mouth. In front of her, there was a blue and white glow that hovered in mid-air. That radiating light formed into a woman with long blue hair and ice blue eyes. This had to be SnowFire!

The figure before her said nothing but was grim and foreboding. Her eyes conveyed a mixture of anger and sadness.

"I know who you are! What do you want?" Erica shouted in frustration. "Why have you stopped me??"

The Spirit of the Mountain said nothing. She just looked at Erica with some degree of understanding, considering the situation.

Then she pointed in the direction that Erica had come from.

"You—you want me to go back? Why?"

SnowFire did not answer Erica. She just continued to insist, unmoving.

Erica struggled to move forward to no avail. However, when she tried to turn around, she could move. SnowFire literally would not let her leave the area.

She made one more thrust forward, even knowing what would happen. She screamed as she struggled with all her might against SnowFire's invisible force. All her strength, pride, and anger made no difference. In the end, she collapsed to her knees, spent and defeated, wanting to cry.

Despite the outcome of this encounter, Erica would try again sometime soon. She had to, whether she succeeded or not.

Weeks passed and Erica and Vakar started becoming accustomed to their new roles. Erica strolled across the land one morning wearing flowing robes of blue with silver, her wrists adorned with bejeweled bracelets. Vakar was ever at her side. She drank in the beauty of the subalpine forest with amazement and appreciation, its bright blue grasses and flowering plants in every color imaginable gently danced in the afternoon breeze, lifting her spirits. Small creatures with long thin legs, tan fur, and light brown wings fed near a stream which snaked towards the snow-covered mountains in the distance. The air was cold but fairly tolerable to her. The suns were on full display in the nearly cloudless green-tinted sky.

This day, Vakar's expression was nearly unreadable. She tried to start conversation with him numerous times, asking about his family or his role as warrior, but his answers were always abrupt and in few words, giving her little room to develop a dialogue. His eyes mostly looked ahead, except when he was making sure she kept pace with him. He was treating the experience of being in her presence like a duty only. He always stayed within a foot or two of her, ever ready to protect her from any threat with his daggers or raw strength. At least he never complained.

"I am not familiar with all of Algoran's seasons, since I'm always so, um, sheltered and protected," Erica began. "Is it always cold like this? Does it get warmer?"

"This is the warmest time. It will become much colder in the coming moonturns," Vakar responded, his words curt and dry.

"I think Algoran would make Colorado seem warm."

"Kolloh-RA-doh?" Vakar attempted to repeat. "A village on your world?"

Erica smiled with her eyes, taking care not to laugh. "Well, it's a part of a vast land there. It is where I was born."

He turned to look at her, as this subject did interest him.

"Do you . . . miss that place?" he asked.

"I do not," she responded. "I chose to leave there, and I do not regret that decision."

"I see. That is good. Many of the villagers already consider you Ullvarr."

Erica gave a wan smile. "Thanks."

"Concerning the change of seasons, I will have our best clothes-maker prepare proper robes and dresses for you before the colder days arrive."

"That is very kind."

Vakar grunted in acknowledgement.

"You are the leader of all the warriors," Erica noted. "You teach them exercises and stretches, yes? To help them become better at what they do?"

"Yes."

"Do you think you could teach me?" Erica asked, her enthusiasm evident, pleading with her eyes. "I think it would help me. I am not very active and the village gives me so much food and drink. I know I was not a thin woman before, when I arrived, but now . . . "

Without thinking about it, she rested one of her hands upon her widened stomach. Lowering her gaze and slightly blushing as she awaited his reply, surely Vakar could see how self-conscious she was and how awkward it was for her to make this request. Could he see her need for training, to instruct her? Had he been ordered not to?

"I would, if it were permitted," Vakar replied stiffly, his eyes looking at the trees ahead. "But I am not allowed to risk injury to you."

Erica lowered her head, feeling obstructed and dejected once more. "I should just accept my walks and shut up?" she scowled.

"I would not have worded it that way, but—"

"I get it," she interrupted. Then she sighed.

A short while later, Erica and Vakar walked through the stone archway which marked the west entrance to the Ullvarr village. She glimpsed the simple but enduring efficiency of the huts. Each was single story but varied in width and function. Some were for storage but most were for families. With Erica now inside the safety of the community, Vakar excused himself as he saw Daraz walking nearby. With a nod, Erica let him go. She watched the two men walk off, no doubt to discuss village business or security.

———

Vakar followed Daraz Vakar into the Leader Chamber. He closed and secured the door behind them.

"The princess did not seem very pleased upon your return," Daraz scoffed. "Did you say or do something to upset her?"

"I answered her questions with the information you provided me," Vakar replied. "Can I help it if she did not like it?"

Vakar did not bother to hide his resentment from Daraz about being forced to comply with the rules and instructions he was given. He and Daraz had been friends for many years before Daraz came to power. So, Vakar felt he could be honest, even blunt, if he needed to.

"She would not be focused on what she *cannot do* if you shared your heart and pursued her. Those were my *orders* to you," Daraz fumed.

"If you had followed them, she would only be concentrating on being your mate and the mother of your children!"

"I cannot give my heart to that—*thing!* She disgusts me!"

"Remember your place, Vakar!" Daraz barked, standing to his full height, glaring at him threateningly. "You are the head of the warriors, but I am Leader."

Vakar clenched his fists. Stress lines furrowed into his brow. But as he contemplated Daraz's words, he had no choice but to acknowledge their truth. His body relaxed.

"I . . . ask forgiveness," Vakar remarked, chastened.

Daraz had to be an example to the whole village. Vakar backed down. But he still needed some convincing.

"Ere-Kah appeared to us from the skies almost a cycle ago, a gift from the twin stars," Daraz insisted. "You could be mated to an avatar for SnowFire! Do you not see the honor given to you?"

"What I *see* is that she is pale, weak, whiny, and fat!" retorted Vakar. "And worse, since she is a host for the one called SnowFire, I see that she is a monster."

"We can turn that to our advantage," Daraz countered. "With her presence, the other tribes and villages will fear us. We can conquer them with hardly a battle. Ere-Kah will secure the Ullvarr's place as a great people on Algoran."

"The Ullvarr are *already* a great people, Daraz."

"Not in number or power. We are not even the sole masters of our land."

"The Kastadi are a powerful ally, are they not?"

Daraz looked down as though contemplating Vakar's words. "Yes," he admitted. "But we should not have to depend on anyone."

Vakar nodded. "So, what should we do now?"

"You need to put aside your dislike for Ere-Kah and ask her to be your mate. Then keep her satisfied and begin your family."

"I would die before having offspring with her!" Vakar said, outraged.

Daraz backhanded Vakar across the face with his hulking fist, hammering him back and to the ground. He then stomped on Vakar's chest, vacating the wind from his lungs.

"You are a fool! That female possesses more power than you could ever hope to have—and Kalami tells me that she already *favors* you!" Daraz raged. "Any child you have with her will be valued above all Ullvarr who have ever lived! Can you not see that? You should want as many offspring with her as possible. You would be securing your own future!"

Vakar was stunned silent.

"Are you, a warrior, going to tell me you are ruled by your own worries?" Daraz continued. "You should *have* no fear!"

Vakar clamored to his feet, anger still simmering behind his eyes.

"I understand your words and purpose, Leader," Vakar wheezed, slightly bent forward as he tried to recover from the pounding he'd received. He made himself look up and into Daraz's eyes. Vakar's sweat accented his pallor. "But hear me on one thing."

"What is it?"

"My only fear is that Ere-Kah SnowFire will one day be the *death* of the Ullvarr people."

Daraz had no answer for that.

1

CEREMONY

HE WATCHED THE MOKTA MOUNTAIN Village from the safety of a tree, hidden between the leaves, branches, and the darkening twilight sky. Like a zala beast, he bided his time patiently. There seemed to be more of these people than he had ever seen previously. They were gathering together for some kind of festival or ritual. The smell of freshly baked delicacies and scented candles filled the air and whetted his appetite.

A bird suddenly left its nest, rustling what seemed to be the entire tree, startling him. He did his best not to cry out or move, hoping the creature hadn't revealed his location. For many long seconds, he held his breath and sweat fell in single beads from his brow. His heart pounded ever more loudly in his chest.

Footsteps. He heard them crashing through the spring grass, drawing closer to his position. Distinct from any other motion nearby, they seemed deliberate.

Even if they get close, they cannot to see me.

The sounds ceased, and then a woman cleared her throat.

"Are you going to be late to your own birthday party, Arrow?" Jordan said in the Mokta language.

"How do you *find* me, Gemta?" Arrow released an exasperated breath. "You know I am not going to tell you, right? Come down here. Now."

The young boy leaped from where he perched and landed like a cat twelve feet below on solid ground, a handful of paces from Jordan. She gave him a scolding stare but in her heart was a deep love and admiration. He was an incredible blend of herself and her mate, Bopol. She believed her Arrow would grow up to be tall and athletic, just like him. Her son had her temperament, though, quick to any emotion. And he was as clever and stealthy as he was stubborn. His hair was a mixture of Mokta white and SnowFire blue, the scleras of his eyes were black but his irises were the color of ice. His face was somewhat long like Jordan's and he had her nose and lips. His skin had been light-colored at birth but now resembled burnt sienna, deeper than Jordan's olive complexion but lighter than Mokta red.

They walked towards the center of the village. He was almost waist high to Jordan, walking at her side in his animal hide clothes, keeping perfect step with her long strides. She wore a full green ceremonial dress which complimented how pregnant she was with her second child. Her slightly rounded cheeks were painted with traditional Mokta symbols in shades of red, yellow, and purple while her rich blue hair, which she had grown to mid-back length, was flowing behind her. She wore a deep green headband with ice blue beads. She was also adorned in earrings embedded with red jula crystals. It was customary for Mokta of all tribes to honor not only the offspring but their parents when a child reached the ages of five, ten, and finally fifteen, which was called The Dawning Time.

"I see you found young Arrow!" Chieftess Kitranor chuckled. "And just in time, too. We were about to start without him."

"Really, Chieftess?" Arrow spoke up, stunned.

"Look around you, young one," Kitranor instructed, appearing solemn. "Do you see all these people from your tribe?"

Several dozen people surrounded them and even more were present. They ranged from children younger than Arrow to the eldest Mokta, who was nearing one hundred cycles.

The boy nodded. "Yes, Chieftess."

"And more importantly, do you see all of these wonderful foods, prepared to honor your fifth cycle of life?"

Three tables held an assortment of foods, one displaying desserts like berry-and-jam-filled spiced dainties and sweet breads, another with various meats, and the last with grilled vegetables and creamy dipping sauces.

The boy nodded again, contritely this time. "Yes, Chieftess."

Kitranor let the moment linger a moment longer, then she grabbed Arrow and pulled him into a hug. She and most of the people around them broke into laughter.

"Did you think I was being serious? How could we *possibly* start your celebration without you, boy?"

"But, Gemtabana, what you said—"

"Relax, Arrow, enjoy this time. It is for you!" she interrupted, smiling widely as she released him. "Now excuse your Gemtabana while I talk to the adults."

Kitranor stood up and put a steadying arm around her daughter-in-law while she motioned to her approaching son, Bopol. He wore a robe whose colors matched his mate's, and his cheeks were similarly painted but instead with brown, blue, and green colors depicting fatherhood.

"Now we see where young Arrow's behavior comes from," Kitranor announced, jesting but not entirely. "His father never much liked ceremonies, either!"

That brought more laughs from those present. It also had the intended effect upon Bopol, denting his pride to send him a message not to avoid the rituals.

"Six cycles ago, these two made the wise decision to become mates while on a great and dangerous quest to find the Qui Tol. They succeeded," Kitranor declared loudly to everyone. "And no sooner had they made it back to this village than Jorr-Don learned she was expecting a child, their son. Now we congratulate the boy on achieving five successful cycles of life. And we praise his parents for how they have raised him!"

That brought cheers and whoops of joy from their fellow villagers. Normally, it was only the immediate and extended family who participated in birth celebrations. But since Arrow was the grandson of the Chieftess and the son of the next Chieftess, nearly the whole village's population turned out this day. Kitranor waited for them to quiet down before she continued.

"We also are grateful and happy for the life which will soon join us!" Kitranor continued, gently stretching her hand before Jordan's abundant belly, eliciting more animated responses from those gathered. "Now, let us lift up and encourage this growing family tonight in a way they will always remember!"

Over time that night, Jordan lost track of who said what to her. She made sure to thank everyone for their kind words and for attending. She knew the importance of such social functions, but they made her feel awkward. It helped that Bopol and Arrow were with her, because after standing so long in her condition, she was becoming exhausted. Finally, they had to assist her in sitting down in the softest spot she could find.

"Congratulations, bluehair!" a voice boomed from behind her.

"Zoska!" Jordan replied as she turned her head, elated to see her best friend walking towards her.

Zoska was accompanied by Lynsha, a mutual friend. Lynsha was in her early twenties, a tall and proud huntress. She bore scars on her left cheek which extended across her nose, a reminder of a successful hunt against a very aggressive Sasstonn which had also broken several of her ribs and her left leg.

"Do not stand up, Mah-mah, you will hurt yourself," Zoska mused. "My parents are watching my younger ones. They knew my daughter and I wanted to be here for you . . . and your 'growing family,' as Chieftess said."

"It is true, Jorr-Don," Lynsha agreed. "She was eager to see you."

"Thanks," Jordan replied. "So, Zoska . . . you finally get to see me this huge with child. Happy?"

"Jorr-Don, I said I wanted to see you that way maybe two—"

"Hundred," Jordan added.

"—times," Zoska completed her thought. "I mean, it is true, I was disappointed that you did not, well, *blossom* as much with your son, but I suppose that was understandable."

"I was so sick and nervous with Arrow; I could barely keep anything down."

Lynsha stood close by, shifting in place, her eyes gravitating between the two mothers and the ground. With a loud sigh, she stepped forward.

"You two make me afraid to take a mate and have *any* children," Lynsha admitted. "Between the stories of your symptoms and the way Zoska teases you for . . . um . . . "

"For how fat I have gotten," Jordan insisted, extending her arms on either side of her stomach.

"How you have *bloomed*, Jorr-Don," Zoska deflected, putting her palms together and separating them outward. "It is truly marvelous."

"You are strange, Zoska." Lynsha stared at her. She glanced briefly at Jordan then back to Zoska. "Why do you not tell her what you are really feeling?"

Zoska looked uncomfortable, even displaying a hint of fear in her eyes.

"Will you tell her, or should I?" Lynsha dared.

Zoska sighed. "This is my reward for trusting you?"

"I am your friend. This is what friends do. You know Jorr-Don thinks you are making fun of her when you are not."

"Will one of you please make some sense?" Jordan interjected.

Zoska took in a sharp breath before speaking, turning in Jordan's direction. "You know how I also bloomed when I had Maska."

She dropped her arms to her sides and bit her lip as she looked down. "Even though you were sick and I felt bad for your suffering, I was jealous of how little weight you gained . . . compared to me. However, I have been able to better share in your second pregnancy, Jorr-Don. I may tease you now, but please forgive how I felt before."

Zoska's embarrassment was evident in her awkward attempt to smile. It noticeably contrasted with her sincere relief and regret. Lynsha stood back and seemed content in her silence.

Jordan looked at Zoska for several moments, absorbing the fullness of her words.

"You are like my sister, Zoska. I am so happy you shared your heart with me about this," she asserted. "There is nothing to forgive."

She gave Zoska a tender hug. Then she turned her gaze skyward and smiled, pondering something for a moment. "Have you considered that maybe I am having twins like you did two cycles ago?"

"No. It is one baby. I can tell," Zoska insisted, holding up an index finger.

"Did you become a seer and not tell me?" Jordan asked.

"'Zoska knows all,'" Lynsha quipped. Her arms stretched apart as she looked toward the sky, making Jordan giggle.

Zoska harrumphed in semi-irritation. "I do not have to read the stars to know this. I think you will give birth to a very healthy child."

"Thank you," Jordan responded.

Zoska rested her thumb and forefinger at her chin, looking contemplative. "You have come far from the scared girl who I helped train. The one who thought she should wait ten or fifteen cycles before having any young ones of her own."

"You are never going to let me forget that, are you?" Jordan muttered under her breath.

Lynsha slapped both of her own hips in satisfaction. "Thank the twin stars! I am not the only one who has not felt ready!"

Jordan looked thoughtfully at the younger hunter. She understood the woman's reluctance but had hindsight to guide her now.

"I hope you change your mind about taking a mate and having children someday, Lynsha. It took some time, but I found someone who made all of the risks and changes worthwhile."

Zoska nodded in agreement. "Well said."

"Maybe," Lynsha replied shyly. "It could be a while . . . but thank you. Now I should probably get some rest."

"May the stars light your dreams," Zoska imparted.

"May the stars light your dreams," Lynsha and Jordan repeated.

As Lynsha walked off, Jordan couldn't help but notice the younger woman's limp, which she was clearly compensating for. It drew attention to the physical pain she was obviously still enduring.

"I hope she feels better tomorrow," Zoska added, prompting a nod from Jordan.

She watched Jordan in the flickering torchlight, and then put her arm around Jordan's shoulder and smiled.

"As active as you tend to be, Jorr-Don, I think you will have the form of a huntress again in a cycle's time."

"I will never be a huntress again, though."

"No," Zoska professed. "You will be Chieftess."

Jordan nodded but attempted to change the subject. "You and Reiban did a wonderful job with this dress!"

"It is my mate who makes the clothes. I only design them."

"Well, your designs are flawless!"

"I am glad you like it. How goes your learning with Chieftess and the elders?"

Jordan winced at her friend's easy redirection of the discussion. Zoska gave her a "don't even try to dodge this" look, so Jordan quickly relented.

"I have been taught the entire history of the Mountain Mokta. But I have only managed to commit about half of it to memory so far," Jordan replied. "Chieftess has been letting me assist her in handling tribal matters like settling disputes and assigning common tasks among the villagers. Next week, I will preside over the joining ritual of Kelov and Hasda."

Zoska seemed satisfied with Jordan's words. "Your child is not due for what, another thirty moons?"

"Arrow arrived early but he was so active, almost hyper. This one is active but seems more content."

"It is a girl then. My daughter was the same way. This one will arrive when she is ready."

Both of them watched meteorites stream across the sky, burning away harmlessly like sparks in the atmosphere. A few other villagers observed the stellar phenomena but, of those who still remained at the birthday celebration, most were engaged in socializing, eating, or both.

A cold breeze made Jordan and Zoska both shiver and look at one another. Jordan could sense an unspoken question from her friend.

"What is it?" Jordan asked.

"I do not think you have aged one day in the last six cycles," Zoska replied, her expression one of fascination and curiosity.

"Why do you say that?" Jordan retorted with some apprehension.

"I have lived twenty-nine cycles and I look it. I know I am still young, but I have changed over time," Zoska answered. "I have lines on my face that were not there before and such."

"That makes sense."

"Jorr-Don, you have lived nearly twenty-eight cycles and experienced all of the same things, but your face has barely changed since the day SnowFire saved your life. Chieftess may have been right. You could be immortal now."

"I hope you are wrong."

Zoska's confused expression showed that she neither agreed with nor understood Jordan's reaction. "Why? Living forever young, forever beautiful?" Zoska continued. "Is that not an incredible gift?"

"You think so? What is so incredible about it?" Jordan responded bitterly. "I have noticed the same thing as you, how I have not aged. It worries me whenever I think about it."

"I do not understand?"

Jordan simmered for a moment then she released a breath through her nostrils. Her mood shifted from anger to sadness. "Why would you want to stay young but watch your mate and children grow old and die?" Jordan shared, on the verge of tears. "Then you would have to do the same with their children and grandchildren, all while you live on, still looking the same. I suppose I could find a new mate, have more children, since I would be young—but that would make everything start all over again."

"Jorr-Don, I did not mean . . . anything," Zoska replied softly. She looked wounded by her friend's anguish.

"I can think of no greater curse than being immortal in a mortal world," Jordan added. "Perhaps that is why SnowFire became the way she is. Maybe she went insane from grief, losing everyone she had ever loved."

"Jorr-Don, forgive! This is your night of celebration. I do not want to ruin it for you."

"This is my son's night," Jordan acknowledged, following her nearby child with her eyes. Watching him, her smile returned. "As long as he is happy, I will be happy. My problems will wait for another time."

———

She thought he was funny and brave. She liked the darker blue streaks in his white hair. Approaching him from behind, she was determined to catch him by surprise while he was distracted eating a piece of sweetbread and talking with his other friends. Through the crowd, she moved slowly, taking very light steps until her little fingers were so close, she could almost touch his hair.

"Hi, Maska," Arrow said nonchalantly.

"You heard me? How?" she retorted, flustered.

He turned around and flashed a poker-faced grin. "My secret."

Irritated, she shoved a small cloth pouch in his face. "Your gift."

Arrow was visibly surprised. "Really? Thanks. What is it?"

"Open it and see," she pouted.

The boy untied the thin cord which held the little bag closed and reached inside. He pulled out a polished, black Taba stone the size of his index finger. It had a white symbol painted on it. Some red strokes had been added around the symbol for impressive flair. Arrow grinned, looking down at the stone in his right hand. Seeing Arrow's positive reaction boosted Maska's mood.

"This is a good gift! What is this?" Arrow asked, pointing at a symbol on the stone.

"It means friend. You are my good friend," she replied, humbly.

"Thank you!" Arrow answered, sincerely touched.

"I made a hole in it. It can be a necklace . . . if you want," she said, handing him a necklace strap.

"Yes, I do," he said, accepting the second gift.

Arrow took a moment to run the strap through the hole in the Taba stone and tied the ends together. Then he put on the necklace and looked at her. She nodded approvingly.

"You made this, Maska?" Arrow asked.

"Yes. It took seven moons to polish it," Maska boasted. "It took five moons to paint it."

"You honor me. I will wear it forever!"

Just then, some of Arrow's male friends dragged him away to play games with them. But Maska savored the moment, silently basking in her best friend's praise of her handiwork. Then she ran after them.

"What game will you play?" she asked.

"This is not a girl game," a muscular boy named Foonta scoffed.

"Really?" Maska narrowed her eyes as if personally challenged.

"You should not say that, Foonta," a smaller boy named Lasta interjected, tapping Foonta's shoulder.

"Why not?" Foonta replied harshly.

"Do not say that. Trust me," Lasta added, pointing at the faint remnants of a bruise surrounding his left eye.

Foonta looked around at everyone, apparently looking for approval.

"Am I wrong? *Elget* is not a girl game," Foonta said more aggressively. "She should not play it. She is not special."

"She is special. She is Maska, daughter of Zoska," Arrow announced her name as if it were a formal title.

"So?" Foonta strutted, puffing his chest. "Will she—"

Before he could finish his sentence, Maska had kicked the side of his knee, knocking him off-balance. Then she threw herself directly at him, smiling all the while. Her momentum knocked them both over and the instant they hit the ground, she drove her right elbow into his stomach. He squinted his eyes, grabbed his belly and groaned in pain.

"Yes," she answered as she stood up and dusted herself off.

Foonta had not been seriously hurt. But in a matter of seconds, she had completely humiliated him in front of his friends and every villager within eyeshot. To add insult to injury, she offered to help the large boy stand back up. He knocked away her hand and got up of his own accord. Eyes narrowed in frustration and almost fighting tears, he stormed off in the other direction.

"You can play with us!" Maska taunted, calling after him and enjoying his discomfort.

"Stop, Maska. Let him go," Arrow insisted.

"She just—your daughter just made a fool of Hosp's son, Foonta!" Jordan observed.

"That is not difficult," Zoska replied. "Besides, Maska is the equal of any child her age."

Jordan continued to marvel at Zoska's daughter. "That is true," she agreed. "You taught her how to defend herself well."

"I cannot take all the credit for that," Zoska stated. "Reiban showed her many things and she learns well from him."

"It was nice of her to make Arrow a gift. What inspired her to do that?"

"She cares for your son. She would slay a Sasstonn for him . . . if she knew how."

Jordan balked at that. "He is five!" she exclaimed. "How can she *like* him at five?"

"I said she cares for him," Zoska rebutted. "Not that she wants to be his mate!"

Jordan breathed a sigh of relief. "I am glad. It is too early to be worrying about those kinds of things."

"I agree."

"Good."

After a moment's consideration, Zoska chuckled. "But if they are still this close in ten or twelve cycles, I think she *will* become his mate."

"Zoska! Why are you encouraging this?"

"What am I encouraging? I am talking with my closest friend, that is all. We are mothers and we must consider these things."

———

Bopol had been speaking with Chieftess Kitranor and his older sister, Miitas, for some time. She was slightly taller than Kitranor and also in charge of village security.

"How certain are these reports?" Bopol asked.

"Two of my best scouts confirmed the sighting," Miitas replied. "The Gulstaa have increased the size of their military and are arming for battle."

The Chieftess looked very troubled. She paced for a moment then stopped.

"If the Gulstaa leaders are planning on expanding their territory through conquest, there is no question what they will do," Kitranor asserted. "They will attack the Kastadi lands and then they will come for the Mokta Mountain to secure the region."

"I agree, Chieftess. We must prepare," Miitas answered, resolute. However, her half-frown revealed her lingering concerns.

"I must also agree," Bopol added.

"Could our scouts determine how long it will take them to fortify their forces and begin?" Kitranor asked.

"It depends on whether they want to increase the size of their forces even further," Miitas replied. "We do not know yet."

Kitranor's face twisted in reaction to the dreaded news. Without looking at him, the Chieftess put her hand on her son's shoulder.

"Bring your mate to me in the morning tomorrow. Whether she is ready or not, I must teach her how the Mokta go to war."

2

SERPENT'S TEETH

ZOSKA HELPED JORDAN TO STAND up.

"It is late," Zoska said, looking up at the moons and stars. "I need to find my daughter and go home."

"I will go with you," Jordan answered. "We both know exactly where she is. I will retrieve my son and do the same."

"Jorr-Don—" Zoska started to say, then stopped herself.

"What is it, Zoska?"

"Even if you are immortal . . . " Zoska gently gripped Jordan's shoulder and looked into her eyes. "I will be your closest friend, closer than family, as long as I live."

Jordan smiled but Zoska's words tore into her. She clasped her hands around Zoska's and nodded her head.

"Always." It was all Jordan could manage in response, her voice strained.

Zoska walked ahead, but Jordan looked down at her palms. Next, she peered back at her friend. Jordan imagined Zoska gradually changing over the next four or five decades, eventually resembling Jordan's grandmother and great-grandmother. Jordan attempted to humor herself, thinking Zoska would be just as clever, feisty and strong, even at her eldest. Yet no matter how close to reality that could someday be,

Jordan felt pieces of her heart break at the mental sight of being with Zoska at her moment of death.

Zoska continued walking but Jordan stopped, unable to pull away from the phantasm her fears were manifesting. Jordan imagined participating in Zoska's burial ritual, herself still looking the same age as she did now. Would Bopol still be alive then? Would her children?

Mere feet away, Zoska realized her friend was no longer following. She turned to Jordan. "Jorr-Don, your son needs you."

The words "your son" immediately snatched Jordan's attention away from her visions. Speculation and fear were luxuries and they would have to wait.

"Do you know where he and Maska are?"

"I think I have a pretty good idea, yes."

"You are going too high," Maska warned, her arms and legs wrapped around the tree's trunk. "We should head back down."

"It is close. Come on!" Arrow reached down with his left hand as his right held on firmly to a branch above him for support.

Maska let him pull her up. The trunk branched outward to the left and right, creating a stable area wide enough for both of them to stand or lean on. From their vantage point on this wooded giant, the entire village could be observed, along with the rest of the mountain leading to its peak. Peering out, it was an impressive vista not far from the celebration grounds.

She heard leaves rustle nearby but couldn't see movement or anything else out of the ordinary. Remembering her parents' training, she tensed her body, trying to be ready for anything. That's when she felt the akasva wrap itself around her leg. Maska stifled her gasp, but Arrow heard her. He turned his head and stiffened when she mouthed the word "akasva." He nodded once, his expression somber.

Moving only his eyes, he located the narrow but long serpent, whose glistening skin was a sickly green-gray that bore thin black stripes etched down its body like tattoos. Its head was small, but its mouth was open and almost disproportionately large, fangs ready to strike, to drive its venom into its prey. It made a sharp, internal screeching noise, meant to frighten away anything threatening it.

Every Mokta youth was taught the dangers of the mountain creatures, including the akasva. Hesitation or a wrong action meant death. Faster than Maska's eyes could follow, Arrow's hand grabbed the reptile directly beneath its head and yanked the two and a half-foot beast from her leg.

The akasva flailed, stretching its neck and worming its way from Arrow's chokehold. It looked determined to bite him in the next few seconds and return its attention to her.

It never got the chance. Within heartbeats, the snake ceased all movement and sound, transforming into lifeless blue crystal in Arrow's hand. Startled, the boy dropped the creature and it fell to the ground, shattering on impact.

Maska was astonished. "How did you *do* that?!"

"I do not know!"

"You saved me!" she exclaimed. "Thank you!"

"We should climb down," he suggested.

Maska nodded.

Soon, they had descended to the ground. Maska searched below the tree, and seconds later, she squealed in delight, squatting down to pick up what she had seen. She excitedly showed it to Arrow, cupped in her hand—the crystallized head of the akasva, frozen in its final expression.

"May I have it?" she asked.

"It is a SnowFire gem," Arrow replied hesitantly. "Chieftess said we do not take them."

"But it was an animal! Chieftess also said our kills are ours, so it is your choice. Will you give it to me?"

Arrow pondered her request. "You really want this?"

"Yes, I do! It is special," Maska announced. "I will make it a necklace—like yours!"

Arrow looked down at his own new necklace, Maska's gift to him. Then he looked at her and nodded.

"Okay, you can keep it," he replied.

She smiled but then hesitated. For a brief moment, she wondered if she might have made a mistake in this request. But when she looked on this prize once more, her happiness banished the thought.

Zoska cleared her throat. She was about twenty feet from her daughter and Arrow, looking as intimidating as possible. Inwardly, she was somewhat amused as both children turned, startled and scared by her presence.

"Gemta!" Maska exclaimed.

"You two are up very late. The celebration is over, everyone has gone home," Zoska spoke loudly enough for Jordan to hear, never turning her attention from the youths in front of her.

Jordan, driven by determination, made her way to them with surprising swiftness, considering her very ponderous state. She picked Arrow up and hugged him tightly, her concern not needing words to be felt.

"We are okay, Gemta. Do not worry," Arrow said.

"You took Maska up in that tree, right?" Jordan replied, her brow furrowed, and eyes riveted on her son demanding the truth.

"Yes," Arrow admitted, standing up straight like his father. However, his eyes showed regret in disobeying his mother.

"How many times have I warned you? It is so tall and there are akasva!"

"Arrow kept me safe!" Maska blurted proudly.

A brief but severe look from Arrow discouraged Maska from saying anything else.

"Whether Arrow kept you safe or not does not make it less dangerous. Do you understand?" Jordan had crossed her arms over her abdomen with one eyebrow raised in annoyance.

"Yes," the girl replied.

"And you, Arrow?" Jordan added.

"Yes, Gemta."

"We are going home now. We will talk more about this tomorrow," Jordan stressed.

Zoska put her hand on Jordan's shoulder as she passed by, stopping her. "Are you going to be okay?" Zoska asked quietly.

Jordan looked at her with an expression of "I have no idea" and then sighed, lowering her head.

———

The morning suns' light was stark and unwelcome as it taunted Jordan's eyes. Still exhausted, she wanted to go back to sleep. But during her years as a huntress, she had trained her body to wake up at this time, regardless of her condition. And now, despite being eight months pregnant, she knew she would remain conscious, whether she wanted to or not. A cool breeze entered the hut through its open doorway. It rushed over the kelkono and caused her to pull the fur blanket closer.

As she awkwardly rolled to one side, Jordan saw that Bopol was already up and checking on their son in his kelkono. Bopol had also prepared some freshly-squeezed irta fruit juice for her. The tangy, thick, and slightly sweet beverage was refreshingly smooth and nutritious, one of her favorites. Its sight and smell were motivation enough for Jordan to navigate her way out of the hanging bed and get to her feet. She ambled over to the table where a large stone cup awaited, filled with the beverage. She smiled at her husband's thoughtfulness.

"Dayshine, Bopol." She smiled.

"Dayshine, Jorr-Don," he replied. "Did you get enough sleep?"

Jordan's eye roll was its own answer. "I will be fine."

Bopol walked over to her and put his arms around her, gently hugging her.

"Did you get to talk with Zoska last night?" Bopol asked. "She was looking for you."

"She found me. Did you know she thinks we are having a daughter this time?" Jordan replied, one hand over Bopol's and the other softly stroking her belly.

"I hope she is right. But I will be happy either way."

That made Jordan smile again. "I know."

She heard her son half-stumble across the floor towards them. When she turned to see him, he was rubbing one eye and looked like he was stifling a yawn.

"Torkomm, do I have to go bathe?" Arrow asked, using the Mokta word for father.

"Yes, Arrow. It keeps you clean and builds your strength," Bopol answered.

"Foonta says he only has to bathe once every seven moonturns," Arrow rebutted.

"Yes, and Foonta smells like it, too," Jordan quipped. "Now go. Not another word."

Arrow obeyed. Jordan elicited a kiss from her husband before he headed outside their hut to join their son.

———

Bopol, carrying a medium-sized bag containing homemade bar soap, shampoo, a drying towel, and Arrow's change of clothes, led his son to the stream.

"Torkomm, did you do this at my age? Torkommta took you?"

"Yes. Your torkommta was diligent with me and my brothers and sister," Bopol replied. "We never missed a day. If the weather was bad at dayshine, we waited till the storm passed. And if the storm lasted all day, we went at night."

After they arrived at the brook and made preparations, Bopol sternly observed Arrow walking into the waters. They rose to the boy's chest when he was fully immersed. Following his father's routine, Arrow then squatted, fully submerged. As he rose out of the water, he vigorously shook his head. Bopol handed him the cleansing herbs and he began to scrub his chest and arms.

"Torkomm," Arrow continued. "Was Chieftess stern with you?"

"You know your Gemtabana," Bopol smirked as he leaned forward. "What do you think?"

Arrow gulped. "She was more stern than Torkommta?"

Bopol nodded. "But it was for our good. She had five children, all within one or two cycles of each other. We were . . . challenging to our parents. We worried them many times . . . like you worried your gemta last night."

Arrow dunked himself again to rinse. Bopol imagined his son was taking a moment to think of a response before he rose up.

"You . . . knew that?" Arrow asked.

"Your gemta tells me everything."

"I wanted to show Maska the High Place. She made me this gift," he crowed, proudly showing his father the Taba stone jewelry. "I wanted to thank her."

"It is good work, a fine gift. I understand," Bopol acknowledged. "But the High Place is dangerous. You know that."

"Yes, Torkomm." Arrow looked downward with the admonishment, frowning.

Then Bopol offered Arrow the shampoo and took back the cleansing herbs.

"I took my share of risks when I was your age, Arrow. How do you think my friends and I found the High Place?"

"You were the first to find it?"

Bopol smiled. "Three of us set out exploring one day and we saw the tree. The oldest of us was probably eight cycles. I was six. One of my friends, Kesal, started climbing the tree before we could warn her."

"What happened?" Arrow asked.

"As she was climbing, going very fast, she brushed by a den of akasva. Two of them wrapped around one of her legs and bit her."

"What?"

"There was no way we could help her. She passed out and fell," Bopol shook his head slowly, still grieved despite the passage of time. "Kesal was dead before I caught her."

"That is very sad, Torkomm. I am sorry your friend died."

"It was long ago, son," Bopol acknowledged. "Though last night, Maska could have been bitten the same way as Kesal."

Arrow nodded wistfully, his face paling in response to his father's verbal imagery. Arrow finished rinsing his hair and emerged from the stream.

"You were fortunate that neither you nor Maska were struck," Bopol stretched out his hand to give Arrow the drying cloth.

"I will be careful, Torkomm."

"Good. That is what your gemta and I hope for."

After Arrow got dressed, he stopped and looked at his father. "How often do you think about Kesal?" Arrow asked.

"I will always regret not doing more to save Kesal," Bopol said. "But if I can help save you . . . "

Arrow nodded in understanding. Bopol returned the cloth to the bag. He put his arm around his son and they returned to their hut.

3

A NEW LEADER

ILSKETH JARTAF DID NOT CHOOSE to be the leader of the Gulstaa. A daughter among eight other male siblings, she was the only one born with the Clansign, a long red birthmark on her pale-yellow right cheek, roughly the shape of a scythe's blade. She was taken by members of the Ruling Council to be educated and trained when Ilsketh reached the age of four. Her parents were well-compensated for their sacrifice.

The rulers, governing factions, and warriors lived separate from the rest of the Gulstaa. They resided in a harsher, more difficult to reach region named Kamethla. It was there that the Ruling Council devised elaborate strategies while the warriors forged their strength and increased their prowess in the art of battle.

Ilsketh spent most of her childhood in Kamethla. As future leader, she had to learn the thousand cycle history of the Gulstaa and their many laws. She also was required to sit in on tactical sessions with the Council. Furthermore, she was expected to become a military leader and the fiercest warrior among their people. As a result, Ilsketh went through more stringent mental and physical training than anyone else.

For fifteen years, she endured a punishing schedule which began before daylight and went well into each evening. She held the title of *Heng Da* or "High One" in the Gulstaa language—but absolutely no disobedience was tolerated. Any signs of rebellion were quashed immediately. And under the guidance of the Ruling Council and the Warrior General, Ilsketh was molded into a tempered, perfect sword: their beloved future leader. Outside of the Ruling Council itself, she was the most powerful person in the region.

One morning, as she was finishing some stretches, a scout ran towards the village, his feet kicking up pebbles, dirt, and snow as he approached. His uniform was torn and disheveled from the long trek. Intrigued, Ilsketh walked toward the front gate, her dark brown bangs blowing into her eyes by the icy winds. Observing the scout's short, lean stature and bald head, he appeared to be in his late twenties to mid-thirties. In contrast, while the back of Ilsketh's hair was short, even severe, it was shorn in line patterns demarking her position. She was tall for a Gulstaa, reaching about six feet, athletic but trim. She had grown accustomed to seeing the dark yellow circles beneath her incredibly sharp eyes, which were the color of lavender. In front of her, the short and thin scout was panting, clearly exhausted from traveling far. His bulging eyes declared his fear, haunted and unsure. The imposingly strong guards helped him remain on his feet and catch his breath.

"The battle—did not go well," the scout gasped. "The Leader took four squads . . . but it wasn't enough!"

"What happened?" one guard demanded.

"The Leader fell . . . so did most of the squads," the scout lamented. "Only a few warriors made it back . . . to tell of the battle before taking Final Sacrifice. The last of them sent me."

The guards nodded with dire certainty.

"You did well. We will alert the Ruling Council," one guard told the scout.

"Thank you. I request Final Sacrifice," the scout said, eyes lowered.

Only warriors could perform the task, either for themselves or anyone else.

"For your service, I will grant your request." The guard landed a killing strike with his sword.

The scout fell to the ground, relief frozen on his face. Both guards gave a slight bow.

"I will go inform the Ruling Council," one guard said. "When I return, perform the death rites for the scout."

"It will be done," his counterpart acknowledged.

Ilsketh saluted the guard as he neared her. He returned the gesture.

"Heng Da?" the guard asked.

"I will accompany you," she said.

"Yes, Heng Da."

———

The Ruling Council was in a state of chaos that Ilsketh had never witnessed before. She sat in the Council Chamber, a circular hall hundreds of cycles old, built with large gray stones and having wooden pillars throughout. At the center of the room was a long, wide and sturdy table crafted from the same rock as the walls. A bright fixture resembling a timbered, candle-lit chandelier was suspended from the ceiling. Fresh air permeated from two small bay windows, one on the eastern wall as well as its opposite.

Normally reserved and deliberate, the eighteen members were loudly arguing with each other, following the news delivered by the guard. Most seemed to be in shock while others were clearly vying to increase their own political power. Anger and disgust rose from within Ilsketh.

She went and grabbed the ceremonial war hammer from its honorary place on the northern wall. She took its hilt firmly in both hands and slammed it into the middle of the ancient stone deliberation table.

"ENOUGH!" she screamed. "I will have order in this room!"

She succeeded in getting everyone's attention. They turned and faced her, stunned by her audacity and display of authority. However, she was Heng Da. Legally, she was the only one with the right to command them, especially now. But they had not expected her to do so.

"I know I have seen only nineteen cycles and have much to learn," she growled, pacing the room like a cat, occasionally looking at various council members. "But even I know that now is not the time to fall apart."

"Heng Da is wise!"

That voice belonged to Segim Artol, the Chief of the Ruling Council, an elder who had presided since before Ilsketh's birth. Tall and stout, he appeared astute but weary—and perhaps wary as well. His hair was long, gray, and well-groomed. Like the rest of the Council, he wore a midnight blue robe and ornamental jewelry made of local crystals and refined metals.

Ilsketh looked at him with contempt but kept her speech respectful. "Who were we fighting?" she said.

"The Mountain Mokta," Segim replied.

"I had heard that the Mokta were good fighters," Ilsketh affirmed. "Did our people die well?"

"Their Chieftess offered them the chance for peace, to retreat."

Ilsketh made a low murmuring sound, her expression twisting into one of disgust.

"That is *not* our way," she demurred coldly.

"Yes, Heng Da. Our people fought to the last warrior, including the Leader."

"Good."

Ilsketh knew Segim was not one to miss an opportunity and was clearly still upset by the Heng Da embarrassing the Council. He cleared his throat and looked her in the eyes expectantly.

"You are now Leader, Heng Da. What shall we do?" Segim asked.

"Do?" Ilsketh repeated.

"I will explain. Should your people punish these Mokta for their arrogance or should we set our sights on new territories?"

His tone had been splendidly reverent but Ilsketh had participated in enough Council meetings to see the trap he had laid for her. Fortunately, she had anticipated his actions before entering the chamber and devised a plan of her own.

"The Mokta acted within the confines of their laws and traditions; they were not arrogant," she uttered slowly, even defiantly. "However, I will not let our people—and our former Leader—go unavenged. In the Early Days, did we not learn from the example of Daltath? Her father, Kintosh, surrendered four provinces to the Wendana to wage peace. The Wendana returned a cycle later and attempted to take all of the Gulstaa lands.

"But Daltath, also born with the Clansign, slew Kintosh and took command. Her cunning and savagery not only repelled the invaders but she spent the rest of her life hunting them down. Now there are no more Wendana. Daltath taught us that surrender is never an option. So, do not ask me if I will act in a way that sounds or looks like surrender. If I ignore what the Mokta did, it says we are weak and invites them to attack us, to believe they can conquer us. Obviously, that is not so!"

It was sickening to see Segim smile at her. Did he believe he had snared her? They both knew a battle now would not go well. The warriors would still be demoralized by the death of the previous Leader. They also would not have much good will or rapport built with Ilsketh. Following this path would force her to rely on the Council more. It would increase Segim's influence over her future decisions. And Ilsketh would not be so easily manipulated.

"But now is not the time for renewed conflict," Ilsketh continued, addressing the entire Council and making eye contact with each member as she turned. "We will bury our dead and heal from this loss. We will grow our forces and properly prepare for battle. I will show you that your efforts in training me have not been in vain. We will attack in overwhelming numbers from all sides, striking down their defenses and use their own people as hostages. When we take the Mokta Mountain, it will be *they* who surrender—or die!"

Segim's expression burned with indignation at the ease with which Ilsketh had evaded him. She had actually turned the situation to her advantage. Her words were met with praise and thunderous applause from the Council. Not only that, but she knew her plan was sound. She could tell he knew that, too. And he was not happy about it.

———

Exiting the Council chambers, Segim approached Ilsketh. Without a word or even a visual acknowledgment of his proximity, she walked upstairs to the roof, indicating she wished to talk privately. Arms folded, she looked at the sky which threatened more snow, ignoring the mountains in the distance and the rugged, barren landscape which surrounded them, lacking trees and even grass in some areas. Only scavenging animals and insects made this place their home. It was appropriate for training warriors because it was good for little else. Food and supplies had to be brought from other Gulstaa communities.

"What is it?" she asked dismissively. "I know you have more to say."

Resting her hands on her hips, Ilsketh refused to turn around and face Segim. She understood how disrespectful this was, but she didn't care.

"Congratulations. You handled your first challenge well," he replied with a syrupy voice.

Now that he had spoken, she turned to face him and regretted it immediately. His hands were in a submissive pose in front of him, his head slightly bowed, accentuating his already hunched posture from advancing age. The crafty look in his eyes and the width of his smile reminded Ilsketh of a desert reptile, confident and preparing to strike.

"No thanks to you," she scoffed.

"Should I go out of my way to make things easy for you, Leader?"

"Watch your tongue, old man," Ilsketh barked, her eyes narrowing, temper barely held in check. "I know you cannot show bias towards me. But you don't have to go out of your way to make things more difficult, either."

"I treat you the same as any member of the Council."

"Yes," her nose flared as she inhaled through it. "That's not at all comforting, you know."

Segim chuckled hoarsely. "Yes, well—"

"What is it you want, Segim?" she interrupted him. Her facial features may have felt calm, but her eyes burned, betraying her dwindling patience.

The older man appeared to appreciate her directness. "You made a unique choice. The first of many, I am sure," he continued. "Still, you have also given yourself time."

"Time?" she repeated. "For what?"

"You are a Leader from a new family line," Segim said. "You will need a potential heir."

Ilsketh momentarily recoiled at what Segim was suggesting. Then her training took hold and she forced herself to consider his words carefully. Her life was not only hers, it belonged to her people. She had a responsibility to them first. Her own desires were an afterthought at best.

"Has a mate been chosen?" she said.

"Yes, Leader."

"When is the ceremony?"

"At nightfall."

"And . . . how long to rebuild and strengthen our forces, Segim?"

"Our losses were significant, Leader. Five cycles to reach previous levels."

"We must be better than before! I want the Gulstaa to be feared and respected."

"That will take seven cycles, perhaps eight."

"Do whatever is necessary, but make it happen, Councilman."

"On my life," Segim said sternly.

Seconds later, his breathing relaxed. She could sense his amusement without looking at him. It was revolting.

"The twin stars favor you, Leader," Segim added, a hint of acidity underlying his mollifying tone. "In eight cycles, you could bear and raise several offspring. Any one of them could bear the Clansign. I would caution you, however. It is perfectly natural to let a mate and motherhood soften you. And I do not just mean emotionally. Having children will change your body."

Not taking his bait, she smiled mischievously. "Will you also remind me that snow is cold?"

"No, Heng Da. But since you were taken from your own family at such a young age, I will remind you that you will be tempted to reclaim what you lost. A shame such sentiments have no place in leadership . . . or your heart."

"You can speak on matters of ruling, Segim," Ilsketh said in a dangerous whisper. "But you will never speak for my heart. Do you understand?"

"Yes," Segim replied, deliberately leaving out her title.

It was a punishable offense, another lure from the crafty old man. But she knew Segim would never be foolish enough to endanger his own power. To accuse him, Ilsketh would have to make his action—and her response—public record. That would sully her reputation, making her look petty and weak at the start of her authority. Anything short of his banishment would not be worth the personal cost to her.

If looks could impart violence, the councilman would have been battered senseless from Ilsketh's wordless fury. She clenched one fist and her jaw tightly for several seconds. Then she took in a deep breath and released it slowly.

"Very well. You have performed your task. And you can be . . . assured that all is as it should be," Ilsketh relented, forcibly restraining her own tears towards the severity of Segim's cruel words. "I must prepare."

"Yes, Leader."

As she descended the stairs, Ilsketh considered several ways to respond to his insolence in the future, some of which included disposing of her former mentor. But she decided against that, since he did not have many years left anyway and his knowledge and experience were occasionally useful.

4
RESPITE

BOPOL HELPED TO STEADY JORDAN as they slowly walked out of the village into the nearby forest. The twin stars were obscured by the overcast afternoon sky which threatened sleet or snow. The steady cold breeze was a hindrance, but they were not deterred. She stumbled when one of her feet sank into a small snow-covered hole, throwing off her already precarious balance. Bopol swiftly angled himself in front of her, stopping her fall. He waited for her to recover her equilibrium.

"I do not think we should continue, Jorr-Don. The weather is not good for this and you are so—" he stopped to correct himself. "You could have the baby at any time."

"Alright," Jordan conceded. "I just wanted to spend more time with you before she's born."

"Why did you not say so earlier? I will spend every moment with you," he added. "And that would make me very happy!"

She pulled him into a passionate kiss, grateful for his devotion.

"This is why I wanted another child with you, Bopol. It amazes me to have you, someone with so much love inside, for a mate. To know that you hold me so dear in your heart, I cherish it—and you."

"You won my heart long ago, Jorr-Don."

The wind carried his braided snow-white hair behind him. The amber in his loving, tender look was brought out even more by the rich crimson robe he was wearing. Jordan was near-entranced.

"A treasure greater than the Mountain," she replied.

"Yours exceeds the Twin Stars to me."

"Careful with that charm, mister," Jordan added, winking. "I might go 'Hosp' on you."

"I do not understand?" said Bopol.

"Nevermind, my love," she chuckled. "I am ready to go back home."

Without a word, he surprised Jordan by gently sweeping her up in his arms. He held her there for a moment, looking all around to see which path he wished to take. She relaxed into his embrace.

"Can I stay in your arms for the rest of the day?" Jordan asked, looking up at him.

"Of course, if that is what you want," he responded.

"I do," she answered, earning a quick smile from him.

He walked slowly, even more carefully, back towards the village. With each measured step, he avoided anything that would jostle or potentially injure her and their unborn child. He felt warm against her skin and when she leaned against his semi-covered chest, she thought she could hear his heartbeat. To her, this was almost paradise.

Only you, Bopol. You are the only one who could make me abandon my fears. You were the one I risked everything for, the only man on this world I could have taken as a mate. You made it worth what I endured having our son. And I'm proud to carry your daughter, with as much tenderness as you are carrying me now. I love you!

Bopol looked down at Jordan in his arms and smiled as he continued towards their destination. He seemed to almost read her thoughts.

She realized she must have been projecting her feelings rather intensely. Or maybe he just knew her that well.

Several minutes later, they crossed over the threshold of their hut. Arrow sat at the back of the hut on the floor, playing with a hideskin-covered drum that Hosp had crafted for him as a birthday gift. Bopol suppressed a laugh, as it sounded like their son was trying to attack the drum more than make music. But there was no doubt he was enjoying the cacophony. Jordan looked at Bopol then at Arrow and returned her gaze to her husband, motioning her head towards the door. Bopol cleared his throat loudly to get his son's attention.

"Yes, Torkomm?" Arrow replied.

"Has Maska heard you play the drum yet?" Bopol asked.

"No, Torkomm."

"I think you should go and spend some time with your friend. We will come get you for the community supper."

Arrow's eyes could barely contain his excitement. "Yes, Torkomm! Thank you!"

The boy ran out of the hut, holding the racket-maker at his side. Bopol and Jordan watched in amusement.

"Nicely handled, husband." Jordan grinned.

"He could smash rocks together and Maska would enjoy it," Bopol added.

"I doubt Zoska and Reiban will be thrilled."

"That is their problem. I want to have you to myself."

"And you will," Jordan answered, raising an eyebrow.

———

Two hours later, Jordan awoke in Bopol's arms. He was still asleep, lightly snoring and she did not want to wake him. She was relieved that her baby seemed unconscious, too.

Just enjoy this. There may not be many more opportunities like these for awhile.

Jordan considered that even if she was not in line to become Chieftess, her children would take up most of her and Bopol's time for several years to come. And yet, she knew she was going to be Chieftess. And she would have even less time for herself and Bopol.

Without meaning to, she sighed loudly. Bopol stirred, making an incoherent sound before opening his eyes and looking around the hut. Jordan sank down a little, embarrassed.

"I am sorry, my love. I did not want to wake you," she confessed.

"It is all right," he answered. "What is troubling you?"

She pulled his arms closer to her, resting her arms and his on her belly. She wanted to snuggle into his chest but simply rested her left cheek and the side of her head against it instead.

"I was thinking about when I will be Chieftess someday. And I worried that I will not have as much time with you. I did not like that idea."

"I understand, I would not like that, either. But as Chieftess, you can give me a position that requires me to be with you most of the time."

"Would that not be abusing my authority?" Jordan asked.

"No. I can give the example of my parents. My mother is Chieftess but her mate is the Village Healer. She can see him whenever she wants. And he can go anywhere with her at any time."

"I see. Yes, you are right. But what kind of position should you have? Miitas is the military adviser and, as you said, Latas is the healer."

Bopol nodded.

"I can be your protector," he advised.

"You mean, like a bodyguard?" she asked.

"Not exactly. I would protect more than your life. I would be there to talk with you, help you relax, keep your morale up. I would care for your heart as well."

She took his hand in hers and kissed it. Then she leaned back against him again.

"You get the job. You will be my Protector when I am Chieftess."

"As my Chieftess commands."

"I am not Chieftess yet."

"You are the Chieftess of my heart."

Jordan blushed, her smile beaming.

This is paradise.

5

PEAKS AND VALLEYS

REIBAN WALKED ALONG THE PATH through the middle of the Mountain Mokta village, waving at both adults and children as he went. He was wearing a tan leather vest over a cloth shirt dyed a deep blue and brown cloth pants fastened to his waist by a black leather belt. All of these he had made, a manifestation of Zoska's designs. Wearing them around the village sparked interest and that often led to more business. So, he was content to advertise in this manner, as was his mate.

He made his way to Bopol and Jordan's hut, although he was not in a rush. He stopped a few times to look at the displays of his fellow merchants.

"Those karfis fruits are making my mouth water, Asfana," Reiban nodded to the middle-aged woman. "What do you want for ten of them?"

"Looking to please the whole family?" Asfana replied. "That is wise, they will thank you for it. I would trade ten for one of your soft cloth robes in yellow."

Reiban smiled. "Please do not take offense, but I would have to ask for fourteen karfis as a fair trade."

"Eleven," she replied in a semi-stern voice.

"Twelve," Reiban interjected with a slight tilt of the head and a smile. "Final offer."

Asfana relented with a mock huff of defeat. "Very well. Twelve."

"Stop by tomorrow morning with the fruits and my mate will take your measurements. It will take a few days to make the garment."

"That is fine, Reiban. Tell Zoska I look forward to seeing her."

Reiban nodded and continued on his way.

"How old are your twin boys now, Reiban?" a strong and stout man of Reiban's age asked as they passed each other. He was the village blacksmith.

"Two cycles, but I think I have wrestled with weaker Sasstonns!" Reiban replied jovially, eliciting a laugh from his neighbor.

Finally, he arrived at his destination, a hut on the west end of the village. He stood outside the entrance, not wanting to be rude, even though he wanted to peer inside.

"Bopol, are you there, my friend?"

"Yes. Come inside, Reiban."

Bopol walked closer and clasped both of his friend's shoulders in a welcoming gesture. Reiban was silently glad that Bopol had learned restraint over time, as he had once fractured Reiban's arm when they were teens. Now he looked at the man his friend had become and was happy for him. Still, the slight furrowing of Bopol's brow alerted Reiban that all was not well.

"Did I interrupt anything?" asked Reiban.

"Nothing that I do not mind being interrupted," Bopol replied. "I was preparing for my next meeting with Miitas and the Chieftess."

"Village security?"

"That and more."

Bopol seemed distracted to Reiban, who had seen his friend in every conceivable mood over the years. No, not just distracted. Bopol was worried. He sat in his favorite chair contemplating something that looked unpleasant.

"Is there a problem, anything I should know about?" Reiban asked. "Maybe I can help."

"I do not think it is an immediate concern, but we always try to plan for numerous . . . possibilities."

Reiban frowned. "No, that is not troubling, not at all."

Bopol took a few seconds to manage a new smile.

"I did not mean to worry you," Bopol consoled. "I must need a break more than I realized."

"I guess you do, eh?"

"What can I do for you, Reiban?"

Reiban was still concerned but not enough to force the point.

"I am always looking for new sources of material for the clothes I make," Reiban disclosed. "I was considering a trip to the mountains in the Kastadi lands. They are fabled to have unique gems and plants for brilliant dyes. I wondered if you could tell me the safest route and any other security concerns in the area."

Bopol nodded. "I am glad you asked this. I think you should delay any plans to go to the Kastadi lands for now. But you could go south of the Mokta Mountain and find another good source for the plant dyes at least. I will see if I can recommend another source of gems for you."

Reiban wondered what could be going on in the Kastadi lands that Bopol felt he had to protect him from it. Nevertheless, he trusted Bopol's judgment. Reiban conceded that if Bopol did not think it was safe there, then it must be so.

"Thank you, my friend," replied Reiban. "I will owe you a pair of boots."

"I will collect that debt when you return," Bopol answered pleasantly. Reiban waved as he exited the hut.

The peak of the Mokta Mountain was thirty-five hundred feet above the ground and snow-covered. Winds were near-constant and treacherous at best. Few traveled here, as there were not many resources that could be obtained at this level which could not be mined or gathered elsewhere on the mountain. Nothing grew this high up and only jagged rocks, snow, and ice awaited anyone who traversed this way. Even the tisa birds were not foolhardy enough to brave the currents at the summit. There was more than one reason why the tale of the first Mokta Chief claiming this mountain was a legend.

At nearly one thousand feet below the peak, light blue grasses mixed with the rock, snow and ice, the winds still harsh but survivable. A few hearty animals like the karlam, a three-foot-tall muscular creature similar to a goat but with orange fur, three eyes and sharp teeth, made dens in small caves. From this elevation, one could see the top of the Grand Icefall, a monstrous waterfall descending two thousand feet, half of it encased in its own glistening frozen shell.

The Mokta village began just under halfway down the mountain on its west-facing region, in the midst of a forest. Most fruits and vegetables could be grown close to the village. But there were also more predatory animals to guard against, such as zala beasts, the slithering akavsa, and the Sasstonns. The village had grown in recent years. It now had a population of over seven hundred people and was still growing. Newborns to pre-Dawning Time children comprised about one-half; twenty-five percent were elders over fifty; and the rest fell in-between. Over the last twenty cycles, the village had been experiencing something of a baby boom. After decades of warding off other tribes, they had seen an extended peace under Chieftess Kitranor. Now each cycle, there was an average of about one hundred live births contrasting with sixty deaths due to illness, animal attacks, accidents or old age. The village had more than doubled in size in the last ten cycles.

At the base of the mountain, there were streams on the western and southern ends, byproducts of the plentiful waterfall. A variety of fish thrived there, ranging from pebble-sized to the length and thickness of a man's arm. There were also water carnivores such as the iimdi, a long thin reptile with blue scales, green eyes and piranha-like teeth, and the dazka, a fish that mimicked a white aquatic flowering plant with light blue pads that rested on the water's surface. But once a fish, animal, or person passed under it, the pad would ensnare it and release a caustic fluid to kill and dissolve its prey before digesting it.

Even now, as the cold season moderated into a warmer one, the hibernating creatures emerged from their slumber, beginning new mating cycles. The Mokta villagers planted new crops in hopes of a bountiful harvest and planned the Festival of the Warm Season, a celebration which often led to the choosing of mates and the start of new families. Rain and storms would come but even if the Mokta were away from the village and got caught in the soaking deluges or lightning, they could take refuge in the caves near the lower precipice.

In the surrounding greenlands, all manner of flora, fauna, and animal life flourished. All of this natural wonder existed in harmony under the protective presence of the majestic Mokta Mountain.

6
PROMISE

JORDAN LOOKED DOWN AT THE two-month-old child in her arms, a daughter she and Bopol had named Jasta, the Mokta word for *promise*. She had a deeper red skin tint than her brother, but the first showings of her hair were a mixture of white and deep blue. She was a big child, strong for one so young. Her eyes were piercing, with the black scleras of the Mokta and ice blue irises, a trait she shared with her mother and brother. Her face resembled Bopol's more than Jordan's—wide with a blunt nose. Unlike her brother, Jasta had fully pointed ears, also like her father. It was a bit strange to see the child giggle and laugh so much, a contrast to the quiet yet conscientious and mostly self-contained nature of her father.

Kitranor tapped at the entrance to the hut, eager to see her newest grandchild again. It was early afternoon and Jordan motioned for the Chieftess to enter.

"How is little Jasta?" Kitranor said.

"Every bit as hungry as her brother was at this age," Jordan mused. "I am just glad she is healthy like he was."

Kitranor nodded. "It has been a long time since we have seen this blend of Mokta and Errrth traits in young ones. Your children are beautiful and wondrous."

Jordan pondered a moment. "When was the last time the Qui Tol brought people from Earth, before me and my mother?" she asked.

"It was before my time, more than sixty cycles ago. But one of those males from Errrth became mates with a Mokta female," Kitranor answered. "Their son was my best friend from childhood."

"Is he still among the tribe? Could you point him out to me sometime?"

"He died from the Shilvaba fifteen cycles ago," the Chieftess mentioned sadly. "But he became mates with a Mokta female and they had a son, who is now married to Hosp."

"I just thought he was light-skinned, as some are," Jordan remarked. Then she gasped in surprise. "Wait! Then that means all of their kids—"

"Are a blend of our people and yours, yes," Kitranor affirmed. "As I told you before, all of the Mountain Mokta have some of your people's blood. Through our oral history, we can trace the Qui Tol's abductions back hundreds of cycles."

Jordan nodded thoughtfully at her mother-in-law's words. They intrigued her.

"I think that is one of the reasons the Qui Tol brought your people here, to see if we were compatible," Kitranor continued. "Obviously, we are."

"The Qui Tol will probably always be a mystery to me," Jordan said. "As advanced as their technol—um, their machines were, able to open doors to other worlds, why did they use them to separate families and experiment on people? Even Zeetra does not know why they did that and she grew up in that culture."

"Leaders do not always tell their people what they are doing," Kitranor admitted. "But if they do, it must be for a good reason or it will bring harm to everyone. The Qui Tol learned this."

Jordan's thoughts started to drift. Kitranor put her hand on Jordan's shoulder.

"What is it?" Kitranor asked.

"I was thinking about Zeetra and how she lost everyone she knew. And that made me think about Erica. I know she is . . . probably dead."

Jordan had to fight off old tears.

"Even if she survived the trip here, she would not have known anyone, would not have had any help," Jordan added.

"Zeetra knows her people are dead and she chose to join the Mokta," replied Kitranor. "She has survived among us. Your friend left your Errrth, a world filled with people. You and Januss showed me that your people are survivors. Your friend may yet live, probably with some other tribe on Algoran. Perhaps you will see her again someday."

Jordan's brow furrowed and she blinked away tears. "I wish I could share your hope . . . but it is too hard."

Jordan turned her attention back to her daughter, who needed burping. Once Jordan accomplished that, Kitranor offered to hold the child. She handed Jasta to the Chieftess, who pursed her lips and made a sound like the witiv insect, a high-pitched chirping rhythm. The baby reached for her grandmother's face, giggling in delight as Kitranor caressed her cheeks, gently swaying.

"I meant to ask you, Jorr-Don, why did you and Bopol name your daughter Jasta?"

Jordan smiled. "When I was pregnant with Arrow and we did not know whether it was a boy or girl, we came up with names for both.

If it was a boy, he would be called Arrow. That was what my father was called when he was a soldier."

"Was he an archer?" Kitranor asked innocently.

That amused Jordan. Of course, Kitranor wouldn't know its meaning.

"Er, no," Jordan explained. "It is a title of sorts, one meant to honor him. Some people on Earth call a person like him a 'straight arrow.' My father followed all the rules very strictly. Everyone in the military got a special name—and Arrow was his. Even after he was no longer a soldier and started a new life skill, he kept that special name. He was proud of it."

"So, you wanted to honor your father in naming your son?"

"Yes."

"What is the story of your daughter's name?"

Jordan lowered her eyes, blushed and smiled, slightly turning her head away. She cleared her throat and returned her gaze to Kitranor, motioning for the Chieftess to return her baby to her. Jordan pulled her daughter close and kissed her forehead.

"I had a lot of difficulty deciding on a girl's name and Bopol had only a few suggestions, but we could not agree on anything. At one point, I turned to Bopol and said, 'I want us to promise each other that, whatever we make her name, it will show her our love and devotion to her as a family!' So, being Bopol, he decided to name the first girl we had Jasta since that is the Mokta's word for promise. He felt that one word was enough . . . and I had to agree."

"You bring out the romantic in Bopol."

"He does the same in me."

"And that is a big part of why your union makes me very happy and proud, my daughter."

Just then, Jordan saw Kitranor's expression subtly change. She had come to recognize when her mother-in-law was carrying a heavy burden, one she was reluctant to share. Jordan lovingly placed the infant in her cazta, a round and wooden baby bed with a hollowed-out center cushioned by blankets and other soft fabrics. Surrounded by the softness and warmth, the child fell asleep within seconds.

"What news do you bring, Chieftess? You do not have to hold it back from me. I want to help."

Kitranor sighed and nodded. "You know I have been teaching you for some time how the Mountain Mokta prepare for battle, even for war. I will now tell you the reason why."

Jordan nodded her acceptance slowly and inwardly steeled herself for what the Chieftess was going to tell her.

"Our scouts have given me troubling reports about the Gulstaa," Kitranor continued. "They have built formidable troop levels and have a strong leader. It is now only a matter of months, perhaps even weeks, before they move against the Kastadi and then us."

As Kitranor shared this information, her words instantly made Jordan fear for her son and infant daughter. She inhaled loudly through her nose then abruptly stifled her reaction. Calming her breathing, she looked at the Chieftess.

"By how much do they outnumber us?" she asked.

"They have at least twice as many warriors, perhaps far more than that," replied Kitranor.

Jordan thought for a moment before responding.

"We have the advantage of the Mountain itself. We know it better than they do. We also know the best places to attack from or hide."

"Yes, Jorr-Don, but there will be no escaping from this foe. The Gulstaa scouts have gained knowledge of our lands over the cycles. They know our hiding places and would use them against us, taking hostages or just killing us."

"Very well. Then the elders and youngest children will need to be sent somewhere outside the Mokta Mountain, when the time comes."

"Yes, when the time comes."

"You have already made a plan to accomplish this, Chieftess?"

"No, Jorr-Don. You will do that."

Jordan's eyes widened, and she gasped. "Me? Why me? That is putting a lot of lives at risk, depending on someone without much experience!"

"Consider it your first test as Chieftess," Kitranor declared.

Jordan looked at Kitranor for several seconds before responding. She could not believe what she had just heard. "What? No! I am not ready for that!" Jordan exclaimed.

Kitranor chuckled. "Child, do you think I was ready when my uncle was killed in battle? I had two small children, just like you—and I had much less time to be taught. You are as ready as you will ever be."

"I do not understand. Why can you not lead this battle and just let me help? I can learn a lot from you still!"

"I will answer any questions you have, but you are no child. You do not need to be protected anymore. You have all the skills I had when I became Chieftess and you have been taught our history."

Jordan felt the proverbial weight of the entire village fall upon her shoulders. It was daunting and terrifying. She didn't understand how Kitranor could carry it, much less pass it along so easily.

"Do not worry. This is not official yet; I still carry the title of Chieftess for now," Kitranor added. "But the elders and I know. You will lead the Mountain Mokta against the Gulstaa when they attack, and you will help us prevail."

Jordan didn't even know that her mouth was agape. She was blinking slowly and deliberately, trying to process everything and not fully succeeding. This was an astonishing responsibility, one that could shape the future of their people—or end it. A question kept repeating in her thoughts.

"Why do you have so much trust in me, Chieftess?"

"I have watched you since the first day you arrived on Algoran. I took you and your mother into my heart as easily as the Mokta took you into this village. I saw you overcome obstacles that would have defeated or destroyed others. And I beheld you change from a girl into a woman, then a mate and a gemta. You have made me very proud. That is why I have such trust in you. I believe you can do this."

Jordan looked at Kitranor's eyes and expression and took solace from them. She inhaled slowly through her nostrils and exhaled through her mouth, firming up her resolve.

"Based on what you've told me about the Gulstaa, they seem highly adaptive in combat," Jordan considered. "We will need to be the same way. Since they outnumber us, we will have to be more clever and attack in ways that catch them off-guard."

"I agree," Kitranor replied, looking pleased. "What did you have in mind?"

7

TRANSFUSION

THE THREE OF THEM SAT by the river's edge, where they had been fishing for more than two hours. Bopol had only intended to have some time together with his son but Maska had practically begged to accompany them. Most times, he couldn't help but see both Reiban and Zoska manifested through their daughter's pleasant smile, insistent eyes, and sharp wit. It was like having both of them along at the same time and that was strangely comforting. Arrow certainly didn't mind her company; she was his best friend in the world.

However, she looked somewhat pale this day. Both Bopol and his son asked her about it but she just grinned and insisted nothing was wrong. Arrow accepted her words but Bopol was more cautious. He had been in too many situations where not dealing with things had quickly led to dire consequences.

"You have one, Maska!" Arrow almost shouted. He watched her fishing pole jerk. Surprise etched across his face that she hadn't noticed. "Pull in the fish!"

"Right," she replied, turning her attention to their potential dinner. "I will not lose it!"

Maska made the right moves but her strength was rapidly abandoning her. Arrow grabbed her from behind as she lost consciousness,

73

letting the pole fall into the water. Bopol put his hand to her forehead then her neck.

"She has fever, a strong one." Bopol kept his voice calm. "We must try to help her now, even before we take her to Torkommta."

Bopol laid the girl down on the ground. He grabbed the empty bag which would have held fish and dipped it in the cold water. He laid it over her neck to try and help her with her elevated temperature. That's when he saw the akasva head necklace, which was also hot and slightly glowing. Bopol's eyes widened in alarm. But he gently removed it from her and placed it to the side. Arrow was silent but his eyes broadcast his embarrassment at this discovery. He was also deeply concerned for Maska.

"Do you know when she got this SnowFire gem?" Bopol asked as calmly as he could.

"Yes, Torkomm. The day I turned five."

"That was over sixty moonturns ago! Did you give it to her?"

Arrow turned his head away nervously. "Yes . . . kind of."

"What does that mean?"

Arrow sighed and returned his gaze to his father.

"It was a real akasva," Arrow replied. "I—grabbed it and it became like this. Then it fell and broke. Maska wanted its head. So I gave it to her."

"So . . . you made an akasva become a SnowFire gem?"

"Yes, Torkomm."

Bopol blinked several times, slowly processing his son's words. Then he picked Maska up, held her close, and ran back to the village as swiftly as he could. Out of the corner of his eye, he saw Arrow shove Maska's necklace into one of the bags. Then he grabbed it by its strap and sprinted after his father.

Zeetra was near the river collecting plants for dyes, shampoos, and hair softeners. In the time since she joined the Mountain Mokta village community, she had become a hairdresser. She enjoyed styling tresses, which gave her a purpose and encouraged her to talk with people. She had first experimented on herself to learn some basic hair do's and don'ts. As people saw the results of her efforts, they took interest and asked to talk with her about her methods. Within a cycle, several villagers even volunteered to have her develop a new appearance for them. And with their satisfaction, Zeetra gained a good reputation as a Winto—Mokta for the equivalent of a hair stylist—eventually developing a regular clientele.

She heard someone running through the nearby grasses. When she turned to look, she spotted Bopol carrying Zoska's daughter. Worried, she chased after Bopol and his son. They soon approached the healer's hut and Bopol laid the girl down on the main floor mat and looked around for his father, Latas.

"Healer Latas must be out for a walk. I will go find him." Bopol looked at Zeetra and Arrow. "Stay here until I return."

"Yes, Torkomm," Arrow replied. Zeetra nodded.

With that, Bopol rushed out of the hut. Arrow and Zeetra sat down next to Maska.

"It is my fault Maska is sick," Arrow admitted, looking sorrowful.

"Why is she sick? What happened?" Zeetra asked.

Arrow explained what he knew. Zeetra listened with intrigue and concern.

"I have seen this kind of sickness before," Zeetra shared.

"It is not Shilvaba. Her eyes have not changed," Arrow added. "It is strange."

"No, this is caused by radiation. It is poisoning her."

"'Ray-dee-AY-shun?'"

Zeetra inhaled slowly before she continued. "It is a kind of energy, like what the twin stars send out into space, er, kotpi," Zeetra explained, using the Mokta word for the sky beyond the world. "From a far enough distance, a world's, er, ring of clouds protects us from it. And when this energy gives off light or heat from a distance as the stars do, it can be very good. But up close, without anything to block the, um, harmful parts, it is deadly to people and animals."

"I see!" Arrow responded. "But . . . we have SnowFire gems on our mountain. Why did no one else become sick like Maska?"

Just then, Latas entered with Bopol and a very worried-looking Reiban, who rushed to his daughter's side and held her hand. Latas looked upset but he mastered his emotions before responding.

"You have answered your own question, Arrow," Latas replied. "The SnowFire gems we have known are very old and the people have always been warned not to touch them. The first chiefs were all children of SnowFire. They would not have been affected by the gem's unique . . . energies. And as time passed, the crystals became less harmful. They probably have no power at all now. But the one you formed is still new . . . and very damaging."

Arrow looked stricken with guilt. "Is Maska going to—"

Before he could complete the sentence, Jordan and Zoska entered the hut. Jordan looked sad but Zoska almost collapsed when she saw how ill her daughter was. Reiban helped steady his mate.

"Maska will not die. There is a way to save her," Jordan insisted.

"Her condition is advanced, Jorr-Don," Latas warned. "I do not know if my herbal treatments can help the child."

Kitranor walked into the hut and visually assessed the situation. Her demeanor was grim.

"With respect, healer, she was not referring to your treatments," Kitranor clarified.

"I can give her some of my blood. It could help heal her the way SnowFire's blood did for me," Jordan offered.

"Would that not change her, make her like you?" Reiban asked.

"I cannot say what might happen after I give her my blood, Reiban. But I do know what will happen if I do not."

"Do it," Zoska pleaded, her voice low and trembling. She was crouched over her daughter, stroking the girl's sweat-dampened hair. "Save her, please."

Arrow walked over to his mother and looked at her with a pained expression. "Gemta, let me do it."

"What?" Jordan replied.

"I did this to Maska. I want to save her. My blood is also like yours."

Jordan's smile was bittersweet. "Our blood is not exactly the same. Half of your blood is your father's. No disrespect to either of you, but it might not work as well as mine."

"I want to try, Gemta," Arrow continued. "If it does not work, you can give her your blood."

Jordan nodded. "All right. I just hope that is not necessary."

Zeetra was aware that Latas had performed some blood transfusions over the years. She had been impressed with some of his inventions, such as a basic syringe made and tested from available materials. Looking at it now, it wasn't enough to handle major hemorrhages, only smaller amounts. It was a thin hollow tube crafted from metal ores with a similarly forged needle tip. He sanitized it with a surgical spirit made from fermented herbs. However, the syringe was intimidating to behold, despite its beneficial purpose. She saw Jordan take it, turning her attention to her son.

"Your torkommta will use this to take out some of your blood," Jordan instructed, showing the syringe to Arrow. "And then he will put it into Maska to share your blood with her."

"Will it hurt?" Arrow asked, gulping.

"Yes," Jordan answered sympathetically. "I am sorry."

"It is okay. I want to save Maska."

Latas approached the boy and rubbed some of the herbal fluid onto a visible vein on his arm. He inserted the syringe, and Arrow gritted his teeth, closed his eyes and endured it with a few silent tears. Jordan put her arms around her son to comfort him. Soon, Latas removed the syringe, now filled with the boy's blood. Kitranor bandaged the boy's arm. At the same time, Latas applied more of the disinfecting liquid to the syringe tip, then cleaned it with a thin cloth. He inserted it into the girl's arm and released its contents into her system. Zeetra was fascinated by the entire process but kept silent.

At first, there appeared to be no reaction. But after several minutes, Maska no longer seemed to be in pain. Then the color slowly returned to her skin and she began breathing more normally. She remained unconscious but Latas verified that her fever had gone down significantly in this brief span of time.

Zoska leaned against Reiban, holding him tightly. She turned to see Arrow next to her. He was on his knees, gripping his arm near the tip of the transfusion entry point.

Zoska put her hand on his back, getting his attention. "You did it. You saved my daughter. Thank you!"

His response was only a nod, eyes full of tears in relief.

Two hours later, Zeetra was relieved when Maska began to stir. She coughed once and turned to her side. She tried to sit up, but Arrow had to help her, since she didn't have all of her strength back yet. She kept her eyes closed as she still appeared woozy. Her parents, who had been sleeping across the hut, were alerted by the movement and got to their feet. Leaning against Arrow, Maska seemed confused but comforted. Zeetra walked a little closer to get a better view.

"What —what happened?" Maska asked, her voice raspy.

"You were very sick," Arrow replied.

"I was sick? I feel okay now."

"I gave you some of my blood. You got better."

"Oh!"

Maska lifted her head and opened her eyes to look at Arrow.

They were ice blue.

8

THE INTENDED

MASKA SAT ON HER KNEES, peering into the waters of the river. She had expressed intrigue to Zoska about the change in her eye color. Slowly, she tilted her head from side to side, her mouth slightly agape. She touched the side of her face with her left hand.

"I do not understand," Maska began. "Are my eyes all that changed? I do not feel any different."

"It was a small amount of blood," her gemta answered, standing nearby. "It saved your life and gave you light blue eyes. Is that not enough?"

"But Gemta, I feel like there should be more."

"Like what?"

"Will my hair change color, like Arrow?"

Zoska considered what her daughter had said. "Maybe it will and maybe it will not."

"Will I be able to make SnowFire gems?"

"I truly hope not. That would make others sick, like you were." Zoska watched as her daughter nodded and frowned.

"Yes, that would be bad," Maska agreed.

"Besides, not even Jorr-Don has shown that ability," Zoska continued. "It might be something only Arrow can do, something he will need to learn to control."

"He feels very bad about what happened to me."

"In that way, he is like his father. He cannot help it."

Maska ran her hands through the stream's waters, then splashed the liquid on her face and pushed it through her hair with her fingers. It appeared to refresh her. As if having an epiphany, she suddenly turned to look at her mother, a wide smile on her face.

"Arrow gave me his blood! Our blood has become one," she exclaimed. "Does this mean we are now mates?"

Zoska was momentarily bewildered by her daughter's inquiry, which was profound in its implications. She looked at the girl, initially cautious. Her nostrils flared as she exhaled. Zoska's brow furrowed and she licked her lips, at first not sure what to say. She cleared her throat to gain another second or two.

"Well, it was a special situation. He was trying to save your life," Zoska said.

"But when we were at Ispo and Avipa's joining ceremony, Ispo cut his hand and gave his blood. Avipa did, too. When they grabbed each other's hands, their blood became one and Chieftess said they were mates!"

"That is . . . true, but they knew what they were doing. They both wanted to become each other's mate," Zoska added, attempting to curb her child's enthusiasm. "They were also old enough to become mates. You and Arrow are still children."

"So, we are too young to be mates?"

"Yes! I am glad you—"

"But we are now promised to be mates!" Maska continued, excitedly interrupting her mother.

"That is . . . not quite what I meant," Zoska replied.

"But our bloods have mixed, my eyes are the proof!"

"Maska, do you not think that it is too early for such thoughts?"

"I am so happy! I must go speak with my future mate! I will be back by evening meal, Gemta!"

With that, Maska bolted away towards the village, leaving her stunned and perplexed mother struggling to comprehend what had just occurred. Zoska put her hand over her mouth and turned to the river. Watching its flowing currents helped settle her own mood.

"She has Reiban's eagerness and my inzda," she spoke to herself, using the Mokta word for *confidence*. "I doubt I will be able to turn her away from this dream."

She sighed and then laughed.

"Jorr-Don, it seems our families may one day be more closely tied than we imagined."

———

Arrow was walking by himself in the forest near the village. Images of his dear friend being so deathly ill continued to plague his thoughts and drag down his mood. The low growl of a zala beast suddenly alerted him that he had been too distracted and wandered an unsafe distance from home. The creature was young but deadly. Arrow turned his head and saw that its yellow eye was narrow, focused on him. It began to crouch, looking hungry.

The boy slowly lowered his hand towards the short blade sheathed on his belt. But he knew that, if the animal attacked now, he was at a severe disadvantage. Even a zala beast cub was faster and stronger than him. Would he be able to change the animal into a SnowFire gem before it killed him? He wasn't even sure he knew how to do that again.

Just then, Maska leaped from behind a tree toward the zala beast. With a savage scream, she plunged her own short blade into the creature's neck. Being given a moment's reprieve, Arrow dove forward and attacked from the other side, stabbing upwards, directly into its heart. Overwhelmed, the animal collapsed to the ground, blood pooling around its dying body. It snorted its last breath and closed its eye.

"Are you all right?" Maska asked, winded.

"Yes. You saved me," Arrow wiped his short blade on the grass. "That was dangerous!"

"My mate was in danger. I had to protect you!"

"Your . . . mate? Me?"

"That is why I was looking for you," she declared proudly. "We are promised to each other!"

"What? Why?"

"We have shared blood, just like Ispo and Avipa."

Arrow's thoughts raced, trying to absorb the meaning behind Maska's words. He sat down on a large rock and rested his hands on his knees. Maska sat down on the ground next to him. He didn't know what to say yet.

"We cannot be mates yet. But we are promised," she continued. "Do you not feel that?"

Arrow shrugged. "I am just happy that you are safe."

Maska looked confused, even disappointed. "Does that mean you do not want to be promised to me?"

"Ah!" Arrow said, sitting up straight and lifting his fist skyward. "Yes, Maska, we are the best, like family!"

Maska looked around, slightly confused. She was quiet for a few seconds as she thought about something.

"Do you believe we can pull the zala beast back to the village?" she asked. "It is too much meat to waste."

"Hm, I think it is too heavy for us," Arrow replied. "But my torkomm could lift it with one arm."

"We should go get him then."

Arrow nodded, and they ran back to the village.

————

Arrow and Maska ran into the hut and abruptly stopped themselves a few feet shy of Bopol. Jordan was standing nearby, her daughter sleeping in her arms. Bopol tried to gauge his son's intent before speaking, but Arrow addressed him first.

"Torkomm, we need your help!" Arrow gasped, slightly out of breath.

"What is wrong?" Bopol asked.

"We killed a young zala beast," Maska interjected. "It wanted to kill Arrow, but I attacked it first!"

"What?" Jordan exclaimed.

Bopol turned to Jordan and gave her a reassuring look. He gently touched her cheek before returning his attention to his son and Maska.

"It is all right, Gemta," Arrow added. "Maska wounded the beast. I stabbed it in the heart. It died right away!"

"Good," Bopol replied. "But if the beast is dead, what help do you need?"

"We are not strong enough to bring it back," Arrow admitted. "Could you help us do that, so the meat will not go to waste?"

Bopol turned to gaze at Jordan, who nodded approvingly. He smiled in response.

"Of course, my son."

"Thank you, Torkomm!"

———————

Jordan stood in the entrance of their hut, careful not to disturb her infant as she watched the trio leave. Once they were out of sight, Jordan put her child in the cazta.

With the rest of her family away to retrieve their prize, her focus turned inwards, as it always did when she was alone. Jordan then sat down in the center of the hut, closing her eyes in an attempt to relax and sort out her thoughts. This had become part of her daily routine, whenever she could make time.

I am not even close to seeing myself as a Chieftess. With everything I have been taught by Chieftess Kitranor and the village elders, I still feel like a child in high school learning government and math. The only difference is that I am married now and have two children of my own.

I am so confused. How am I supposed to lead this tribe? How are others supposed to believe in me when I am not sure about myself? And how do I send people to fight and die against an enemy like the Gulstaa?

Jordan heard someone approach the hut. As she turned, she saw that it was Kitranor. She stood up, greeted her in a soft voice and pointed to her sleeping daughter. They stepped outside to talk.

"Is there news?" Jordan asked.

"A Kastadi scout reached us at starsrise," Kitranor replied. "They have seen Gulstaa soldiers cross their borders and they are mounting a response."

"Are we sending help?"

Kitranor waited a moment before responding. Her mouth curved slightly upward on one side and she arched an eyebrow knowingly. The action stretched the few wrinkles near her eyes.

"I do not know. Are we, Chieftess?"

Jordan felt her anxiety flare and became lightheaded. Adrenaline sent needle-like pinpricks throughout her body. Her doubts roared and threatened to overwhelm her.

In that moment, she heard a still and small voice in her mind say "Will you trust me?" It reminded her of six years ago, when she had been dying from the Mosdon poison. She presumed it was God or His angel. She knew the voice meant well for her. But did she have the time to wait on Him? It was one thing when the only choices were to trust Him or die. In contrast, Jordan remembered all she had been taught by Kitranor. Those tactics were clear and could be used immediately. Jordan reasoned they would be sufficient to protect the Mokta. Did it really come down to a choice between trusting God or Kitranor?

Only seconds had passed but she knew she had to respond quickly. To Jordan, being Chieftess meant depending on yourself. So, she marshaled every ounce of strength from within her being. She pushed past her discomfort with the title of Chieftess, past the soft, still voice—and made a decision.

"Yes. I will send twenty-five of our best warriors to aid the Kastadi," Jordan declared. "I will also send a few scouts to provide them intelligence on the Gulstaa's movements. But I want to keep all of our archers and the rest of our scouts in reserve."

"Good, good," Kitranor replied. "You have a strategy in mind to protect the village then?"

"Yes," Jordan continued. "I just hope some of it is not necessary."

"You must be ready for anything, so do what you must."

"Then I need to ask something of you: will you stay with Jasta while I go talk with Zeetra?"

"Had you not asked, I would have offered anyway. I would spend every waking moment with my grandchildren if I could."

"I know," Jordan replied with a wink and smile. "Just remember, they are my children first."

"Go."

———

Zeetra had finished with her last client for the day and was cleaning up her hut when Jordan knocked at its entrance. The Onchei woman brightened when she saw her friend. Zeetra was wearing a dark green long-sleeved robe which contrasted well with her pale skin. Her long white hair was loosely braided and pulled into a ponytail that flowed down her back. Her shop had two wooden chairs; their seats were covered with soft fabrics that approximated cushions. She had painted the wooden walls with deep hues of purple and overlaid surreal patterns with lighter colors. It spurred conversations and took her clients' minds off anything that might be worrying them. There was also a ceramic basin on a wooden table where she mixed herbs and dyes. She kept her styling utensils in a wooden cabinet near the basin. A window and the doorway provided most of the lighting, but she added a few candles for ambiance and aroma.

"Jordan! This is a surprise! Are you finally going to let me work with your hair?"

"I might, but that is not why I am here."

"Have a seat then, let us talk," Zeetra responded, motioning towards the chairs. "I have some kintras tea ready. Would you like some?"

"Yes, thank you."

Zeetra grabbed the tea pitcher from a counter in her kitchen area and poured the beverage into two cups. The scent of the drink reminded Jordan of peppermint. But after she graciously accepted the cup and took a sip, the taste was more citric and tropical than Jordan expected.

"Thank you, it is very good!" Jordan complimented.

"I am glad you like it. It has become a personal favorite of mine," Zeetra added. "Now tell me, what can I do for you?"

"What I am about to say must be private between you and me," Jordan commanded somberly. "Understood?"

Zeetra's eyes momentarily widened. "O-Of course."

"I am Chieftess now—and we are going to war with the Gulstaa."

At first, Zeetra's face showed delight for Jordan's good fortune. But when Jordan spoke of war, it felt like ice surrounded her heart. In that moment, she knew why Jordan had come to her and it filled her with dread.

"How can I help?" Zeetra asked, her voice numb and uncertain.

"I would like you to advise me," Jordan replied. "I know you left behind the technology of your people, but you were trained to be military, right?"

"Yes."

"You know how to form strategies and suggest defenses?"

"Yes. But why me? Surely you have Mokta military advisers?"

"That is true. And I will be talking with them. But from what I have learned of the Gulstaa, they are a formidable opponent the Mokta have fought before. They may be able to anticipate our actions and compensate for them."

Zeetra nodded. "But no one knows the methods of the Qui Tol. There is no way for them to prepare for that."

"Exactly."

Zeetra saw the wisdom in Jordan's approach. With the odds seemingly against the Mokta, their best option was the element of surprise.

Zeetra also considered another way to assist her Chieftess and the Mokta.

"I did not entirely leave behind Onchei technology, Chieftess," Zeetra admitted hesitantly. "I still possess the knowledge and skill to recreate some . . . and possibly improve on it, make new things."

"What did you have in mind?" Jordan asked.

Zeetra looked down for a second. Then she looked back into Jordan's eyes intently.

ACT TWO

ACTS OF WAR

INTERLUDE

THE INCANDESCENT GLOW ATOP TEN wooden pike torches reflected softly in a shallow pool in the center of the azure-hued ancient cavern. The sound of their solemn flames licked the air. SnowFire was kneeling at the water's edge, her hands folded across her lap, head lowered with eyes closed. She took in deep breaths and released them slowly.

"On this single day, once every cycle of the twin stars, I honor you, my children," she declared, her voice reverent and loving yet torn by time and loss. She spoke in her archaic language, one no longer remembered by the people of Algoran.

"SkyWings, my firstborn son. You were handsome like your father but had my disposition. You led the Mokta well as Second Chief. You chose your mate wisely and your bloodline continues to this day.

"WiseEyes, my daughter. You comforted me when I raged against one or one thousand. You stayed by my side throughout your life, even after you took a mate. Your heart has been in every Mokta Chieftess for ten thousand cycles.

"DeepHeart and EverLove, my twin daughters. No one could tame your spirits, certainly not me. I was so proud of you! You loved life and people. Yet you convinced so many of your brothers and sisters to leave the Mountain and carve their own paths. You are the reason there are Mokta throughout this world.

"MorningLight, my son. You loved your father so deeply, only wanting to make him happy. And you succeeded. You were the first of my children to die, protecting your father in battle. I destroyed the Castozi to avenge you.

"SnowLion, my giant and kind-hearted son. You took your sisters' cause of leaving the Mountain and made it your own. You uprooted your mate and children and crossed the barren wastes. Your descendants mated with the people of that land and became the Kastadi.

"WinterSky, my daughter. You forged peace across many lands. You walked this world longer than any of your siblings. You outlived three mates and had many children, raising Chiefs and Chieftesses. I was with you when you took your last breath. You were so beautiful that even old age could not diminish you.

"MountainSnow and BrookStone, my twin sons. You set out to the East and the West and created mighty empires. You still live on in the legends of your people.

"CoarseWinds, my son. My lastborn, sired when your father was old. I did my best to ease your troubled heart but not even your mate, whom you loved so tenderly, could do that. You led a hopeless battle against a superior force and won, even though you did not survive. The Viltarka felt my wrath and are no more."

SnowFire lifted her head and focused her eyes on the stalactites hanging like daggers from the cavern's roof. Then she looked at her hands.

"Was it necessary to end so many lives?" SnowFire softly asked herself. "At the time, I thought so . . . but what was it for? Vengeance? Only killing the one who slew my child would have satisfied vengeance. Yet

I slaughtered all their people without mercy . . . even the children. I would not let myself hear their cries or pleas."

SnowFire squeezed her eyes tight and wailed in frustration. The mountain shook, some of the stalactites broke off and shattered on the ground. Small animals skittered away from the sound, running closer to the surface. Above the surface, birds fluttered higher to escape the danger and larger animals descended the peaks to find safety.

"How does this honor you, my children? The only legacy I have given you is the blood, bones, and dust of strangers. And why?"

With those words, SnowFire prostrated herself, overcome with grief. Her children had been deceased for millennia, but she suffered as though they had perished only yesterday. Still on all fours, her tears began to drop onto the rocky floor.

"It began with a desire," she continued, eyes still closed but managing a small smile. "I took this form and became woman. I felt the same emotions as mortals. Our love was so strong! And when we had our first child, we were both so happy."

Her smile faltered.

"I did not think about what it meant for a mortal and immortal to become mates. I had such a short time with him. And only a little while longer with you, my precious ones. You will never know your new sisters. And someday, they will join you in death, too. What have I been doing? What do I do now?"

She cried out, sobbing and projecting her pain outward, making the mountain tremble once more. And the echoes of blue and white flames danced throughout the cavern. Steam rose from newly formed cracks along the inclining surfaces, melting ice and snow close by.

Then SnowFire ceased all movement. Only the dripping of water from the roof of the chamber, as it splashed onto the floor, resonated throughout the cavern. Then a cool breeze wafted through the corridors and into the room. SnowFire lifted her head and turned to look. There was no one physically there but she sensed a presence.

"Who—" she began to say but stopped herself. Something about this was familiar and formidable.

There was no audible answer to her half-spoken question but SnowFire gasped as if she heard something. And then she bowed quickly, in reverent fear and obedience. Her eyes widened with amazement, even though she was still looking down. She spoke in a hushed whisper.

"Father of Spirits!"

9

WARCRY

ILSKETH WOKE JUST BEFORE THE twin stars' light appeared on the horizon. Her eyes were greeted by the familiar wooden ceiling and thick stone walls of the fortress she resided in but had never considered home. It was two stories tall, had eight rooms, and was forged in the center of Kamethla. Despite the comfort of her bed, long-instilled routines and duty forced her to stand up and grab a robe to wear over her night clothing. Her mate, Gothmarl, continued to slumber. She allowed it, as he had tended the youngest of their four offspring late into the night.

She had come to respect Gothmarl's attributes and talents over the last six cycles. He was physically strong but not a warrior, handsome in a brutish sort of way and amusing, if not overly intelligent. She knew he was sincere in his feelings for her, which ranged from admiration and love to deep passion. In contrast, she appreciated him but had never felt romantic love for anyone. She understood that he was not ambitious, therefore he would always be content with his role in her life. He was an exceptional father who would defend any member of his family to the death. She gazed at him silently for several moments and smiled. Under normal circumstances, she would never have chosen him as a mate, but she was glad she had accepted him.

Leaving her sleep chamber, she visited the children's room. Anci was her eldest, a daughter who was tall and stout for her age. Strong-willed, charismatic and decisive, she was a natural leader. Kintoth was born a year after her. He was slender and fast, crafty and centered. His little sister, Lithtar, was short, quiet, exceptionally beautiful and caring. And Ilsketh's youngest son, Mistig, was barely two cycles old. He had been sickly since birth, requiring diligent and skilled attention. He had been feverish overnight but had recovered and was now dozing peacefully like his siblings. Despite his challenging condition, he was a happy and loving child, displaying his own form of strength and determination. These four were her pride and future. And she was immensely relieved that none of them had been born with the Clansign. They would be spared the burden she carried.

Keeping an eye on the budding eastern horizon glow, Ilsketh changed into a thick cloth shirt, leather bracers, pants, and boots. She walked through the fortress' brick-hewn hallways and past the occasional guard, eventually descending the stony stairs that led to the courtyard. She took that time to clear her thoughts.

Waiting for her was Himstras, the man who had resided over most of her warrior training since childhood. She also considered him a surrogate father figure. Well into middle age, he was of average height and able-bodied, surprisingly fast given his musculature. He was bald and bore many scars from battle, which had cost him his right eye and two fingers on his left hand. Despite his gruff countenance and scowl, she could always tell when he was pleased to see her. His eye gleamed in a certain manner that acknowledged her in a positive way.

Without a word, she grabbed her preferred cutlass from the weapon rack. He was already practicing with his scimitar. As soon as she was within five feet of Himstras, he charged at her. She easily evaded him but like a zala beast, he turned suddenly and sliced across her upper right arm. Despite the sting of the wound, Ilsketh rolled forward and faced him, slamming the hilt of her sword up into his chin. Then she kicked him in the chest, knocking him off-balance. Menacingly, she held the tip of her blade to his throat before he could recover.

"I yield, Heng Da," Himstras conceded.

Ilsketh nodded. She winced briefly and checked her arm. There would be a small scar but it was not bleeding much.

"You usually wait a while to cut me," she noted, returning her gaze to Himstras.

"I felt inspired this morning." He smirked.

Ilsketh laughed. "Shall we go again?"

"It's your blood to lose, Heng Da."

"Splendid."

———

Sometime later, Ilsketh refreshed herself and had a small meal before changing into more formal attire. As she approached the Council Chambers, she steeled her mind for the experience ahead. The morning spars allowed her to vent any of the previous day's frustrations or concerns while spending time with Himstras usually put her in a good mood. Upon entering, she alighted on her ceremonial throne, centered between the seats of the Council members. She could feel elevated tensions and expectations. All of those present were looking to her—or more precisely, the way she would lead—especially Segim.

The old man had become frailer and lost some weight in the passing years, but his eyes gleamed and his tongue was as sharp as ever. As he crossed the room to open the day's discussions, he held his stomach with his left hand and his eyes winced as he shuffled along. Ilsketh made certain not to show any hint of satisfaction at his discomfort, as she may have instructed Segim's personal chef to make some modifications to the Councilman's diet. Undeterred by his internal distress, he leaned on the thick walking stick in his right hand and slithered forward until he reached the ideal spot to address his peers.

"Heng Da and my fellow Council members, I am pleased to announce that our military forces are now at peak levels, stronger than they were before our last major conflict!" Segim disclosed in a strong voice, eliciting cheers from the Council and a smile from his leader.

"That is excellent news, Councilman," Ilsketh replied. "When can they join the advance group we sent into Kastadi territory?"

"At your discretion, Heng Da. They are yours to command."

"Very well. I will hold a ceremony to honor them this day at the main gate, before the twin stars reach their full height. Then they can depart knowing they are our trusted defenders."

"I'm sure that will please them greatly, Heng Da," Segim gushed in his sweetest tones, masking the irony of the words which he did not believe. "I will see to it as soon as we recess."

For a seemingly interminable period, the elderly statesman outlined the day's business concerning trade as well as which tribes and peoples were allies and who was considered an enemy. Segim also recommended increasing soldier deployment along the Gulstaa borders to stem any retaliatory strikes by the Mokta or anyone else. That resolution swiftly passed a Council vote, with the added benefit of restoring a semblance of active consciousness to Ilsketh. She had been extremely bored by Segim's love for the sound of his own voice.

As soon as she could, Ilsketh called Himstras forward to discuss the long-term strategy for isolating the Mokta and then surrounding them with overwhelming numbers. Acknowledging their enemies' formidable fighting skills, Himstras projected it would take from half a cycle to nearly two cycles to ultimately defeat the Kastadi, the Ullvarr and finally the Mokta. He also warned the Council that, while enemy casualties could be as high as seventy percent, the Gulstaa themselves could expect casualties between thirty and fifty percent, making it a costly war, both in resources and lives.

Ilsketh sympathized as she saw the somberness in his comportment, the heaviness in his soul, knowing he would be sending good men and women to their deaths. But she could also see that Himstras took some solace from the fact that they were soldiers; this was their job and their existence. They would do what needed to be done without question.

Still, she understood why this affected Himstras so deeply. All but one of his five grown children had perished in Gulstaa conflicts over the last two decades. It had driven his mate, their grieving mother, to take her own life. And it created distance and estrangement between him and his surviving son. Himstras had raised Ilsketh as his own daughter and she was likely his sole remaining reason to live. Knowing this, Ilsketh was deeply motivated to make him proud and help him feel useful, even if she could not voice these feelings.

As the twin stars approached their zenith, the departing Gulstaa regimens were gathered near the main gate as ordered. Ilsketh had donned her battle armor and helmet. She stood on a balcony above hundreds of her soldiers. She was gratified. They had been standing still, awaiting her commands. Her troops were young but hardened. Not only did they look prepared for combat, she could sense their total commitment to this war effort. It invigorated her.

She took a deep breath and raised twin warhammers in her hands, symbols of her reign as Heng Da. The flat bludgeoning ends of each large weapon had been coated in a special metal alloy, making them incredibly durable. The other side bore spikes and had been prepared the same way. A portable stone platform lay at her feet. It was two feet tall by four feet wide, with a metal frame beneath it, including short, thick legs for support. There was a hollowed-out area one inch deep at the center of the platform.

Her attention focused entirely on that fixture, Ilsketh hit its center with one hammer and then the other, instantly quieting those gathered. Then she repeated the action again, taking time to make contact with the soldiers' eyes in-between the crashing sounds. She created a rhythm only the Heng Da could perform, announcing the Gulstaa's declaration of war. She closed her eyes, moving instinctively as she continued the melody for another minute. She concluded by lifting her arms up vivaciously, pausing momentarily as she held them above her head. Then she swung both hammers downward, hitting the platform at the same time. That action completed, she stopped and opened her eyes. She was sweating and slightly winded yet completely enlivened by the thrill. With a delighted grin, her excited eyes greeted each of her warriors. The rapport they shared was enticing, almost feverish in its intensity.

For the final part of this war ritual, Ilsketh gave a deep guttural cry as she slammed the blunted metal ends of the hammers into one another, causing a tremendous spark. The impact rang out cacophonously through the area and its echoes continued for some time. The warriors observed in abject silence, but she could see a unified reverence in their expressions and demeanors.

When the echoes ceased, a massive roar erupted from the soldiers, who raised their fists and weapons.

She laid down the hammers before continuing.

"I will be with you, fighting and bleeding!" Ilsketh shouted, interrupting them. "I live and die for this land—my people, my mate, my children!"

She was so proud at this moment, exhilarated to be their leader. The adrenaline rushing through her veins made her feel invincible.

"Six cycles ago, the Mokta fought well," she continued. "They held their lands and our previous leader fought to the last soldier. We honor their memory!"

She clenched her right fist before shooting it into the air. "Now, we go forth, forged like metal and harder than stone! We will take the lands of the Kastadi and the Mokta! We will show them what it means to be Gulstaa—THAT WE ARE THE STRONGEST!"

Over the next several minutes, cheers and shouts resounded. The soldiers dashed their swords and axes deep into the ground and shouted "Tokranah atba ivomos!"—the Gulstaa words for "force that spares no enemy!" Then they ripped their weapons from the soil in a single motion, holding them skyward and screaming "Tijka Gulstaa astimka usk kestors!"—Gulstaa for "No Stopping Gulstaa Victory!"

Even Ilsketh felt the fires within her belly, the desire to charge into battle and shed blood. She grabbed her warhammers once more and raised them high above her head.

"Open the gates!" she bellowed. "The twin stars themselves are our witnesses! We go to war!"

10

KITH AND KIN

DARAZ SAT ON A LARGE rock, peering down at the three other Ullvarr village elders who stood before him. They were all in the midst of the forest, the twin stars shining overhead through a nearly cloudless sky. It was the warm season and flowering plants were opening, sharing pleasant aromas. The trees swayed in rhythm with the refreshing breeze, insects chirped and buzzed, birds soared overhead, and a brook splashed nearby.

Even hunched over from advancing years, Holaz was taller than everyone gathered. He spoke first, his long, faded moss-green hair covering his drooping shoulders, in contrast with his balding scalp.

The elder had mentored Daraz in village politics not long after his Age of Emergence, a year before he took Kalami to mate. And Holaz had comforted Daraz like a father when Daraz received news of his own mother's demise. Holaz's voice brought him out of his musings.

"We have the support of the Kilnok, Toff, Wata, and Dizu tribes, covering the four regions of the Kastadi lands. They believe in Ere-Kah SnowFire and want to please her," Holaz insisted, his voice raspy but easily heard. His green eyes were wild with excitement and gave him a youthful air. "When we call on them to move against the Mokta, they are with us."

"And what of the Kastadi and their Chief, Teebor?" Daraz asked.

Ilkamie, a middle-aged woman, slender and short-haired, met Daraz's gaze. "Teebor of the Kastadi wishes to meet Ere-Kah SnowFire. He is intrigued by her story and could probably be convinced. I did not tell him that you plan to move against the Mokta."

"That was wise. We do not want to provoke him," Daraz replied.

A younger man shifted in place nervously, his deep green hair shaved on both sides. He was wide and fleshy with short legs and arms. His untrusting eyes made contact with Daraz's, but he said nothing.

"Speak your thoughts, Untarr," Daraz welcomed. "Why are you troubled?"

"Great Daraz, I wish to know about Ere-Kah SnowFire herself."

"What do you mean?"

"When we do our part on your behalf, will she be ready to do hers?"

"What do you think she is supposed to do?"

Untarr cleared his throat, appearing somewhat uncertain. "She may look—somewhat—like SnowFire," he continued. "But does she have the power of SnowFire?"

"You want her to be able to tear our enemies apart with the sword or perhaps her bare hands? Burn them to ashes if they dare to oppose us, as the stories claim?"

"Well . . . yes," Untarr confirmed.

Daraz looked mildly amused for a moment. Then he laughed. "Ere-Kah can do that and more!" Daraz declared with a confident smile. "You know she came to us from the sky. But did you know that when she becomes angry, fire flashes in her eyes?"

"I—I have never seen her angry," Untarr answered, somewhat fearfully.

"I have, and you should hope you never do, my friend," Daraz continued.

He leapt off the rock he'd been perched on and strutted around everyone. He paused to take a moment to eye each individual as he spoke.

"I have no doubt of this. Ere-Kah is strong enough to tear apart a Deathwing or break mountains," he boasted, stretching out his arms and making gripping motions with his hands. "I pity anyone she calls an enemy! This is why we have been so good to her. We want to keep her happy and see that we honor her."

"I did not know, Great Daraz!" Untarr responded. "You are wise."

Holaz stood by silently, clearly amused by Daraz's tactics.

"Fear not, Ere-Kah is one of us now," Daraz added. "And when it comes time to use her, she will do exactly what we need her to do!"

The meeting dispersed and Daraz returned to the village with Holaz. At the entrance gates, they clasped hands. He favored Daraz's plan to use Erica as a means to attack the Mokta, avenging himself on Jordan.

"Do not worry about Untarr," Holaz soothed. "He makes much noise but says little. And when it is time, he will follow you."

"I know, old friend," Daraz responded with a laugh. "All will be well."

Holaz smiled and returned slowly to his hut, leaning laboriously on the thick petrified stalagmite which he used as a walking stick. Daraz heard one of his children playing close by, which always brought a smile to his lips. He turned, only to see a mild spectacle occurring.

———

Kalami watched as Erica pretended to howl like a zala beast, tilting her head back and closing her eyes, the sound bellowing from deep within her somewhat heavy build. Kalami's daughter, Makazi, was completely captivated by Erica's imitation, along with three of her female friends. Erica was their teacher, but the Learning Time had ended earlier in the day. Right now, they were celebrating Makazi's tenth cycle of life. Kalami was admittedly impressed with Erica's efforts. Bringing refreshments for her daughter and guests, she feigned delight. Vakar stood motionless behind Erica, his expression guarded as always. Were it not undignified, Kalami believed he might have shaken his head in disbelief. Or perhaps he would have allowed himself a chuckle.

"I was in no danger, though," Erica confided with a grin, continuing her story and pointing to the warrior. "Vakar killed the creature with his dagger. It was over in seconds!"

"Vakar is your mate, isn't he?" Makazi added, giggling.

"No," Vakar stated, his stone-faced expression unchanging.

"He is not, but everyone seems to think he is, don't they?" Erica replied, leaning in close and whispering to the girl.

"But he is always with you!" Makazi prodded. "He must care about you a lot!"

"He is my protector. Of course, he stays by my side!" Erica replied.

"Enough teasing, Makazi," Kalami warned before shifting her grimace back to a practiced smile. "Everyone, I have more achama!"

The last six years had been extremely difficult for Kalami. Prior to Ere-Kah's arrival, she had been the sole recipient of lavish gifts and attention by the village, as the Leader's mate. And yet, Kalami had never felt close to the people in the village, though there were many she called friends. She did not trust anyone. Kalami was surprised then aggravated when Erica showed genuine gratitude and appreciation for all the hospitality being shown to her by the villagers. It made Kalami covetous of that sincerity and trust, something she would never possess. Seething with annoyance, Kalami had tried to delegate the task of maintaining Erica's satisfaction. And though several people had tried, their attempts had failed from Kalami's viewpoint: they were afraid of, too distant from or too accommodating to the blue-haired prize of the Ullvarr.

So, she had resumed her role as Erica's closest companion, the liaison between Erica and Daraz. Kalami had even arranged several pairings between Erica and some of the village's most handsome and available young men but none had resulted in a lasting relationship or any offspring. That was extremely disappointing. It meant that Kalami had to continue preparing precise dosages of the herbal powders she slipped into Erica's food and drink, which was burdensome.

During those years, Daraz had been away more, fulfilling his part in a Great Plan he had devised to unite the tribes against the Mokta. He attended many meetings and earned the political favor of many allies, at the cost of time with his beloved. He had told her to expect this. He also promised he would reward her grandly and personally for her sacrifices when they had completed this endeavor. She believed in Daraz almost as much as she loved him. She would do anything for him, which she had proven time and again. But the stress had cost her over time.

Since Kalami's mate could not be there to listen to her and share her joys, heartaches, and deepest secrets, she took her fourteen-year-old son Binoz into her confidence. He could not possibly fulfill Daraz's role, but she simply needed a friend whom she could be completely honest with and not fear consequences. Binoz was loyal to her and understood what was being asked of him.

It was Binoz who had suggested she use cooking and baking as an outlet for her displeasure and nervous energy. And while food preparation had never been her strongest talent, she made a goal to improve steadily. There was satisfaction in being able to taste the end results and, once she achieved some success, to receive compliments. There may have also been some spite towards Daraz in this choice. She was desperate enough that, if she added to her figure from partaking of her handiwork, that was acceptable. In the last five cycles, she had done just that, hoping that Daraz might finally pay attention to her again. She determined that even making him upset would be better than not seeing him at all. It was even more frustrating when he did not.

Kalami had spent most of this morning working near the wood-burning stove and then carried several baskets' worth of achama treats halfway across the village in numerous trips. It had left her sweating profusely and looking somewhat winded.

The children rushed to her to receive the bite-sized achama pastries. She let them reach into her weaved basket, which was filled to capacity. They were a light-yellow color, cake-like, smelled like berries, and tasted like the nectar of the Iptal insect. Kalami enjoyed making treats for the young ones and they cheerfully filled their bellies with them. The crumbs on her clothing indicated that she had sampled more than a few herself.

She set the basket on the ground and leaned against a tree.

"Take a rest, Kalami, you've earned it," Erica offered, sincerely.

"I only need a moment," Kalami wiped some of the perspiration from her forehead. "I did not expect it to be so hot already."

"You've been near the stove for too long," Erica insisted. "If you don't cool down, you will become ill."

"I would love to take a relaxing soak in the river and then a short sleep," Kalami replied sarcastically. "But I have supper to prepare for my family."

Kalami stood up but was still unsteady. It galled Kalami as Erica moved to help her remain upright and centered. However, for the sake of maintaining the illusion of friendship, Kalami gave her thanks.

"Let me do it." Erica looked concerned. "You've been teaching me a few of your recipes. Let me put that knowledge to use. You go relax and take that soak. I will stay with Makazi and her friends."

Nearly exhausted, Kalami decided to stop caring for a moment.

"I should let her," she thought. "Ere-Kah can manage my duties for a change." She nodded.

"Thank you, Ere-Kah," Kalami attempted a genuine smile. "I think you are correct. I should take this time for myself."

"Good! I am glad to hear it. Enjoy yourself!"

Kalami waved at Erica and then turned to walk in the direction of the nearby river. Erica headed towards Kalami's hut.

Like a boy half his age, Daraz followed her, taking care to stay out of sight. That might have worked with many others but not Kalami. She knew he was behind her and had to force herself not to laugh at his amateurish attempts at stealth. She could not repress her smile, though, so she proceeded away from him towards the water ahead. When she reached the stream, she walked in, still clothed, until fully submerged.

The waters that fueled this brook descended from the melting snows of the nearby mountains, so they were still icy cold. It felt refreshing to Kalami. She swam for a moment, then turned and floated on her back. She gracefully lowered her feet to the riverbed. As she stood up, only her neck and head rose above the stream.

"Hoping for a better view?" Kalami teased.

"Yes," Daraz replied.

"You haven't tried something like this since our first year of being mates."

"You're just as beautiful now as you were then, my Heartpath."

"Now who is the sorcerer? You speak very convincing lies," she answered, counterfeiting shyness with a smile. "But I am grateful."

"It is no lie," he added.

She walked closer to the shore, her body now visible from the waist upward. "I do not much resemble the girl I was fifteen cycles ago, Daraz."

"And I do not look like the boy I was then, either. We have both changed."

Kalami scoffed. "You have less hair, a few more scars and lines on your face. But you are still the strong and ruggedly handsome man I took as my mate. I do not think it is a fair comparison when I—"

"You have birthed and raised two children and cared for us. And since her arrival, you have cared for Ere-Kah, despite your . . . reservations. Yet even with all that, you have hardly any lines on your own face. You carry your body with elegance and dignity . . . as the mate of a leader."

"Continue to spoil me with your words like this—"

"And what?"

Kalami walked the rest of the way out of the water, put her soaking wet arms around Daraz and leaned on him. "Just continue to spoil me with your words," she finished.

He could not say anything in response, however, because she had already begun kissing him.

Makazi's friends had already left her home as the evening mealtime was rapidly approaching. In her parents' hut, she and Ere-Kah had finished off the last of the achama.

"You are making the next dessert, one of my choice," Erica stated.

"That is not fair!" Makazi protested.

"Why?"

"You always want egisban," she announced unhappily. The multigrain bread, with a berry pudding inside, was topped with a sweet glaze made from Iptal nectar. It had become Erica's favorite sweet treat.

"There is a reason for that. It is very good!" Erica replied.

Makazi looked at Vakar. "Do you like egisban as much as Ere-Kah?"

"*No one* likes egisban as much as Ere-Kah," he answered.

Kalami opened her eyes and watched the blue-green skies overhead. She was still resting her head on Daraz's chest. He had been awake for some time and was skygazing as well. The suns had set, and the last remnants of their light was fading on the horizon of the mountains.

"I did not mean to rest for so long," Kalami fretted. "Do you think the children will be worried?"

"You said they are with Ere-Kah. They will be fine."

Kalami closed her eyes and smiled. "You are right. And we did need this time together."

They lay there in silence for a few moments. Then a realization sparked within Kalami and she frowned. "When are you leaving next?"

"Tomorrow. It is for a hunting quest. It will be myself, Horok, and Sefar. We will be back in two star-turns."

Kalami turned toward Daraz and sighed.

"Then we will stay here tonight," Kalami imposed, her voice soft but with a hardened gaze towards the distance. "So, I can make sure you stay by my side until dayrise."

"Nothing would please me more," he responded, sitting up and pulling her close.

The sound of the stream continued to splash against rocks and the shore. As the winds picked up again, a zala beast howled in loneliness in the distance.

11

REVERSALS

DARAZ KISSED KALAMI WHILE THE twin stars' light pierced the darkened sky and heralded the dawn of a new day. She sat up but said nothing.

Minutes earlier, he had gone to their hut and grabbed what he needed for his hunting quest while Kalami waited outside. He knew his travel companions would be waiting for him at the Southern Gate. He saw that she could barely keep her eyes open.

"I do not think you will catch much this day. You are as tired as I am," she whispered. "Are you sure you want to go?"

"Someone would not let me sleep," he replied, also whispering. "Still, I must go."

"Really? Must you?" Kalami folded her arms.

Seeing the hurt in her sleep-deprived eyes, he considered his options briefly. One answer came to his mind. "I must set a good example. I am Leader," he declared.

Obviously not satisfied, she nodded in acknowledgment. He had made his decision. He saw that she would abide by it. With some twinges of regret, Daraz walked toward the Southern Gate.

———

An hour later, Erica began to stir. She was momentarily startled to realize she wasn't in her own hut, until she recalled why she had remained at Kalami's. At the same time, her senses were unusually acute: The vibrant scents of grass, flowers and trees—even the fragrances of the leftover meat, vegetables and half-eaten egisban—were extremely crisp in the mild morning air, along with the more abrasive tangs of her own body odor and bad breath. Erica had to squint at how bright the sunlight glare was to her eyes. And as she put her hands to the ground, preparing to stand up, her sense of touch redefined the smooth finish from the texture of the wooden floor in a way she'd never noticed before. When she did manage to get to her feet and moved forward, she felt the pull of gravity. Lastly, she became aware that the slight buzz in her skull and thoughts, which had been a constant companion from her first day on Algoran, was completely gone.

She couldn't be feeling this different just from sleeping in another hut. She was aware on some level that what she was experiencing now was normal, that her perceptions should have been like this all along. But they hadn't been, and she wanted to know why.

Erica was happy to see that Kalami had made it home and couldn't help but snicker a little at how loud her friend was snoring. She made eye contact with Vakar, who had woken up when she did. They left the hut and Vakar followed Erica as she headed towards the nearby stream. She greeted fellow villagers as she passed them. Breathing in the morning air, Erica's senses began to return to normal levels. Even so, they were still considerably more focused than she was accustomed to.

Near one of the farming structures, an elderly, bald Ullvarr man was milking a domesticated Oltusa, Algoran's cattle. It had long blond fur, short tusks, and six strong legs to carry its considerable mass. He talked to the beast like an old friend and the animal responded positively, swishing its tail and grunting in a way that sounded like a laugh.

The man's mate patiently prepared plant matter to become animal feed. Erica had seen her many times. But she had never realized how beautiful the older woman's hair was; the graceful silver strands complimented the light green ones, especially in the simple long braid that flowed over the woman's left shoulder. And even though time, the sunslight and weather had lined her face, she was picturesque to Erica: a living work of art. Erica hoped she would age so well someday.

Passing the village gates, Erica continued walking for a while toward the river. When she and Vakar arrived, she looked at her own reflection in the water and was perplexed. She considered whether she was seeing things. She had known her hair was blue but now she saw the deep and vivid shades of it. It felt like she was seeing them for the first time. Was this a dream?

She pinched the skin on her left hand and scrunched her face from the pain it caused. Erica closed her eyes and leaned her head back, gripping her own upper arms in frustration.

Was I under some kind of influence? Was it something I ate or drank? But I don't eat or drink the same things every day. What's changed?

She contemplated these thoughts for a few moments. Had someone kept her drugged? Erica shook her head, not wanting to accept the possibility that any of the tribe may have betrayed her.

I will have to confirm this. I'll make my own food over the next couple of days. If I continue to feel clear-headed like this, I will have my answer.

Without a word, Erica returned to the village and her hut. Vakar followed her. She could tell that he knew something was troubling her, but he stayed silent.

Erica focused her attention that day on teaching the village children, including Makazi and her friends. It was rewarding to see them progress in writing and develop new skills like simple pottery sculpting. Most of them were attentive and receptive to her methods, although a few of the boys required sterner instruction.

That night, she feigned illness and told Kalami and Vakar she would have some supper later, but she never did. Her desire to test her theory was greater than her hunger. She awoke the next day still lucid, a bittersweet and almost unwelcome confirmation. As a final test, she went for a morning walk and took a fresh kalbaza fruit from one of the trees on the edge of the village. Its flesh was tender, sweet and juicy. There was no way anyone could have spiked it with a drug of any kind. It helped curb her hunger as well. More importantly, it did not cause the lightheaded feeling to return.

As she worked with the children that morning, Erica had to fight a growing sense of resentment. She also wondered if Vakar or Kalami—and presumably Daraz—knew what was being done to her.

She froze as one of Makazi's friends screamed.

"What is it?" Erica asked.

"Y-y-your hair, Teacher Ere-Kah!" the girl exclaimed. "It was like fire! And your eyes glowed!"

"What?" Erica looked around. "Did anyone else see this?"

Makazi and two of the boys nodded fearfully. "Do not be afraid," Erica insisted with a reassuring smile. "I am sorry. I don't know why that happened. But I will try to make sure it does not again."

Erica felt a rushing, tingling sensation fading in the back of her skull.

"Let's just keep this between us," she added.

Erica ended the Learning Time early that day. She walked to the community well and took a drink of fresh water. Vakar was never far. When she turned to see Vakar, he was looking away. And for the first time, Erica sensed fear from him.

This is one of the few times I wish I could talk to SnowFire. She scares me, but she's the only one except Jordan who could answer my questions.

She looked at her hands.

What am I now? Were the drugs holding back whatever it is I have become?

She touched the gems fused to either side of her neck. A tear ran down her cheek.

Am I a danger to everyone here?

Erica wiped the tears from her eyes. She took several deep breaths, to clear her head and prevent herself from hyperventilating.

Kalami added a few dashes of mitubi spice to her kocha dumplings, which bobbed about in the bubbling stovetop kettle in front of her. She looked at Binoz with admiration. He resembled his father, tall and strong. In two years, he would go through his Age of Emergence and pick a new mate soon after. Kalami treasured the time she still had, both with him and his sister.

"Binoz, will you check the Southern Gate for your asta? He should be returning at any time."

"Yes, Kacheela," Binoz answered dutifully.

As she spoke, Kalami spotted Makazi outside the hut. "I see your sister out there. Tell her to come to me."

———

On the other side of the village, Erica paced inside her hut, as she had for the last ten minutes. Despite her procrastination, she knew she was ready. Her breathing was quick, and her heart pounded.

Vakar stood by the doorway, eyes straight ahead. She pondered how much he knew, since he was with her all the time and saw everything she did. She decided to test him.

"I still can't believe this. I suppose this is what I get," Erica complained, stopping to lean on a tabletop.

"What do you mean?" Vakar asked, intrigued. He looked her way.

Erica turned her head to face him. "If I had not followed Jordan through a hole in the air to this world, none of this would have happened."

He narrowed his gaze. "I still do not understand."

Erica sighed. "Nevermind. You always do your job, so you have nothing to worry about."

Turning her attention to Kalami, she accepted that she had to confront her. She knew it might destroy the only life she'd known since arriving on Algoran, but she could no longer avoid this. She had to tell Kalami what she had learned about being drugged and see if Kalami was aware of it.

And what if she did *know all along?* Erica wondered. *What if she was responsible? I guess I'll confront that, too. I've just got to do something—now!*

She exited her hut. Her tension rose as she felt Vakar following her.

———————

Vakar and Erica were suddenly distracted by shrieks of pain and screams from close by. A legion of Gulstaa soldiers were smashing through the Southern Gate, terrifying the villagers. Ullvarr sentries converged from every corner of the village. The Gulstaa cut down most of them without slowing; they had better armor, weapons, and unmatched savagery.

Erica ran to Kalami's hut and Vakar was relieved. That might keep her out of harm's way long enough for him to deal with this threat. He unsheathed the daggers from his belt and slashed at one Gulstaa while kicking another, breaking their shin. He fluidly demonstrated his fighting prowess, strength, and speed. But the sheer numbers of the opposition reduced his effectiveness. One Gulstaa soldier moved in close with a mace. Vakar took a glancing blow to his left side, not having room to maneuver. Another Ullvarr warrior moved in to defend him. Despite his pain, when he saw Binoz running from two Gulstaa, Vakar limped as fast as he could to intercept them.

On the way, he caught sight of Kalami emerging from her hut. She bounded in the direction of her son, but Erica stopped her, grabbing and holding her arms. Erica strained as Kalami struggled, trying to wrest herself free.

"What are you doing? My son—"

"Vakar will protect him. You'll only get killed!"

However, one massive Gulstaa knocked Vakar over through sheer might and held him down, giving an opening to his companion towards Binoz. The other soldier impaled the teen through the chest with a short sword and blood splashed in all directions. As he struggled with the

Gulstaa soldier, Vakar heard a horrified Kalami scream her son's name. He saw Binoz fall to the ground lifeless, his expression frozen in shock and disbelief. With a strength born of grief, Kalami hurled Erica aside.

Vakar saw Erica run back inside the hut, probably to protect Makazi. Ashamed at his failure to save Binoz, Vakar landed blow after punishing blow against his opponent.

At the same time, without a sound, Kalami closed the distance between herself and her son's killer, picking up a bladed weapon dropped by a fallen sentry. Its sharp shaft penetrated the Gulstaa's back, spilling his blood and causing his eyes to widen as he died.

She briefly looked down at her son's corpse and then turned her gaze to Vakar, who had just killed his own foe. He strained to push himself up on his elbows.

"Why did we not know of this attack?" Kalami hissed.

"This must be an advance tactical group!" Vakar replied. "They want our land, not us!"

"I thought the Gulstaa had been defeated by the Mokta!"

"They were!"

Just then, the next wave of Gulstaa soldiers, a group of archers, entered the village and unleashed a volley of arrows. Kalami tossed a sentry's shield to Vakar and ran back toward her hut to protect her daughter. Energized by fresh adrenaline, Vakar leapt up while covering his vital areas with the shield. He then sliced through two arrows meant for Kalami before his injuries stole his strength again and he collapsed to the ground. Six more arrows embedded themselves in Kalami's upper back when she was mere steps from her hut. They pierced through to her chest, and she collapsed forward.

Huddled in one corner with Makazi inside the hut, Erica's eyes flashed open in alarm as she heard Kalami's agonized cry. The child squinted her closed eyes, whimpering and crying.

"Stay here, Makazi. Don't move!" Erica shouted as she stood up. "I'll save your mother if I can."

"Ere-Kah, no!"

"Just stay here! I'll be back."

Erica cautiously opened the wooden door and peeked outside. At the same time, a lean and athletic female Gulstaa moved toward Vakar, who was barely conscious, an easy target. Erica's eyes darted back and forth in desperation. She grabbed the overturned stone dinner table from the hut and hurled it in the direction of the female Gulstaa.

One moment, it was in her hands and then it immediately impacted the female Gulstaa in her back and right arm, knocking her away. Screaming in agony, the Gulstaa rolled several times and came to a stop on her stomach. Her continuing moans signaled that she was still alive. But it was clear that her arm and perhaps even her back was broken.

Erica looked down at her hands. Next to her, Makazi stood wide-eyed, horrified by everything that was occurring around her.

I did that? No, that wasn't my strength, it's what SnowFire gave me!

"How did you do that?! Your eyes—" Makazi shrieked.

"What?" Erica said.

"They are glowing again!"

Erica had no time to figure out what it meant. Instead, she turned and scooped up Makazi, who was near-frozen with fear.

Erica ran as fast as she could towards the Eastern Gate, which had not yet fallen.

"Vakar, we have to go now!" Erica screamed, not stopping.

"I will not abandon my people!" Vakar shouted.

"If we don't get out of here, there won't be any people to abandon. We'll all be dead!"

Erica spotted Kalami nearby on the ground. Blood was trailing from her mouth and pooling under her clothes. The dead and dying were everywhere throughout the village even as more Gulstaa entered to continue their attack.

Vakar seemed conflicted but evidently, even he could not deny the reality all around him. He nodded brusquely at Erica, forced himself up, and bolted after her. The three of them made their way toward the tree line.

12

WOUNDS OLD AND NEW

ESCAPING THE CHAOS IN THE Ullvarr village alive had been difficult enough for the three of them. But now, keeping Vakar conscious was even more challenging. As the only uninjured adult, Erica had to lead them. She hid them waist-deep in a stream below a shallow rock face a quarter mile from the village perimeter.

It wasn't nearly far enough away.

Her hair was soaked, and strands draped across her face. Vakar's right arm hung over her right shoulder as she held him up, not even thinking about how heavy he was. Makazi clung onto Erica's leg, still in shock. They were all shivering from the ice-cold waters.

I know the territory but Vakar can't walk on his own. I could leave him with Makazi and go for help. There isn't any point, is there? Even if I found someone to help, the village can't be saved. And I can't leave Vakar or Makazi. He's barely getting by with the bandage strips I made from my robe. And we've got to keep moving.

"Will Vakar be all right?" Makazi whispered nervously, her eyes still haunted by the carnage she'd witnessed.

"He is still bleeding. We need to get it to stop," Erica whispered in response.

"We need to find some upoa root," Makazi stated. "That will stop the bleeding."

"Is there any around here?"

"Yes, it grows next to the fipa trees."

"What does it look like? Can you show me?"

Makazi nodded. Despite what had happened, she was a survivor, practical and smart like her mother. Cautiously, she led Erica out of the stream and toward some upoa roots.

Erica used a fist-sized rock to hack off a chunk of the gnarled wooden root. Per the child's instructions, she smashed it into a fine powder. She carried the medicine to Vakar in her hands and spread it over his wound. Within minutes, the bleeding slowed and then stopped. His pain also seemed to lessen before he lost consciousness.

"The sounds of the fighting have stopped." Erica turned her head in the direction of the village. "We have a chance now to get to a safer place."

"Where will we go, Ere-kah?"

"Once Vakar is able to travel, we will head to the western border of our lands. Perhaps the Kastadi will take us in and protect us."

"Do you think they can defeat these Gulstaa?"

"I don't know. But there is no other choice."

————

Several hours later, Vakar woke up, and Erica fed him fiba tree berries and water. He was weak but able to stand with her help. Erica had gathered additional upoa root to take with them. He used a thick broken branch to walk, since he was having trouble with his balance.

By nightfall, they found a cave for shelter. She checked for any predators, large or small, and determined there weren't any. As a preventive measure, she cleared out some old arachnid webs and abandoned insect nests. She and Makazi secured additional berries from nearby as well as kindling wood to create a fire. The evenings could be brutally cold and there had been no chance to bring blankets or warmer clothing. To survive, they would have to huddle close together on the ground and keep the flames lit.

"Ere-Kah, do you know any stories?" Makazi yawned, rubbing her left eye.

"I do not know any Ullvarr stories. I am sorry," Erica replied.

"What about stories from where you come from?" the child asked.

"From my world? I can probably think of a few," Erica considered.

"What is your world like?" Makazi asked. "Is it like Algoran?"

"In a few ways, it is. Earth has trees, caves, and water like here. But the animals are different and so are the languages. There are . . . villages there that are as big as one hundred villages here!"

Makazi's eyes became like saucers. "One hundred villages? I cannot imagine that! So, um, there are a lot of people in those villages?"

"Yes, many thousands, sometimes millions—"

"What is meel-yuns?"

Erica briefly contemplated how to answer that.

"Er, many, many thousands of people," Erica responded. "There are tall buildings that reach up to the clouds and . . . machines that take people to the top of those buildings and back down again."

"There are machines on your world?"

Erica nodded. "Yes, there are lots of machines. Some that take people great distances, flying like a bird. Other machines tell you what time it is or help warm up your food without fire."

"You are telling stories now, aren't you, Ere-Kah?" Makazi laughed.

"No, what I am saying is the truth."

Makazi didn't seem to know what to think of that at first. "If you speak the truth, it sounds like you come from a wondrous place," Makazi continued. "Why would you want to leave there?"

Erica paused a moment before responding. "There may be machines that do incredible things on that world . . . but people are people, wherever you go," Erica answered, sighing. "There are good people and bad people. Good and bad things happen. And sometimes bad things happen to good people. It can make you feel like you want to get away."

"And that's what you did? You left your world to get away?"

"Yes."

There was silence for a minute.

"Ere-Kah?" Makazi asked.

"Yes?" Erica replied.

"I am sorry that bad things happened to you on your world. And then bad things happened here."

"It is all right."

"Thank you for saving me and Vakar."

"You are welcome."

There was another short silence.

"Are . . . are my kacheela, brother, and asta still . . . alive? Will we see them again?"

"No," Vakar spoke. He was unable to move but he was fully conscious. "Your brother and kacheela are dead. Your asta would have been hunting near the border. He is probably dead, too."

Makazi's mood visibly deflated and her eyes became fearful again. Erica sat up and gently pulled the girl into a hug.

"Was that not too harsh, Vakar?" Erica snapped, turning her head to look at him.

"She is the daughter of a leader. She deserves to know the truth," he replied.

"I know you are a warrior and maybe warriors can take such truths, even at a young age," Erica scolded. "But she is just a child and you told her that her family is . . . gone."

"It is . . . all right," Makazi replied softly. "Vakar is right. I needed to know."

Vakar looked satisfied but Erica stared daggers at him.

She's trying to be brave. But she's got a long, hard road ahead of her that I know all too well. She shouldn't have to do that alone.

"There is an Ullvarr custom," Makazi shared, her voice quivering. "Whoever takes in an . . . orphan . . . becomes the new parent—or parents—of that child. They are family . . . for life."

Erica looked at Vakar to confirm this was an actual custom. Vakar nodded slowly. His furrowed brow expressed his conflicted feelings, but his eyes were soft, signaling his acceptance.

"I know you are not Ullvarr, Ere-Kah, but you have lived among us. You have learned our language and ways," Makazi continued. "Will you honor this custom?"

Erica wasn't sure how to react. Instinctively, she held the girl close. "You want me to be your mother—your kacheela? Are you sure?"

"Yes, I am sure," Makazi answered, returning the embrace.

A moment later, Erica stood up and went to stoke the fire and add more wood.

She had known Makazi for most of her life, but Erica wondered if she was ready to be Makazi's guardian. The child was only ten years old.

Can I raise her as my own, with Vakar as her father? This will radically change my relationship with him. He can barely stand me most of the time!

But this isn't about him . . . or me. Or even Makazi. This could be about the future of the Ullvarr people!

Erica shook her head in disbelief.

This is crazy! I'm just one human being, an Earthling. Why am I the one who has to decide the fate of an alien species? But if I abandoned them, neither one would last long out here. I would live but the Ullvarr people might be gone forever and I'd be responsible.

Erica looked back at the girl, who was patiently awaiting her answer.

All I know is my parents' example of raising a child, and they were terrible! Is that what this comes down to? Do I trust myself to be a mother?

The fire, now properly tended, would last for another hour or two. Erica lay down on the ground, pulled Makazi close, and covered the girl with the thick sleeves of her robe. She backed up against Vakar, both for warmth and to be reassured by his presence.

"Makazi, I don't know how well I'll do, but yes," Erica answered. "Vakar, what about you?"

"I will do this . . . for Makazi," he replied sincerely. "And the Ullvarr."

"We are in agreement. We . . . will be your parents," Erica added.

Erica could feel Makazi's smile without seeing it. The girl relaxed and leaned into Erica more.

"Then . . . I will ask you to give me a new name, Kacheela," Makazi declared, calling Erica her mother. There was relief and also tears in her voice. "I want to forget who I was. Then I can become your daughter."

Erica was deeply touched by the child's sentiment. She understood it. It reminded her of herself, before she left Earth.

"All right. How about—"

"Can you give me a name from your world?" Makazi interjected.

Erica was surprised by that. "Why do you want me to do that?"

"It is just what I want."

"All right," Erica replied, pondering her options. "As a girl, I had a close friend named Pamela. She was smart and pretty like you."

"Pah-mil-lah?" Makazi repeated.

"Pamela."

"'Pami-la.'"

"Close enough. Do you like it?"

"Yes," the girl answered. "I will be Pami-la, daughter of Ere-Kah and Vakar."

That sounded very strange to Erica, but she didn't want to offend the child. So, she smiled instead.

"Thank you, Pamela. I am very honored."

Vakar started to snore, and soon, Pamela fell asleep in her arms, content. The crackle of burning wood, combined with its heat and the closeness of the others helped Erica join them in slumber.

———

Three days later, the new family crossed the border into Kastadi territory. Since she was the most able-bodied adult, Erica had chosen to scout ahead to secure their path forward. That was when she discovered the body of Daraz and the two other Ullvarr from his hunting party.

Not wanting Pamela to see her biological father with such horrific battle wounds, his face frozen in shock, she disposed of the bodies in their culture's way. She dragged their lifeless forms to a nearby clearing, positioning them in different directions that formed a Y shape, all turned face down.

After taking a moment to catch her breath from her physical efforts, she recited *The Final Journey* from memory. It was an Ullvarr poem meant to comfort the dead and guide them to a place of peace and rest:

> *"Your inner fires burn no more*
> *The hunt is finished*
> *And time has no more meaning*
> *Follow the mountain paths*
> *And the twin stars*
> *They are your companions now*
> *Do not think about us*
> *We will go on*
> *Take our love with you*
> *The place you go*
> *The world you now know*
> *Call it home*
> *Ussah."*

After several minutes of silent observance, part of the ritual she had witnessed a handful of times, Erica bowed in respect to the deceased. Then she quickly doubled back to Vakar and Pamela, leaving the dead to be returned to nature.

Vakar and Pamela sat on the ground talking to one another. She was pleased to see them conversing normally.

"—maybe we could combine the berries with some gifpa root and okspa to make a soup?" Pamela shared with Vakar. "I saw some growing nearby."

"Good," Vakar replied. "Okspa can taste bitter . . . but the berries would help."

"I'll ask Kacheela when she gets back," Pamela added.

Erica walked up to them, but she could not conceal the emotional impact of what she had experienced earlier.

"Is everything all right, Kacheela?" Pamela asked.

"Everything is fine. I found three Ullvarr hunters. They were dead," Erica relayed, her voice cracking on the last word.

Vakar tensed in surprise but he stifled his response and asked instead. "You honored them in our manner?"

Erica nodded, too overcome with emotion to speak. Pamela hugged her silently.

"Thank you, Ere-Kah," Vakar said humbly. "You did not have to do that."

"Yes, I did," she whispered. "The Ullvarr gave me a home when I got here. You made me feel welcome."

Vakar looked at the ground silently.

Pamela squeezed more tightly around her waist.

"In your heart, you have become Ullvarr," Vakar stated. It was a supreme compliment from the warrior.

Erica was still too emotional to respond to the praise, but she acknowledged it with a nod. She cleared her throat before continuing to speak. "I think I saw a Kastadi village in the distance," Erica shared. "I didn't see any smoke rising from it. Maybe it was spared?"

"How far was it?" Vakar asked.

"I think we could get there by moons-rise, if we start now. But we will have to walk faster than before."

"Asta, you are still hurt." Pamela looked at Vakar. "Do you think—"

Erica smiled at Pamela's use of the Ullvarr word for Father.

"I enjoy such challenges," he replied confidently.

"Then it's settled," Erica added. "We will go."

13

ENEMY OF MY ENEMY

THE THREE MOONS WERE HIGH in the Algoran sky when Erica, Vakar, and Pamela arrived at the edge of a dense forest. They were several hundred feet from the village, which was mostly deserted. A small fire was visible. There was a savory aroma of roasted vegetables in spices, indicating that a few Kastadi remained. Observing from behind a large tree and some bushes, the trio were surprised to see a dozen short and muscle-bound, red-skinned strangers with white hair, pointed ears, and amber-colored eyes present among the Kastadi.

"Those are Mokta!" Vakar whispered. He stood behind the tree and peered around it.

"Mokta? Why are they here?" Erica asked, also whispering. She was fascinated to see a new species she had only heard about in passing.

She and Pamela were crouched behind the bushes, looking through an open spot in the middle of one of them.

"They are longtime allies of the Kastadi," Vakar declared. "The fight must not be going well if the Mokta have already been called."

"But we are also allies with the Kastadi, right?" Erica replied.

Vakar nodded. "Yes, but—"

Before he could complete his sentence, Erica stood up, taking Pamela by the hand. She and the child started walking towards the village.

"You can get medical help." Erica beckoned confidently, stopping to look back at Vakar. "Join us."

The Ullvarr warrior grunted as he made himself move forward, forced to set his pride aside and acknowledge the truth in Erica's words. She smiled briefly before continuing her walk towards the village.

One of the Mokta, a woman close to Erica's age, pointed her torch in their direction. She spoke loudly in her own language, sounding excited. That Mokta woman, a male Mokta, and a Kastadi ran the short distance to them. The woman gasped when she saw Erica. She spoke again in her native tongue.

"What did she say?" Erica asked in Ullvarr. "All I understood was Ullvarr and Earth!"

Vakar replied to the female Mokta, surprising everyone by speaking her language.

———————

"I am Miitas of the Mountain Mokta—and my brother's mate is from Errrth. Her name is Jorr-Don!"

Vakar was intrigued to learn this information. He knew he would have to relay it to Ere-Kah and Pamela in Ullvarr soon but wanted to know a little more first.

"She knows Jordan!" Erica shouted.

"Ere-Kah, what is going on?" Pamela asked, tugging at Erica's arm.

"Eree-Kah?" Miitas repeated, adding Mokta inflections. "We looked for you! You were with the Ullvarr?"

"She appeared from the air about six cycles ago," Vakar answered in Mokta. "We welcomed her into our village. She is one of us now."

Miitas nodded with some enthusiasm, clearly excited.

"We have much to discuss," Miitas stated.

———————

Miitas had one of her Mokta soldiers, the equivalent of a field medic, treat Vakar's wounds in one of the abandoned Kastadi houses. He also gave him a strong herbal sedative to ease his pain and allow him to sleep. Erica and Pamela sat on the ground next to a campfire outside the house, along with Miitas and a male Kastadi soldier named Caador, who spoke Ullvarr.

Assured that Vakar was going to be all right, Pamela lay her head down in Erica's lap, snuggling contentedly against Erica's soft stomach. Closing her eyes, Pamela quickly drifted into slumber. Erica gently stroked Pamela's long green hair, looking on her fondly. She sighed with a sense of relief.

"Her parents were killed in the attack on our village," Erica shared quietly. "She is my child now—and Vakar's."

Caador conveyed Erica's words to Miitas in Mokta. He did the same for Erica in Ullvarr when Miitas responded.

"You and Vakar are mates?" Miitas asked.

"No . . . not exactly. But we have taken responsibility for Pamela," Erica replied.

"Pah-meh-lah? That does not sound like an Ullvarr name?"

"The girl asked for an Earth name."

"You must be kind, to take this girl as your own. On Algoran, it is one of the highest honors."

"Pamela needs us," Erica offered, looking down at the child in her arms with newfound love and affection. Then she glimpsed into the house where Vakar was recovering. "And maybe we need her, too."

Miitas nodded in acknowledgment.

"This is your first child?" Miitas asked.

"Yes," Erica replied with some reluctance.

Miitas' words had reminded Erica of Hal Nowak, her ex-fiancé. Years ago, she had hoped for a future with him, including children. But after she unintentionally sabotaged that relationship, he had moved on without her. Now they were literally worlds apart.

"I have a son who is a little older than your daughter," Miitas shared.

"Do you ever get used to it—having a child?" Erica asked, genuinely curious. "Does it ever feel normal?"

Miitas' pride beamed through her eyes and hearty smile. "There comes a time when you will forget what it was like to not be a gemta. Your child will become your world. And that is how it should be."

"And yet, you're a soldier?"

Miitas slowly reached out with her right arm, spread her fingers and then closed them into a fist. "I fight to protect my family and my people. I would gladly give my life to preserve theirs."

"I understand," Erica answered, respecting the other woman's position.

Just then, Erica was forced to muffle a yawn from her own exhaustion. "I . . . should probably get some rest," she added.

"I have one more question," Miitas interjected. "Do you know if any other Ullvarr made it out alive? You are the first survivors we have found."

"I think we were the only ones," Erica replied bitterly. "The Gulstaa were so fast and . . . brutal. It was a slaughter."

Miitas looked momentarily pained to hear that news. She slumped her shoulders and let out a heavy sigh.

"We feared as much but I had hoped we were wrong," Miitas admitted. "Ullvarr and Mokta have been enemies for many generations but we always believed you had the right to exist as a people. Battles should be between soldiers."

"The Gulstaa must not share those beliefs, Miitas," Erica replied. "Do you know what their goal is?"

"We defeated them nearly ten cycles ago. I killed their leader in the last battle. We think they want revenge for that and to take our lands as their prize."

"Can the Mokta defeat them?" Erica asked.

"Yes, with the help of our allies," Miitas responded.

Despite her fatigue, Erica gently set Pamela on the ground and stood up. She surprised Miitas by enthusiastically clasping the Mokta's shoulder with her hand.

"There is a saying on Earth: The enemy of my enemy is my friend," Erica declared. "I don't care about past problems between the Ullvarr and Mokta. If we can help you stop the Gulstaa, we will!"

Miitas smiled after hearing the translation from Caador. She clasped Erica's shoulder.

"On behalf of the Mokta, I welcome the friendship of the Ullvarr!" Miitas beamed. "Pick any empty house to sleep in. When your companion is well enough to travel, I will take the two of you—and your child—to my village."

Erica picked up Pamela, who was still sleeping. She started to walk towards one of the houses but stopped and turned her head to look at Miitas.

"Is Jordan there in your village?" Erica asked.

"Yes. She is well," Miitas answered.

"I have so many questions. But . . . they will have to wait."

"It is all right. We will talk more in the morning and I will explain. May the stars light your dreams, Eree-kah."

"Thank you. Good night, Miitas."

———————

The morning light gradually crept over an open window into the domicile that Erica had chosen. They slept on the ground, as Gulstaa soldiers had damaged the sole bedding and several wooden chairs. There was a stone water basin and a few stone counters. A single smear of blood on one of the wooden walls was the only indication of what had happened to the previous occupant. It had taken Erica some time to quell her imagination and allow herself to fall asleep. The security she felt in the protection of the Mokta and Kastadi was the only thing that allowed her any relaxation at all. Even so, her dreams were not very peaceful.

Since leaving the Ullvarr village, Erica had become quite used to Pamela nuzzling close to her during the cold nights. She was no longer awakened by the child's occasional repositioning. Her presence actually helped Erica sleep a little better.

You call me Kacheela now. I feel like you deserve better. But we only have each other, the three of us.

A tear rolled down Erica's cheek. She couldn't tell if she was happy or sad. She was no longer a trophy princess; she was free from that. Pamela and Vakar were her future now.

She chuckled softly.

Who would have thought I'd wind up here, like this? She looked at her blue hair, having grown long after six years. *And being a parent to someone else's daughter. Now I'm sharing that task with a man who couldn't stand me until I saved his life.*

She looked through the window towards the moonslit sky. Then she smiled again.

Why does it make me feel so good?

When she woke hours later, it felt strange to not see Vakar in the room with them. She had to remind herself that he was in another house nearby. Erica slid free from Pamela, letting her continue to sleep. As she walked outside of the house, Miitas greeted her. Caador approached close behind.

"Dayshine, Eree-kah!"

"And to you, Miitas!"

"Were you able to sleep?"

"Yes. Thank you."

"We do not have much food here, but your family may eat from what we have."

"You are generous. Thank you."

Miitas led Erica to where the morning meal—a hot, soupy mash of grains, water, dried fruit, and spices—was being prepared. She hesitantly grabbed one of the small ceramic bowls and half-filled it with the meal, wary of food being offered. After what she had experienced with the Ullvarr, anything offered by strangers was potentially suspect.

But when she saw everyone get their meals from the same source, she relaxed some.

With no utensils, everyone had to drink from their bowls. That was no issue for Erica. Compared to the berries and edible leaves she had consumed over the last week, this was a feast and delicious. She was almost disappointed when she drained the last of the bowl's contents into her mouth. However, she did not want to appear greedy.

"You may have another serving. It is all right," Miitas offered encouragingly.

"Are you sure? I don't want to take someone else's meal," Erica stated.

"You will need your strength to travel. Do not worry, we have enough."

Not needing any more prompting, Erica loaded up another bowl and savored the experience once more. She felt full by the time she was done with her second helping.

"Do you feel better now?" Miitas asked.

"Yes! Thank you," Erica replied.

"Good. Would you like to continue our talk from last night?"

"Yes, I would like that. Can you tell me about Jordan? Did she look for me? I've wondered that for a long time."

Miitas nodded.

"She was very worried when you did not appear with her when she returned from Errrth," Miitas answered. "But she was injured and had to return to our village from the Qui Tol lands. Those who were with her had no time to search. And we had no idea you were in the Ullvarr lands."

"After she recovered, did she—did the Mokta—search for me?" Erica asked.

"Chieftess Kitranor did have some of our scouts search near our village, on the off-chance you somehow arrived there, but you were never found," Miitas replied. "Jordan could not join the search."

"Why not?" Erica insisted.

Erica could see that Miitas was being careful and deliberate about what information she revealed.

"She can explain that when you see her," Miitas answered. "She is the one who sent some of our forces to help the Kastadi fight the Gulstaa."

"Jordan sent your forces?"

"Yes. She is now Chieftess of the Mountain Mokta."

"Wait—what? She's the leader of your whole tribe?" Erica said, stunned.

"That was determined by SnowFire herself," Miitas said. Then she paused. "Do you know who that is?"

Erica nodded. Then a thought occurred to her. "Why would that matter to your people, the Mokta? Do you not decide your leaders for yourselves?"

"Normally, we would, yes. But SnowFire has . . . a special relationship with our people."

"What kind of relationship?" Erica asked, now very curious.

"We are her descendants. Our ancient stories say that SnowFire was the mate of our First Chief, many thousands of cycles ago. They had ten children who prospered and became our ancestors, the Mountain Mokta."

"That . . . sounds like a good legend," Erica said.

Even though she had seen SnowFire and struggled against her power, there was still doubt in her voice. On Earth, she had briefly spoken with Jordan about SnowFire, but it had been difficult for Jordan to go into many details about her.

It seemed to Erica that Miitas picked up on that and smiled with understanding.

"Like you, we also thought the tales were exaggerated over time," Miitas offered. "We did not think SnowFire was real. But she saved Jorr-Don's life and slew the Qui Tol people in Jorr-Don's defense."

"I know SnowFire is real. But who are, um, who were the Qui Tol?"

"They are the ones who brought Jorr-Don and her gemta to Algoran."

Erica stepped back and turned her head slightly towards Caador, not sure she had understood the translation correctly.

"Why would SnowFire be angry at these Qui Tol for bringing Jordan to Algoran?"

"That is not what angered SnowFire," Miitas said. "One of them tried to kill Jorr-Don."

"And because one of them attacked Jordan, SnowFire got mad at all of them?"

"Yes."

That was mind-boggling. But then she remembered the first thing Miitas had said regarding the fate of the Qui Tol.

"Hold it! Are you telling me that SnowFire slew a whole race of people—by herself?" Erica asked, skeptical.

"Do not look surprised," Miitas replied with a combination of amusement and pride. "There are none that match the fury and power of SnowFire. She is the Spirit of the Mountain. Many on this world fear her from the legends alone. There are no others who are like you —changed to look like SnowFire—except for Jorr-Don and her children."

"'Children?'" Erica gasped, taken by surprise.

Miitas nodded.

Suddenly, there was a clamor among the other soldiers. When Erica looked up, she saw red smoke was rising in the distance. Miitas stood up and grabbed her weapon.

"What is wrong?" Erica looked around, trying to discern what was happening.

"Our scouts have sent us a warning. More Gulstaa are coming. They will be here soon!"

"Do we have time to get Vakar and the other wounded out of here before they arrive?"

Miitas looked at the dissipating remains of the smoke signal.

"No, we will not have time," Miitas responded, offering a hand for Erica to stand up and move. "We will have to defend this village—and you."

Erica swallowed hard, taking her hand. "How long before they get here?"

"I can already hear the warcry of the Gulstaa," Miitas answered, regret evident in her voice. "They will soon approach in formation. Our two scouts have already sacrificed their lives to buy us time. Still, I give you my word: my soldiers and I will give our all."

"Will we make it?"

"Our chances of survival are not good."

Erica pulled out one of Vakar's daggers from her robe. She held it clumsily but with conviction.

"I am no warrior, but I will defend my daughter with my life!" Erica declared. "And Vakar, too, if I can."

Miitas smiled. "I can see why Jorr-Don is your friend. You have fire!"

"I fight for what is mine."

"Well said," Miitas added. "I will have Caador assist you."

As Miitas predicted, it took only minutes for the line of Gulstaa soldiers to become visible amid the fields outside the Kastadi village. Erica estimated there were at least one hundred soldiers advancing in a quick walk. They looked eager to do battle once more.

Erica watched as Miitas spoke with one of her soldiers. Though she couldn't understand their words and there was no time for anyone to translate, Erica could tell that things were not going well by the frustration in Miitas' voice as she asked questions. The soldier pointed at the rest of the soldiers and looked equally discouraged as he gave his answers to his leader. Erica could see only disappointment in Miitas' eyes afterwards. Yet there was also a strength and determination in her posture.

She wasn't giving up, even though it was clear that the Mokta and Kastadi soldiers had superior forces. Nevertheless, this was threatening to be a repeat of the Ullvarr village massacre.

Did we only delay the inevitable? I don't want Pamela or Vakar to die! I *don't want to die!*

Overhead, the sound of heavy wings slowly flapping could be heard. Looking skyward, everyone had to cover their ears and shut their eyes as tremendous, agonizing screeches filled the air. Heat rushed above them as black flames exploded forward, engulfing a portion of the Gulstaa soldiers. They had no time to scatter and were instantly incinerated.

One of the Kastadi soldiers shouted something; it sounded like he recognized whatever these creatures were. The Mokta and Kastadi seemed confounded. The four magnificent, dragon-like beasts were only attacking the Gulstaa! They were all flying in a formation, as if directed.

Erica squinted, thinking she saw a person mounted on the leading dragon. As her eyes adjusted past the morning sunlight, Erica was able to make out more details. There was a woman atop that dragon.

It was Jordan!

ACT THREE
DEFENSE

INTERLUDE II

SNOWFIRE SLOWLY LIFTED HER HEAD, her amazement and apprehension still overwhelming her. She remained on her knees.

"I am not worthy of Your presence," she said softly.

She listened intently. Her eyes narrowed as she tried to comprehend what was being communicated to her.

"Yes . . . of course. O-of course—"

SnowFire stopped speaking, as if interrupted. She tilted her head slightly to the right, as if curious. Then she nodded.

"Yes. It has been a long time. I have seen and experienced much. I have given and lost much."

She continued to harken to the Father of Spirits, dazed and electrified by His every word and ubiquity. Closing her eyes, she nodded. Tears began to well within and she bowed even lower to the ground. Several minutes passed as she humbly received all that His Presence communicated to her. Her mouth felt dry and her skin became clammy, but she endured it without a word. She started to tremble, partly out of reverence and out of excitement.

The power and holiness occupying this area was almost beyond description. On the surface above, even the animals were still and silent. The avians circled the mountain, rising and dipping in formation through the sky. Light snow began falling.

"Thank you, Great Father!" SnowFire exclaimed suddenly, still looking at the ground. "No one has ever understood me before. You have shown me myself. I can never repay Your mercy, which I do not deserve. Thank you! Thank you!"

She began to weep openly. But unlike times past, she did not feel despair. Through this release, she felt consolation and solace.

And she was grateful.

"What would you have me do?"

14

PREPARATIONS

TWO MONTHS EARLIER

Jordan did her best to keep up with Kitranor on their early morning run. Or rather, Kitranor was trotting along and Jordan was bent over, hands gripping her knees and wheezing like a woman many times her own age. In Jordan's defense, she had given birth to her daughter only nine weeks ago.

"You . . . you are just doing this to laugh at me, are you not?" Jordan panted. "I just had a child, you know!"

Kitranor smiled with understanding. "I never said I was not being amused by this. However, you did ask for my help in preparing you for combat . . . "

"Yes . . . I did," Jordan replied.

Kitranor walked over and helped Jordan stand up straight. Keeping one hand at Jordan's back, she used the other to wipe the perspiration from her forehead.

"After the birth of my third child, I increased my activity in this manner, while also keeping up my strength through good foods and drinking much water," Kitranor stated compassionately. "My purpose was to become stronger and healthier."

"And you lost the weight you gained from having kids?"

"No, not really. But that was not my goal."

"You must have been really thin before you took a mate!"

"Yes," Kitranor said with a laugh. "I was! Now come, we need to begin again."

Jordan looked at Kitranor indignantly. Kitranor chuckled.

"You will probably hate me before we are finished," the older woman joked.

"I am learning that very quickly," Jordan retorted.

Kitranor put her hands on her hips and stared sternly at Jordan. "Well, at least you can do *something* quickly. We shall see if the rest of you can catch up!"

"Can I invoke some obscure Chieftess law to make you leave me alone?"

"You could," Kitranor answered, her eyes showing concern. She sighed. "But then, you would fail your people and likely get them all killed. Is that what you want?"

Jordan stared at Kitranor in disbelief. "You were not joking just then, were you?" Jordan asked.

"No, I was not."

"Fine," Jordan responded. She inhaled sharply. "Let us return to the torture training."

"Gladly, Chieftess," Kitranor replied with a smile.

———

Several weeks passed.

Jordan gripped a cliffside. She continued pulling herself up to the next ledge a few inches at a time. Every muscle in her body felt acidic, complaining from the strain she was placing on them. She wore no safety gear and had no one to catch her if she fell. Those were significant enough incentives to keep her from making mistakes or giving up.

When Jordan reached her immediate goal after a few minutes, Kitranor was waiting for her. Fatigued from her efforts, Jordan was eager to get to the summit and return to the ground.

Kitranor tended to a small gash on her left forearm.

"What happened?" Jordan asked.

"I lost my footing and had to reach out to prevent a fall. I sliced myself on a sharp rock."

"Will you be alright? It is bleeding."

"It is not too bad; I will be fine. This is not an excuse for you to stop climbing."

"That was not my intent. But I think you should go back down. I will complete this on my own."

"Are you sure?"

Jordan nodded.

"Very well," Kitranor answered. "I will see you at the village tonight, my daughter."

"Yes, Gemta."

It took two hours for Jordan to reach the summit and four more to descend back to the valley below. She had rationed the water she brought and left another bag of it secured at the base of the small mountain. The suns were starting to set and there was a slight breeze. Even with all her accomplishments so far, the village was another hour away and the temperature would soon plummet.

Jordan was surprised to find Bopol waiting for her, holding the extra water bag for her. Jordan nearly collapsed into his arms, filled with relief.

"This is a pleasant surprise!" she wheezed, exhausted.

"You are Chieftess now. Do you think I would leave you unprotected?"

"You are my hadjta!" Jordan replied, using the Mokta word for true hero. "Were you going to protect me from the rocks, too?"

"If you would have let me, yes. Instead, I could only catch you if you fell."

"Then carry me back to the village, my strong warrior!"

"As my Chieftess commands," he answered as he easily picked her up in his arms, holding her close.

She leaned up and kissed his lips, cupping his left cheek with her hand. Then she relaxed back into his embrace with a satisfied smile. She felt safe as they returned to the village and slept peacefully that night.

———

The next afternoon, Jordan sat on the ground inside her hut facing Kitranor, Healer Latas, and Bopol. The mood was grim, and no one spoke for several moments. Jordan blinked several times, as though not fully accepting what had just been said to her. She was glad that Zoska was watching her children.

"The Kastadi are losing to the Gulstaa?" Jordan considered. "Three thousand Kastadi? Are you sure this is reliable information?"

"Yes, Chieftess," Bopol replied. "The scout who bore this news is under Miitas' command. His word is good."

Jordan stood up, angered and horrified. The loss of life alone was staggering. Frustrated, she began to pace inside the hut. "What are our current options?" Jordan forced herself to remain calm.

"We can commit more of our warriors to aid the Kastadi. If we do so, we can try to halt or reverse the Gulstaa's advance. Or we can commit our forces to defending the Mountain and let the Kastadi fall."

"If we aid the Kastadi, we risk not being able to properly defend the Mountain," Kitranor added. "And if we do not aid the Kastadi, we will not have their support once the Gulstaa attack us."

Jordan continued to walk around the hut. Then she stopped, considering something. A smile crossed her lips.

"We need a third and fourth option," she exclaimed excitedly. "And I have them!"

"Tell us," Kitranor responded, impressed.

"You . . . probably will not like either of them," Jordan continued. "But I believe they have the best chances of success!"

"What is it that you have decided?" Kitranor asked.

"I have already talked with Zeetra," Jordan replied. "She is going to help advise me and build machines to assist the Mokta."

Bopol looked displeased and Kitranor was aghast.

"You want Qui Tol machines to protect our people?" Kitranor confirmed. "You are correct, daughter. I do not like it."

Bopol cleared his throat. "And what is your fourth option, Chieftess?"

Jordan looked through the doorway of the hut and into the skies.

"We need another powerful ally, one the Gulstaa are completely unaware of," Jordan suggested. "And while the reward if I succeed is great, the risk if I fail is even greater. But I think I can do this, now that SnowFire has changed me."

"Chieftess, forgive my ignorance," Latas interjected, finally speaking up. "But what people, what ally do you speak of?"

Jordan turned to face her father-in-law.

"The Deathwings."

15

FIRE BRINGER

JORDAN, BOPOL, AND FOUR SENTRIES entered the Kastadi lands on foot, which had taken two weeks to reach. The sentries followed in a diamond formation to surround and protect the Chieftess and her mate as they proceeded.

Jordan had not seen this place during the warm days. She could hear insects buzzing about as well as birds chirping happily from their perches. The landscape was mountainous and lush with a combination of greens, blues, and ambers from the foliage that thrived only in this region.

"Chieftess, explain to me once more how you intend to, er, persuade the Deathwings to aid us?" Bopol requested, as respectfully as possible.

Jordan held up her gem-infused palms. "There is something about the SnowFire gems. My instincts tell me I will be able to communicate with them and that they will listen to me."

"If you are mistaken, we will not be able to protect you—or ourselves," Bopol added. "This is an extreme risk. Are you sure there is not another way?"

"If there were, do you think I would be doing this?" Jordan turned to her mate and winked. "What is the matter? Do you not trust me?"

Bopol allowed himself another slight smile. "You know I trust you. Why else would I be on this mad quest with you?"

"And that is one more reason that I love you, Bopol."

The sentries remained silent and serious.

Several miles in this distance, Bopol spotted their destination: a Deathwing nest near the base of a mountain. There were four of the dragon-like beasts, but they knew there could be more, either inside that cavern or preparing to hatch.

"We could reach the nest by nightfall," Bopol noticed. "But I recommend that we set up camp and wait until morning to advance."

"I agree," Jordan added, nodding.

At midday, the Alpha sensed movement approaching the den. Cautiously he rose on powerful legs, inhaling deeply through his long nostrils. His round, golden-hued eyes with dark slits for pupils scanned around. His kind could see in light or absolute darkness. The natural pattern which marked him as an alpha formed a light circle with a dark center crowning his scalp. His face sloped down like an avian and his long ears folded back, hugging the sides of his head. He had speckled black skin except along his underbelly, which was more translucent, revealing hazy patterns created by swirling smoke inside. His forked tongue tasted the air, wary of new scents.

He left the central chamber as his mate and brothers continued their slumber. He traversed the pathways which snaked between the rocks, chipped away by wind and water over thousands of cycles.

As he approached the entrance to the den, the Alpha grew more intrigued.

Was this some predator? If so, was it one of the four-legged kind or the two-legged ones?

A deep rumbling from within him emerged as a low roar, a warning for the intruder. He focused his senses and prepared himself to send flames, should this creature not heed him.

Then he sensed something unusual, a power that was both familiar and ancient. With the recognition, his mouth opened with the equivalent of a gasp. Then he exhaled and a small amount of smoke escaped.

'The Cold Woman! Fire Bringer!' He rattled in astonishment. *'How?'*

The Alpha emerged into the piercing morning light. He saw a lone young blue-haired woman walking cautiously toward him, her arms half-raised. There were crystals in her palms, and they had a slight glow to them.

Can you hear me, Great One?

The Alpha was momentarily shaken. The female's voice did not come from her lips, but he heard it in his thoughts. It sounded like it was right next to his ears, a regular voice with a submerged accordance speaking at the same time.

'Who are you? How are you speaking with me?'

The young woman smiled nervously. She heard his answer. Her movements were hesitant and fearful. Beads of sweat were evident on her forehead and cheeks, but her face was a mask of calm.

I am Jordan SnowFire.

'How do you know the Cold Woman, the Fire Bringer? Why do you bear her name?'

I am . . . her daughter.

'Why do you seek my kind?'

A war has come to . . . the people I protect. A large and terrible army wants to destroy us. I need your help to stop them.

'Why? Your power is more than ours. You have destroyed many tribes!'

That was my mother. I am still young and learning. I will do all I can to protect my people. But I must call on allies—trusted ones—who can help me. Please, Great One, will you and your family aid me?

The Alpha stood motionless for many seconds. Then he paced in front of the entrance of the cave for even longer as the twin stars continued to rise. Jordan stayed very still awaiting his response. He walked down to where she stood. He looked her in the eyes and lowered his head to the ground.

'Get on my back, Fire Bringer. Show me this threat. Then I will give you my answer.'

―――――――

The last time Jordan rode a Deathwing, it nearly killed her. This time, the experience was much more tolerable. Flying at these dizzying speeds brought back memories of being on roller coasters as a child. The Alpha relaxed some as he sensed her excitement and joy. She also felt something akin to protectiveness from the giant black dragon. It wasn't anything like what a pet might feel toward its owner. It was closer to what a parent might feel towards a child. And it was as much a surprise to him as it was to her.

They flew deeper into Kastadi territory and already, Jordan and the Alpha had seen four communities wiped out by the fighting. All that remained was smoke, debris, and bodies. At least two hundred people had been exterminated. Even with so much destruction and carnage, Jordan and the Alpha had not yet reached the main force of the Gulstaa.

Jordan respected the Kastadi. Their Chief had saved her life once. It was painful to see these strong but gentle giants laid waste and left as food for beasts. It was especially difficult to see the children. She knew she had to stay strong and focused. But in honor of these proven allies, Jordan did not wipe the tears from her cheeks when they fell.

Still, she knew she had to focus her mind on other things, or she would be overwhelmed by the losses.

How far back does the relationship between SnowFire and the Deathwings go?

'Since the days when my kind were new to this world. Long ago,' the Alpha responded. *'Every hatchling is told the story of the Cold Woman, the Fire Bringer. My mate and I will soon share it with our own offspring when they hatch.'*

Will you tell me the story? I do not know it, Jordan admitted.

'Your mother did not tell you of us?' the Alpha asked, surprised.

My mother has always been . . . distant. We do not speak often, she admitted.

The Alpha let forth a burst of hot gases. Jordan didn't know whether that was a laugh or merely the Deathwing clearing his throat.

'I understand, SnowFireChild,' the Alpha said. *'The Cold Woman can be hard to understand. It would please me to share the tale with you.'*

Thank you.

As they flew through some thick clouds in the green-tinted sky, the Alpha seemed to relax and slow down a little. Jordan could somehow understand that he was immersing his memories in this pivotal story of his people. She could feel his pride at what this represented to them. And at the same time, it humbled him and brought forth many emotions from deep within. She was amazed and supremely curious.

'In those days, so long ago, we were strong and fast but there were not so many of us,' the Alpha began. *'The two-legged ones hunted us for food and sport. They were clever and fierce. They did not have to be strong when there were so many of them. We would kill two or three, yet ten more would take their place and wear us down.*

'Our ancestors lost hope. They feared the next hatchlings might be the last of us,' he continued. *'But then the Cold Woman walked among us. She spoke to us in our own words. She did not fear or hate us. She told us that word of our kind had reached her. And she wanted to help us.'*

That's . . . incredible! Why did she want to help you, Great One?

'She said we were different from all the others on this world, as she was. She wanted us to continue. So, she touched the chest of an Alpha like me. And there was a stirring within all of my kind.'

What did she do? Jordan asked.

'She gave us the dark fire which we have had within us ever since. That is why we call her—and you—Fire Bringer. You are the daughter of SnowFire. We are grateful to the Fire Bringer for helping us defend ourselves, for helping us continue. That is why I help you now.'

At first, Jordan didn't know how to respond. What SnowFire had done was extraordinary, using her own power to help ensure the survival of a species. Did SnowFire feel a singular kinship to these creatures because they were so few in number, on the verge of extinction? Or was it something else?

I . . . am honored. And I am also grateful for . . . my mother's actions. Your kind deserves to continue. You are brave and strong.

The Alpha did not respond to Jordan verbally. But in her mind, she felt the warmth that her words had inspired.

'I have felt your . . . pain at the loss of the allies you call Kah-stah-dee and I have seen what these Gool-stah have done to them,' the Alpha said, resolute. *'I still wish to see their army, to know how many of them threaten you. But know this, Fire Bringer: whether they have one thousand or many hundreds of thousands, we will aid you.'*

Thank you, Great One! I am very pleased to have your family's help!

'You do not understand, so I will make clear,' the Alpha replied more emphatically. *'Not just my family. All of my kind will aid you!'*

What?

'I have shared what I have learned with them. All are as one towards your request. We will aid the Fire Bringer!'

16

EMERGENCE

THE BEATING OF THE DRUMS grew louder, almost thunderous, within the main Gulstaa encampment. Ilsketh raised her alcohol-filled tankard above her head, causing some of its contents to spill on herself and those around her. She shouted her joy to the sky as she danced to the music near the blazing bonfire at the center of the garrison, laughing with the men and women under her command.

It had been a successful day, as far as she and her soldiers were concerned. The Gulstaa army had pushed into another Kastadi province and smashed all resistance with minimal difficulty. Now, they were the only living tribe for miles in every direction. Ilsketh had ordered a feast prepared to celebrate their good fortune in this glorious campaign. She wasn't foolish enough to declare victory, since they had not yet encountered the Mokta. But this feeling was good enough. And the warriors deserved to be commended for their works.

An hour later, she walked away from the festivities, needing to clear her spinning head. She had not been drunk like this in several years. And while it felt good to relax and enjoy herself with the soldiers, she did not like feeling out of control. She motioned a sentry to join her and walked to the edge of the camp. The night breeze was cold and sobering, although she could still feel the warmth from the liquor mixing with roasted meat and vegetables in her belly.

She closed her eyes and leaned upon one of the wooden posts marking the entrance. A moment later, she thought she heard something in the sky. Staring upwards, she saw what looked like a large black bird very high up. It was more graceful than any feathered creature she'd ever seen.

"Is that a dragon?" Ilsketh said, curious.

The sentry focused his eyes where she was looking. Then he gasped.

"Heng Da, that is a Deathwing!" the sentry cried. "We must—"

Ilsketh put both hands on the sentry's shoulders and looked in his eyes, attempting to calm the terrified man with her own peaceful smile.

"Do not worry, soldier, he is too far up. He will not attack us from there," Ilsketh consoled. "And our arrows will not fly that far. Perhaps he is simply as curious about us as I am of him. Let him be."

Her advice was sound. Fighting a Deathwing was never a safe course of action. It was to be avoided if possible.

"Yes, Heng Da."

————

The Alpha could feel everything she felt. And while he did not entirely understand why she was so upset, he knew enough. Inwardly, Jordan seethed with rage. Tears born of her fury streamed down her face and she held onto the Alpha's neck tightly with both arms, unable to speak. The sight of her foes celebrating a massacre tore at her inwardly. The Alpha maintained his silence out of respect, to allow her time. He continued to fly away from the stronghold of the Fire Bringer's enemy, sharing what she felt with the rest of his people. The Alpha could sense that she longed for the comfort of her mate, so he flew back to his mountain.

He landed gently and waited for her to dismount. She had regained some of her composure and resolve, most of her tears having dried. She looked up at the Alpha with gratitude and respect.

Thank you, Great One. I may have need of you tomorrow.

'*I will be here,*' the Alpha replied. '*Just call out to me.*'

Jordan bowed her head towards the Alpha and turned. Then she walked away towards her own camp, somewhat unsteadily.

———

Bopol stood and walked briskly to meet her, visibly overjoyed that she had returned safely. But when he saw her expression, the look in her eyes, he ran to her and held her. They walked slowly back to their camp, Jordan leaning on him. He held her close, occasionally kissing the top of her head and hugging her as they continued.

A moment later, she sat on the ground near the campfire next to Bopol and faced the sentries. She gave them a wan smile.

"I was successful in making contact with the Deathwings," she relayed. "We will have the support of not just this immediate group but all Deathwings on Algoran."

"That is incredible!" Bopol uttered. "How did you accomplish that?"

"I will have to explain in detail another time," Jordan replied softly.

"I know it could not have been easy for you," Bopol said.

"The hard part was flying over the Gulstaa main camp and back."

The memory choked her words and re-ignited her outrage. She looked downward and her mouth twisted into a near-snarl.

"They were so ecstatic with their victory! The whole encampment was one huge celebration." Jordan spat the words. "We flew over village after burning village . . . it took all of my will not to order the Deathwing to attack right then . . . "

Jordan had to stop and put her head in her hands, grieving. She heard one of the sentries address Bopol and hand him a hot drink to give to her.

"Your actions were wise, Chieftess," Bopol interjected, offering the drink but she shook her head. "You lived to report what you observed. We know where they are now and likely where they are going."

Bopol took a sip of the drink and then offered it to her again. This time, she took a sip and tried to clear her thoughts. But she couldn't. Jordan leaned forward to make eye contact with everyone.

"I have never wanted to kill before today," she admitted, the campfire glaring against her eyes. "But these Gulstaa must be stopped. And with the Deathwings, we have a real chance of doing that."

"We will support you, however you lead us," Bopol declared boldly, reflecting the group's loyalty. Then he spoke more softly. "But you need rest."

"Yes," she agreed, looking at everyone. "We will talk again in the morning."

————————

That night, Jordan dreamed of Erica Melendez for the first time in years. They were children again, in Jordan's room on Earth, no more than eight or nine years old. Jordan's long brown hair was pulled into twin tails while Erica's was surprisingly short. They both wore t-shirts and blue jeans. Jordan was sitting backwards on a rolling chair facing Erica, who was lying back on Jordan's bed. Mid-morning summer sunlight was shining through the window, causing the blinds to form unique long shadows on the walls.

"Will it be you or me who gets married first?" Erica asked innocently.

Jordan laughed. "It will be me, of course!"

"Why you? I might get married first!"

"Well, sure, maybe."

"'Maybe?'"

She winked at Erica. "If you get married first, I'll be happy for you!" Jordan assured.

"But you don't think it'll happen," Erica pouted.

"It's not that. I just feel like I'll get married first."

"Why?"

"I dunno. I think he'll be tall and strong, handsome," Jordan continued. "But I don't think he'll talk too much."

"Oooh, so manly!" Erica mocked, rolling her eyes. "Will he cook for you, too?"

"Maybe!"

They both fell into a giggle fit for a minute.

"Well, I don't know what kind of guy I'll like," Erica considered. "But he needs to understand me. If he can do that—and if he loves me—then I'll marry him."

Confused, Jordan replied, "That's not really romantic, but okay."

"You're gonna have a lot of kids, aren't you, Jordan?"

"Maybe. How about you?"

"I dunno. One or two?"

"Okay, I can see that." Jordan nodded.

Suddenly, without changing their positions, Jordan and Erica became young women. They looked the way they did when they reunited shortly before they both left Earth.

"You found your dream guy," Erica confirmed. "And you married first."

"Who knew he would turn out to be an alien?" Jordan quipped.

"Or that you'd be living together on his world?" Erica added.

"Do you still want to get married, Erica?"

Erica smiled as she pondered the idea. "I think so," she concluded. "I almost did, a couple of years ago. But it didn't work out."

"I'm sorry," Jordan responded.

"I don't know if I'd be any good with kids, though."

"Sure you would."

"I didn't have good examples in my own parents. I wouldn't wish that on any child."

"You're not your parents," Jordan assured.

"No . . . I'm not," Erica replied with a slight smile.

Then the room went dark. Jordan felt a momentary sense of vertigo. When the spinning abated, Algoran came into view. At a pace similar to riding the Deathwing Alpha, she sensed herself speed across fields and over mountains into Kastadi territory.

Now feeling like an observer in her own dream, she stood outside a village which had clearly been devastated in a recent skirmish. She saw Miitas in the distance speaking with someone—a human woman! Erica? Erica was alive! She had changed some since Jordan last saw her. She had blue hair and ice-colored eyes like her own, with SnowFire jewels fused to her neck. She seemed strong and self-assured. But she also looked like the conflict had hardened her.

"Our scouts have sent us a warning," Miitas told Erica. "More Gulstaa are coming. They will be here soon!"

"Do we have time to get Vakar and the other wounded out of here before they arrive?" Erica replied.

Miitas looked up and saw a dissipating smoke signal in the distance.

"No, we will not have time," Miitas said. "We will have to defend this village—and you."

Erica swallowed hard. "How long before they get here?"

"I can already hear the warcry of the Gulstaa," Miitas answered, regret evident in her voice. "They will soon approach in formation. Our two scouts have already sacrificed their lives to buy us time. Still, I give you my word: my soldiers and I will give our all."

"Will we make it?"

"Our chances of survival are not good."

Erica pulled out a dagger from her robe. She held it clumsily but with conviction.

"I am no warrior, but I will defend my daughter with my life!" Erica said. "And Vakar, too, if I can."

"Daughter?" Jordan repeated to herself, astounded. No one heard her. It did not surprise Jordan that she understood both the Mokta and Ullvarr languages that the two women were speaking. It was no different than when she communicated with the Deathwing Alpha.

Miitas smiled. "I can see why Jorr-Don is your friend. You have fire!"

"I fight for what is mine," Erica said.

"Well said," Miitas added. "I will have Caador assist you."

Within minutes, the Gulstaa military closed in on their position. The Mokta and Kastadi warriors were prepared to fight with all their might but they were hopelessly outnumbered.

———————

Jordan awoke in a panic, cold sweat matted to her forehead, hair, and back. She was disoriented from not knowing where she was and shocked that it was already mid-morning. She near-tumbled outside her tent, still wearing her Chieftess robes from the previous night. Bopol was not in sight but the four sentries were close. She ran to one of them.

"Why was I not woken sooner?" Jordan shouted.

"Bopol was concerned for you," the female sentry replied. "We were told not to wake you."

Frustrated and haunted by an inescapable feeling that her dream was somehow really going to come true soon, that meant Erica was nearby with Miitas and her troops. And they were all in terrible danger from the Gulstaa.

Focusing her concentration, Jordan broke into a run towards the mountain den of the Deathwing Alpha.

"Chieftess, you should stay here until Bopol returns!" the sentry cried out, running after her. "It will be safer!"

"If you want to stop me, you will have to catch me!" Jordan answered, increasing her pace.

It took Jordan less than a half hour to reach the entrance to the Alpha's den. He was waiting for her, his head lowered to make it easier for her to mount his back. With one leap, she ascended the Alpha and they took off at breakneck speed.

'I will have you to your friend very soon, Fire Bringer!' the Alpha thought to her. *'My mate and siblings are right behind us.'*

Her anger rose as a grimace crossed her face.

I only need you to do one thing, Jordan thought. *Destroy any Gulstaa you see!*

Twenty minutes into their flight, Jordan spotted the ruined village along with the Mokta and Kastadi soldiers posted there. The battalion of Gulstaa soldiers was ready to strike them down.

The Alpha circled once before beginning his descent, targeting the Gulstaa. Understanding what the Alpha was about to do, Jordan leaned against his neck and held on as tightly as she could. When he unleashed his black flames, it was like flying through an explosion. She could feel the heat rushing against her arms, legs, and face. She expected it to hurt but it didn't. Instead, it exhilarated her. She felt an uncharacteristic joy as she watched the Gulstaa men and women catch fire and turn to ash. She lifted her right arm and howled in triumph.

Take me lower! she thought.

'Yes, *Fire Bringer*,' he replied.

She crouched forward on his back as he raced towards the surface, acting on instincts she didn't know she possessed. The Alpha took her towards a large swath of soldiers. With a loud battle cry that shrieked from deep within her, Jordan vaulted from the Alpha towards a man easily twice her size. Consumed by rage and bloodlust, she didn't care that she had no weapon. She slammed into the man, knocking him to the ground. She seized his giant axe and yanked it from his grip with no effort, using raw strength she had never had until now. Then she whirled around and sliced into him with his own weapon.

She sensed that her wide, furious eyes were glowing, as were the jewels in her hands, but that didn't matter to her. Her blue hair flowed behind her, seeming to flicker all around her like flames. Her movements were fluid as she moved from one soldier to the next. She slashed some with her axe and others she slammed her fist into their chests or heads. It caused a sickening crack each time, killing them instantly. Never once did she stop, slow down, or even breathe hard.

She was aware on some level that Miitas, Erica, and the other Mokta and Kastadi soldiers were watching this one-sided battle in stunned silence. She was no longer the gentle and caring person they had known. She had become her SnowFire namesake.

Jordan picked up a sword from another fallen soldier in her other hand and charged into another group of Gulstaa. Using the sword and axe at the same time, she began to almost dance in a circular pattern. Time blurred for her. All she knew was laughter, the spinning of blades, a constant stream of bloodletting and the loud thumping of her own heartbeat. It was an intoxicating combination.

"Jordan! STOP!"

The pleading voice was Erica's, speaking in English. It broke Jordan out of her near-trancelike state and she came to an immediate halt.

Subdued at Jordan's feet was the sole surviving, astonished female Gulstaa soldier. She was six-feet tall and very muscular. The soldier was holding her hand over a deep gash in her right leg inflicted by the heavy sword Jordan was wielding. She was clearly in pain but trying not to show it. And she was clearly afraid, though Jordan had to admire how well the soldier masked that fact.

"Who—what *are* you?" the Gulstaa exclaimed in her own language.

Jordan understood her.

"I am Jordan SnowFire," Jordan answered, her voice sounding like more than one person speaking.

The soldier understood Jordan.

"SnowFire is an old story!" the soldier retorted. "You cannot be her! And yet what you have done—I do not understand!"

Jordan spotted Miitas and motioned for her to come over. Miitas did as she was commanded but looked afraid of Jordan.

"Bandage this soldier's leg and send her back to her people," Jordan commanded.

"Yes, Chieftess," Miitas replied stiffly.

Jordan crouched down next to the Gulstaa soldier.

"I want you to take a message to your leader," Jordan suggested.

The Gulstaa soldier nodded and listened.

A moment later, two Mokta soldiers picked up the Gulstaa warrior and began to take her to receive medical treatment. The soldier lifted her head to speak toward Jordan.

"I will convey your message," the soldier responded. "But my Heng Da will not relent."

"Remind her about the Qui Tol people," Jordan added.

"Who are the Qui Tol people?" the soldier asked.

"Exactly," Jordan replied resolutely. "And that could happen to the Gulstaa if she does not heed my warning."

Miitas remained silently at Jordan's side but the fear remained in her eyes.

Jordan faced Erica, happy to finally be reunited with the friend she'd thought lost forever. However, she did not expect the look of horror in Erica's eyes. It gave her pause, confusing her.

"What is it? What's wrong?" Jordan asked.

"How can you ask that?" Erica responded, her voice just above a whisper. "Jordan, look at yourself! What have you done?"

Jordan looked down at her hair, arms, hands, and clothing. They were soaked in other people's blood. She saw the damaged axe and chipped sword on the ground, still stained with gore. Jordan backed up slowly, now starting to tremble with adrenaline and fear. She could feel where swords and spears had sliced across or pierced her own skin. There was soreness from blunt impacts, but she had no broken bones. Her wounds were already healing at an incredible rate.

Feeling as if the world was moving in slow motion, Jordan turned past her friends and colleagues only to witness the surrounding ground cluttered with Gulstaa corpses, body parts, bones, and blood. Mixed in were ash piles created by the black fire of the Deathwings she had unleashed on the unprepared soldiers. That charnel sight reminded her of the decimated bodies she had seen strewn across the Onchei dining hall in the castle of Queen Amstar. It sent chills down her body. And with that sensation came an alarming realization.

"This is what SnowFire does! This is what she is capable of . . . what I am capable of," Jordan uttered weakly, walking forward with heavy steps. "I really have become her daughter."

Sweat beaded Erica's brow and she covered her mouth with one hand.

"This is what she gave me," Jordan continued. "And this is what happens when I let it out."

The Alpha stood nearby, his expression surprisingly compassionate. The other three Deathwings were perched at a nearby hill.

She sat on the ground, blinking her eyes in disbelief. Her mind was not able to fully process what she had done. She looked at the palms of her hands, still faintly glowing, then she closed her eyes.

"I am a monster," Jordan said flatly. "I have become a monster."

Several long seconds passed. Only the sounds of the wind and the Alpha's loud breathing could be heard. It was as if everyone else was holding their breath and remaining perfectly still.

"No, you haven't," Erica conveyed in English, walking towards her. "You are no more a monster than I am. You're Jordan Lewis . . . and you're still my friend."

"Erica, how can you say that after seeing all this?" Jordan replied in English, lifting her head.

"You came here to save us, didn't you?" Erica asked.

"Yes."

"And the soldiers you killed, they were the same ones who destroyed my people, the Ullvarr . . . and the Kastadi, right?"

Somewhere in the back of her mind, Jordan acknowledged that Erica had called the Ullvarr her people.

"Yes," Jordan answered.

"And you listened to me," Erica continued. "You snapped out of it. You're yourself again, aren't you?"

"Yes."

Erica walked up to Jordan and helped her stand up. Then she hugged her.

"This is war. It brings out the worst—and sometimes the best—in all of us," Erica declared. "And if no one else tells you this, I will: Thank you for saving us, Jordan."

17

PERSPECTIVES

BOPOL RACED ALONG, HIS SUPERIOR physique allowing him to push himself, maintaining a brisk pace that matched the scout which Miitas had sent to him. Her message had been brief and to the point. "Follow the scout, you are needed." When his sister said little, something was terribly wrong. He and the scout made a two-day journey in twelve hours. The sentries who had been with him would catch up at their own speed.

Sweating profusely and somewhat worn, he could see billowing black smoke from quite a distance and once he and the scout got closer, he could smell the stench of burning flesh and bone. With some difficulty, he forced his imagination to remain still, blocking out scenarios that involved Jordan or those with her. He reminded himself that she had departed on a Deathwing and was probably safe. Yet he wondered what could have happened.

As he neared the Kastadi village, Kastadi and Mokta warriors were tending a mass burning of Gulstaa bodies in a cleared field. Miitas supervised them but when she saw her brother running towards them, she delegated her task and walked to meet him.

She looked half-exhausted. Foregoing any semblance of protocol, she embraced Bopol. When he looked into her eyes, he saw a fear that was unfamiliar. It bordered on desperation, which he had never seen in Miitas before.

"What happened?" asked Bopol.

"We should talk in private," Miitas responded.

Seeing that there was no immediate threat, he followed his sister. She led him to one of the abandoned houses. Its walls were damaged, and part of the roof had collapsed. The broken furniture lay in pieces on the ground. Even so, it afforded a degree of seclusion for her purposes. Miitas took a moment to collect her thoughts.

"We met with the Kastadi at this village and then encountered the only three Ullvarr to survive the Gulstaa: an injured soldier, a female child, and Jorr-Don's friend, Eree-Kah," Miitas began.

"The one from Errrth?"

"The same," Miitas acknowledged, nodding. "She is like Jorr-Don, touched by SnowFire. She had been living with the Ullvarr."

"Hm, that would explain why we did not find her," Bopol considered.

"Eree-Kah has claimed the orphaned Ullvarr girl as her daughter," Miitas continued. "As the only qualified adult among the survivors, she also offered peace on behalf of the Ullvarr. She wants to aid us against the Gulstaa."

"Interesting!" Bopol noted. "But it does make sense. A new and present threat would outweigh any old feuds."

"Yes," Miitas agreed. "Then the Gulstaa advanced on us, at least one hundred strong, compared to our thirty. I was prepared to die defending Eree-Kah and her family . . . but Jorr-Don arrived. She . . . saved us."

Miitas was perhaps the most emotionally strong woman Bopol had ever known. She had seen many conflicts and bore many scars.

She could separate herself from the grim tasks she sometimes had to perform in defense of the Mokta. At the same time, she was very close to her mate of seventeen cycles and a loving gemta to her son. She maintained a balance in her life that Bopol deeply respected.

So, when Miitas sunk to her knees and appeared on the verge of tears, it was both unsettling and heart-wrenching to him. Her eyes looked more troubled than before, widening in remembrance.

"What is wrong?" Bopol asked her.

It took a few seconds for Miitas to respond.

"Jorr-Don commanded the Deathwing to attack the Gulstaa and it burned perhaps twenty, killing them. Then Jorr-Don leaped off the beast with a terrifying scream. She tore into the Gulstaa like a rampaging Sasstonn! She had the strength of many Mokta. She destroyed them—all of them—except one," Miitas recalled, her terror evident. "When she fought, it was like nothing I have ever seen. Having heard the legends, I felt as though I was watching SnowFire herself in all her wrath. Her gems lit up, as did her eyes, and brother, her hair was like blue flame! Do you understand what I am saying?"

Bopol fully comprehended his sister's words and nodded slowly.

"Jorr-Don was a different woman. She could not be stopped," Miitas continued. "And she enjoyed the killing! She enjoyed it . . . so much."

Miitas had to take another few seconds to restore a degree of calm to her mind.

"I have killed many times in my life. I have protected the village, the Chieftess, and the mountain. But I have never taken pleasure in it," she added. "I just did what was needed, no more. Chieftess taught us that at an early age. We are at war now, so we will fight to defend our land and our allies. This . . . was different."

His heart raced as he listened to his sister's words. He looked up through the broken roof to the slow-moving clouds traveling westward on the unseen winds.

"Is she herself again now?" he asked.

"Yes. She has been closed away in one of the houses," Miitas replied. "Eree-Kah visits and speaks with her."

Jorr-Don, were you possessed by SnowFire? Or . . . is this what you are becoming? Have we accomplished so much together, only to lose you to whatever SnowFire did when she shared her blood with you?

Just then, Bopol was ashamed at his thoughts. He tried to put himself in his mate's position and wondered how she would feel. He remembered Jordan's remorse at the loss of a single life only a few cycles earlier. That had been an accident and it tore her apart. He knew how angry she had been recently at the atrocities of the Gulstaa. It was not difficult to see her being pushed too far.

Am I truly so easily discouraged? I am the one who should believe in her when no one else does.

Bopol offered a hand to Miitas to help her stand up. She took it and rose to her feet, still rattled. When he spoke, it was with sincerity and conviction.

"I know what you saw has shaken you," Bopol said. "But consider this: as hard as it was for you to see, Jorr-Don did these things. She has to live with that. Can you imagine, knowing Jorr-Don as you do, how much worse this must be for her?"

Now he saw it was Miitas' turn to feel abased. Her eyes raced back and forth frantically. He imagined her comparing her combat experiences prior to the Gulstaa assault to Jordan's during the battle. Her tears welled up, she put her hand to her mouth and gasped.

Erica took a bite from the dry bread, winced, and then dipped it in her bowl of soup before trying it again. She was much more satisfied.

"You should try this, Jordan. It's a lot better with the soup," Erica suggested in English.

They were inside the Kastadi house that Erica had chosen as a temporary residence. Erica had encouraged Pamela to spend time with Vakar. Erica had been trying to get through to Jordan but so far, had not succeeded. Jordan had been lying on the floor for hours, not really moving or talking. They had come here after Erica had led Jordan to a nearby stream to clean off the blood and gore from her person and clothing. Jordan had been in shock, not resisting but not responding, either.

Erica had tried talking about the past: how technology had changed in the four years Jordan was gone; the growing relationship between Jordan's brother, Mark, and Erica's cousin, Kayla; different jobs Erica had held; and even her relationship with Hal Nowak. If Jordan heard any of it, she gave no indication.

Then Erica had some fresh inspiration and brightened at the thought.

"Miitas told me that you have children but there wasn't time to go into detail," Erica shared. "Can you tell me about them?"

Jordan's eyes blinked suddenly, and she looked in Erica's direction. "My . . . children?"

Erica almost startled at hearing Jordan's voice.

"I'd like to know all about them," Erica answered, recovering her smile. "You know, since we're both moms now."

Jordan sat up on her elbows, still looking disoriented. She closed her eyes, as if searching her memory.

"That is right. You told Miitas . . . you would defend your daughter."

"I did tell her that. How did you know?"

"I saw it in a dream," Jordan semi-mumbled.

Erica raised an eyebrow at that. That would make for a strange discussion another time.

"I was taken in by the Ullvarr. The woman who helped me adjust to life here, her name was Kalami," Erica continued. "She had a daughter named Makazi. Makazi's an orphan now. She asked me to be her mother and I agreed. She's ten."

"Makazi?" Jordan repeated.

"Well, she asked me to give her an Earth name," Erica added. "So, I call her Pamela."

Jordan cracked her first smile. It was weak but genuine.

"It's a shame you cannot tell our friend Pamela Leibowitz that you named an alien child after her." Jordan snickered. "She would love that."

"I'll try to remember the next time I'm in the neighborhood," Erica quipped. "Now, your turn."

Jordan nodded, lifting her tired eyes. "I have a son. We named him Arrow. He is five."

"After your dad's nickname? Wow."

"The last time I saw you, before we got separated, I was already pregnant with him. I just did not know it yet," Jordan said. "I also have a daughter named Jasta. She was born ninety moonturns ago."

"And Bopol . . . your mate?"

"My husband is well. He has been very good to me," Jordan related warmly. Then her mood plummeted drastically. "Today, I do not feel like I deserve him . . . or my kids."

Erica recognized where the conversation was starting to go. She put down her bowl and went straight to Jordan, grabbing her shoulders and looking her in the eyes.

"I want you to hear me, Jordan Lewis. You can't blame yourself for what happened today!"

"Oh? Who should I blame then? The soldiers I ripped to shreds? Their leader, who is not here?"

"It's not time for blame! Don't you get it?!" Erica shouted. "There's still a war going on and you're a Chieftess! Your people, the Mokta, need you. The Kastadi need you. We few Ullvarr need you. Your husband and kids need you!"

"But I turned into a monster out there!"

Erica stood up, still maintaining eye contact with Jordan. "Maybe I'm the wrong person to talk to about this but I saw other Gulstaa smash through our village in the Ullvarr lands. They beat and stabbed children, old people, and eventually, everyone. Only Pamela, Vakar, and I survived and fled. To me, the Gulstaa are monsters. And maybe it *took* a monster to stop them. I won't shed any tears that they're gone."

Jordan blinked several times before she found words to respond. "That is . . . pretty cold, Erica."

Erica said nothing else. Jordan stood up and dusted herself off. She took a few seconds to stretch her neck from side to side, eliciting a couple of tension-releasing pops. Then her equally icy eyes looked right into Erica's.

"But you are right about one thing: I do not have the luxury of grieving over my actions right now. Too many people need me."

18

A MESSAGE DELIVERED

TEKALA USMETH GRITTED HER TEETH and continued her slow limp towards the Gulstaa encampment ahead. It was late and the rolling grassy terrain had made the trek more arduous than she anticipated. Worse, the gash in her leg was bleeding again, potentially catching the attention of predators. None of that mattered to her.

She kept her blurring vision focused on the firelight emanating from the walls less than a kilometer distant. Her breathing was labored, and she was probably feverish. However, she could not allow herself to die until she reached the Heng Da.

When she felt she could go no further, she took a small curved metal horn from her belt and put it to her lips. With all her waning might, she blew into that signaling device, which made a shrill pitch sure to be heard by her fellow soldiers at the barracks. As she fell to her knees, she heard commotion from within the camp and smiled. Now, all she had to do was wait for them to come get her. She had to stay alive and hold on long enough to relay the message.

Soon, two hulking Gulstaa sentries reached her position.

"It is Tekala from Advance Squad! She is badly wounded!" one sentry declared.

"Heng . . . Da!" Tekala uttered, her voice straining.

183

"We must take her to Heng Da!" the other sentry exclaimed. "Quickly! Before she dies!"

The more muscular of the two sentries hoisted Tekala over one shoulder and made a run for the encampment. The other sentry followed as quickly as he could and went to locate their leader, rousing her from sleep.

———————

When Ilsketh heard that it was Tekala asking for her, a warrior she had personally trained for Advance Squad, she ran to see what had happened. She was startled to see the young soldier so pale and weakened by her injuries, her blood pooling beneath her legs. Ilsketh crouched down next to Tekala.

"Tekala, I am here!" Ilsketh proclaimed. "Heng Da is here! Talk to me!"

Tekala smiled. "Heng Da . . . I made it. Must tell you—must—"

"What happened to you? Where is the rest of Advance Squad?"

"I am . . . the only one."

"What? Who killed them? The Kastadi? The Mokta?"

"Snow . . . Fire."

That name surprised Ilsketh.

"SnowFire? I thought that was a . . . a Mokta story?" Ilsketh questioned.

"Jorr-Don SnowFire . . . is real," Tekala gasped. "She killed us . . . with our own weapons."

"One woman killed an entire Gulstaa battalion?"

"She also . . . commanded four Deathwings. Those beasts burned and scattered us . . . and she slew the rest . . . crystals in her hands . . . eyes like the ice. Blue hair like fire. She let me go . . . to give a message to you."

"What was her message to me?"

Tekala took some deep breaths between coughing fits. She sweated profusely and Ilsketh could tell the woman did not have long to live. Tekala rallied the last of her strength.

"She said, 'Tell your leader . . . that Jorr-Don SnowFire is . . . Chieftess of the Mountain Mokta. The Mokta and Kastadi lands . . . are under my protection. If the Gulstaa do not want . . . to suffer defeat after defeat . . . like you saw here today, the Gulstaa must . . . depart my lands. No more harm will come to the Gulstaa . . . if you leave.'"

"You have done well, Tekala. Your name will be an honored one," Ilsketh acknowledged, taking the soldier's hand in hers. She squeezed it reassuringly.

"I told her you . . . would never . . . sur . . . rend . . . er—" Tekala released her last breath.

The nearest sentries picked up Tekala's body and took it to another part of the camp. They would prepare it for the Gulstaa death rites.

Ilsketh stood up and closed her eyes. She knew every battle could not be won in a war. But this wasn't just a loss of a single soldier or a portion of a battalion. Advance Squad was one hundred of her finest troops, most of whom had trained under her. For them to be attacked from above by Deathwing fire and dispatched by their own blades through the actions of one woman—it was a devastatingly crushing defeat. And Ilsketh took it very personally.

She clenched her fists in silent outrage. This affront could not go unchallenged.

Opening her eyes, she saw that Himstras had found her. He looked curious but solemn. He had long ago learned to read her moods, although her anger was more than apparent to anyone present.

"What do you know of the SnowFire legend?" she asked.

"SnowFire? I heard it many cycles ago during one of our battle campaigns," he replied. "A traveling old Mokta shared the story with me over some ale and a meal. The tale is said to be many thousands of cycles old. SnowFire is supposed to be some powerful creature from the Mountain where the Mokta now live. She became mates with their First Chief, and their descendants are the Mokta we know now."

"That is all?" Ilsketh queried.

"No, there is much more. This SnowFire is said to be an undefeated warrior with a terrible and frightening rage," Himstras continued. "It is claimed that she has destroyed whole races by sword and fire when they threatened the Mokta or provoked her wrath."

"Interesting. Did the old Mokta say what SnowFire looked like?"

"Yes, he did, actually," Himstras continued, intrigued by Ilsketh's strong curiosity. "He described her in detail. He said she was tall and slender yet very strong, with ice-blue eyes and long, deep blue hair. He even said, when she was in battle, her hair would light up like flames!"

Ilsketh felt ill for a moment. She stumbled backwards a few steps before righting herself.

"Heng Da, what is it? What is wrong?" Himstras wondered, very concerned.

"It seems that today, Advance Squad fought a legend," Ilsketh replied scornfully.

"Is that so? How did they fare?"

"They are all dead. Tekala made it back to give me the news before she perished."

Himstras looked at the fresh blood on the ground. "And she said it was SnowFire?" he asked.

"The woman who wiped out my soldiers called herself Jorr-Don SnowFire, Chieftess of the Mountain Mokta."

"That is not possible!"

"Eyes like ice, blue flaming hair. She killed the troops with their own blades," Ilsketh informed him. "Oh, and somehow, she commanded four Deathwings to attack our troops."

"That sounds like madness!" he exclaimed. "No one can master those beasts!"

Ilsketh then remembered the Deathwing that circled above the camp the night before. And she seethed.

"Last night, I saw one of those creatures high above the camp. It must have been her," Ilsketh fumed. "She knows where we are!"

"Then we should move immediately," Himstras replied. "Where do you want us to go?"

Ilsketh calmed herself and concentrated on her years of experience and training. She searched for the strategy that would best aid her people. And she found it.

"Move two battalions to our South and East to keep the Kastadi from attacking us on those fronts," she commanded. "We will seem to give this new Mokta Chieftess what she wants. We will withdraw to just inside Gulstaa territory."

"Heng Da, I do not understand?" Himstras replied.

"You do not? You taught me this strategy. Once we are inside our borders, I want our troops to send a message back to the Mokta through their actions," Ilsketh answered, her gaze as hard as any stone. "Burn the Kastadi and Ullvarr lands we conquered, make them a barren waste."

Himstras' eyes lit up with comprehension and he smiled. "Very good! You want to see if she will return to aid the Kastadi or if she will let them burn."

"Yes. If she comes to help them, we will attack the Mokta lands. But if she lets the Kastadi burn, she will make an enemy of them. They will not fight for the Mokta when we attack the Mokta."

"You always were my best student," Himstras boasted.

"We will separate fact from legend. We will even slay Deathwings if we have to." Ilsketh warmed inside, even though she could not outwardly show how much his praise pleased her. "Either Jorr-Don SnowFire will die by my hands or I will die by hers!"

ACT FOUR

STRATAGEMS

INTERLUDE III

SNOWFIRE STOOD OVER ERICA, WHO was sleeping next to her daughter. The winds were especially cold and harsh this night. Even with a heavy blanket, they occasionally shivered during deep slumber. The child was used to snuggling closer to her mother to feel just a little bit warmer. SnowFire smiled at the sight.

Heat emanated from her body and the temperature within the house rose to more comfortable levels. Erica slowly opened her eyes, blinking several times. She shifted her position, keeping Pamela behind her. When her eyes focused, she looked astonished.

"You!" Erica blurted in Ullvarr. "Are you here to taunt me like before? Or will you actually speak this time?"

"I am Snow and Fire."

The words were in Ullvarr. Erica looked pleased that she spoke to her this time but SnowFire could also see her resentment.

"Why are you here?" Erica asked.

"I wished to see my only living children, my daughters. I need to speak with you."

"You mean me and Jordan?"

SnowFire nodded.

"I do not know if Jordan will want to see you," Erica continued. "I'm not even sure that I want to see you."

"I understand," SnowFire replied sadly. "But this will be the only time we can talk. So, we must talk."

"What does that mean?"

"It means what it means. There is no more or less to it."

Erica appeared fully awake now. She slipped out of her daughter's embrace and stood to face SnowFire.

"Jordan is . . . very upset right now."

"I know. I felt her rage and passion from battle. She has begun to understand who and what she is, what she can do. And it frightens her."

"It frightened all of us."

"It should frighten you. Such a gift is a tremendous responsibility . . . and burden. The two of you hold the power of life and death. They can serve you well. But if used without understanding, you could lay waste to this entire world."

"Then why do this to us? Why give us these gifts?"

SnowFire allowed herself to relax. Erica looked surprised to see that.

"You remind me of my firstborn daughter. Her name was WiseEyes. She had a sensitive heart, as yours is." SnowFire paused. "And like both you and Jordan, she feared what she gained from me. She hid it away deep within herself. WiseEyes only used its strength to guide her through difficult times."

Erica paced contemplatively for a few moments.

"You must have questions. Ask them, I will answer," SnowFire offered.

"What exactly did you do to me and Jordan? Why do you call us your daughters? I know you saved Jordan's life and then she changed, but . . . nothing happened to me . . . right? I just woke up and was like this."

SnowFire's eyes gazed upon Pamela then returned to Erica.

"I shared my blood with you, just as I did with Jordan. That began a change within you. The scholars from your world might have better words to explain than mine. I have said that you became my daughters and it is true."

Erica did not look either resolved or convinced. She remained silent, encouraging SnowFire to continue.

SnowFire knew that Erica knew little of the Mokta or their history. When she spoke again, she made eye contact with the woman and hoped to convey the warmth and love she felt for her.

"For countless ages, I was merely the Spirit of the Mountain. I had no form, I simply existed and was content with what I was. It was only when the first Mokta, who would become my mate, earned my respect and trust that is when I created a body for myself, one capable of physical interaction.

"I allowed myself to know love and happiness. I bore children and raised them to adulthood. Then I watched them have their own children and grandchildren. In time, I also watched them all die, whether by the sword, disease, or from old age. I watched over my descendants, the Mokta, protecting them from their enemies until it was too painful to be around them. So, I removed myself and returned to the Mountain. But I was no longer a simple spirit, I could not go back to the way I had been before. I did not know how."

SnowFire hesitated briefly.

"Instead, I sought a new path, one that would allow the Mokta to continue and thrive like never before. I sought to increase their years, to live as long or perhaps even longer than my first children. I had been alone for so long; I missed my dear ones. After many failed efforts—with individual females from different tribes of this world—I found hope and promise in Jordan from Earth . . . and you, Erica. The two of you received my blood without becoming ill or dying. My blood replaced what you had been with what I am. Now, I am no longer alone in this world. And your children will inherit what I have given you."

Erica seemed amazed and somewhat bewildered to hear SnowFire speak like this.

"Why are you saying all of this to me? Shouldn't you be speaking with Jordan about this?" Erica asked.

"Jordan is standing outside the window, listening to every word I have said."

"What?"

Erica swung around towards the window. Jordan walked around the house and through the doorway. She did not look happy at all.

"Speak your thoughts, Jordan. I will hear you," SnowFire compelled her daughter.

"I—I hate what you have made me!" Jordan said in English, a tear running down her left cheek.

"You would not be here if I had not made you as you are," SnowFire replied softly in English. "You would not still have your mate or lived to bear children. You would not have returned to Earth or seen your family. Nor would you have met Erica again, who is now your sister."

"Instead, you made me a killing machine!" Jordan shouted. "I destroyed one hundred lives! My actions will grieve one hundred families!"

Pamela stirred. SnowFire sensed that the girl, pretending to be asleep, was frightened.

"You also saved fifty thousand Kastadi and Mokta lives," SnowFire continued. "The Gulstaa fear you . . . and with good reason. The Kastadi will tell new stories about you. You will become legend."

"I do not want to be a legend! I just want to be a good Chieftess, mate, and mother!"

"In my eyes, you already are," SnowFire declared with no small amount of pride.

"If that came from anyone else but you . . . " Jordan started to say, her eyes wild and glowing.

Jordan took a moment to calm herself, and then spoke again.

"My son, Arrow, he changed a snake into a SnowFire gem. And when that gem made his friend sick, he gave her some of his blood to save her. It made her like us."

"That ability is too dangerous for your son or anyone else to use again," SnowFire interjected. "When hordes of the Onchei soldiers encompassed me, I turned some of them and their weapons to crystal and shattered them with my fists!"

The mental imagery seemed to sicken Jordan momentarily. Erica stared at SnowFire in disbelief.

"As for the girl your son saved, she must be the last who receives the blood of Snow and Fire. It is meant for us alone," SnowFire insisted. "I was very deliberate when I chose the two of you. It is only by providence that the girl survived. Your descendants will have it but no one else. As Chieftess, Jordan, you must forbid the Mokta in this. Erica, you must observe it as well. There must be no sharing of your blood from this day forth."

SnowFire's command caused Jordan to visibly bristle with new resentment.

"It is amazing that you use the word *providence*," Jordan said. "Because the only providence that I know is associated with God. He is the one who spared me when I was at the point of death from the Mosdon poison."

SnowFire was confused by this. And Erica looked like she had no idea what Jordan was talking about.

"You encountered the Father of Spirits?" SnowFire asked. "I did not know. Would you tell me about this?"

Jordan's jaw dropped. She and Erica exchanged stunned glances.

"Y-y-you know about God?" Jordan stammered, looking to Erica for support.

Erica shrugged. "I've always been an atheist."

Jordan blinked then nodded, as if to tell her friend "oh, I forgot about that." She turned to face SnowFire before continuing.

"The poison was killing me; I could feel myself slipping away. I started thinking about God. And then everything became peaceful around me. I heard a voice."

"What—what did He tell you?" SnowFire asked.

"The voice asked me if I would be willing to spend the rest of my life on Algoran. It asked if I believed in God's power. And it asked if I believed His power could give me back my life, if I trusted Him. And I said 'yes.' That is the only reason I survived the Mosdon."

SnowFire pondered Jordan's words. It was troubling at first, but as she slowly considered them, she accepted them. Looking down, SnowFire smiled.

"The Father of Spirits bestows great mercy and honor to us." SnowFire paused. "He allowed all of this to occur and bound our lives together."

"Why?" Jordan asked.

"Only the Father knows that, Jordan."

Jordan looked skeptical, as if she could not believe she was having a conversation about God with SnowFire. Erica remained quiet with her arms crossed. She seemed to be carefully processing everything that was happening around her.

"All right. As Chieftess, I will forbid the sharing of our blood. What about the ability to make the SnowFire gems?"

"That is my duty. When I leave, I will take that ability with me. No one will have to bear that burden anymore."

SnowFire looked out the window at the night sky and then turned towards her daughters again. She took in a breath and then sighed.

"Jordan, Erica, I do not regret making you my children. But I did not handle it well. I did not stay with you and share your heritage with you. I did not tell you about your brothers and sisters from long ago, your history or my motivations. I forced you to find your own way, which you have done well. But I should have been there for you . . . and I was not. For that, I feel sorrow . . . and I ask your forgiveness."

Erica and Jordan appeared to be amazed by SnowFire's words. Not entirely sure what to do or say, both women stood there. Moments later, Erica nodded to SnowFire, but Jordan did not.

"Recently, the Father of Spirits visited me," SnowFire continued. "He spoke with me for some time. He reminded me who and what I really am—the Spirit of the Mokta Mountain. For so many cycles before creating a body for myself, I had been satisfied sheltering the lives of the plants and animals on the Mountain. I am the Mountain itself, literally its spirit. In taking physical form and joining with a mortal, I ensured that I would know the joys of life and the pains of loss. I no longer knew who or what I was, and I destroyed my own peace . . . until now."

"Has something changed?" Jordan asked, genuinely curious.

"Yes. The Father of Spirits has offered to help me. I will be leaving soon to return to the Mountain, where He will help me find rest . . . and a new peace."

"Will you be back?" Erica asked.

"No. I will abandon this form and become only a spirit once more," SnowFire said. "However, it would please me if you would visit me at the Mountain sometimes. You two will be able to sense me and perhaps your children will sense me as well."

"I do not have any biological children," Erica said.

"Not yet," SnowFire said.

Erica's eyes widened at the implications. Jordan seemed unfazed.

"SnowFire, I need to ask you something," Jordan said. "Erica and I, are we immortal?"

"You will be long-lived," SnowFire answered. "I do not know if you are immortal, the way I am."

"How long did our siblings live?" Jordan asked.

"Your sister, WinterSky, lived the longest of any of my children. She saw three hundred and ninety-two cycles. The others who died naturally saw between two hundred and fifty and three hundred cycles. I suspect you will live at least that long."

Overwhelmed by that revelation, Jordan fell back against a wall. She slid down to a sitting position. After taking in some deep breaths, she looked up at SnowFire.

"Is there any way you can make me have a normal, mortal life again?" Jordan pleaded.

"I cannot take back what I have given you, Jordan," SnowFire replied. "All I can tell you is that you will accept it . . . in time. You are not the first of my offspring to feel this way."

Erica walked over to Pamela and sat down. Then she looked back in SnowFire's direction.

SnowFire looked on Jordan and Erica with a sense of accomplishment, quietly drinking in the reality of having living children again. It did not matter whether they shared her views, loved or hated her. They existed and possessed their own potential. Jordan was already a protector of the Mokta and a young mother. Erica had survived the manipulations of the Ullvarr and the savagery of the Gulstaa. Moreover, she had adopted an Ullvarr child and been a help and consolation to her sister, Jordan. They were strong and loving. They would be her last offspring and it was more than satisfying.

Across the room, Jordan still looked troubled.

"I do not understand everything that has happened. And I will not pretend that I am happy about all of it," Jordan admitted. "But I am glad that you came here and talked with us."

"I owed that to both of you. I wish I could stay longer."

"I hope you find peace," Erica said sincerely.

"I wish the same for you," SnowFire replied, looking back at her. Then she turned her head. "And you as well, Jordan."

Jordan nodded, still seeming partly overwhelmed by this entire experience.

"My daughters." SnowFire beamed. "Be well."

Then she disappeared and the temperature returned to normal.

———————

Jordan and Erica stood there, occasionally looking at one another. It would take time for each of them to deal with the implications and consequences of SnowFire's visit, including accepting the fact that they had become biological sisters.

A few minutes later, Miitas burst into the house, her face looking amazed and surprisingly pleased.

"Chieftess, I have good news!" Miitas announced. "Our scouts report that the Gulstaa are in retreat! They are returning to their own lands!"

19

LIKE CHRISTMAS ON ALGORAN

ZEETRA FELT THE COOL BREEZE flow over her, the sunslight shining brightly overhead. The trees swayed in those gusts and birds took flight while the insects continued their buzzing and chirping. The young Onchei woman was surrounded by the entire tribe near the center of the village. And for the first time since she had come to live among the Mokta, she felt not only happy but welcome. Still, she was nervous.

She looked for courage in the tender, confident eyes of Jaidos, the Mokta man who had warmed her heart and eased her towards the love they now shared. He was tall and slender, athletic and intelligent. His long white hair was braided in the wavy traditional style of the tribe and he wore a silver matrimonial robe that matched hers. Jaidos had the ferocity of a warrior but chose to craft poetry and song. His velvet voice always soothed her, no matter what troubled her.

Months earlier, Chieftess Jordan had asked Jaidos to assist Zeetra in building the machines which would help protect the Mokta against the Gulstaa. During that time, she and Jaidos had become friends, opening up to one another. They had also learned and adjusted to each of their unique and quirky behaviors, such as her insistence on touching up or playing with his hair, even during work. Or his stopping everything and demanding silence if he had inspiration for prose or a melody. Such things could be irksome in their timing, but they were always short-lived. She found them better endured than resisted. Eventually, she told him how deeply she cared for him. He responded to her that he felt the same way. And now, Jordan was presiding over her wedding ceremony.

Prompted by a nod from the Chieftess, Jaidos pulled a dagger from his robes and quickly sliced across his right palm. He turned the hilt to face Zeetra and handed it to her. She followed his example, squinting at the discomfort but resolved to follow through. Then she placed her palm together with his, symbolizing their union.

"Jaidos and Zeetra, you have followed in the tradition of our ancestors and joined through blood," Jordan declared, beaming with joy. "May your days together be many!"

Many of the gathered smiled widely and shouted in delight at the Chieftess' proclamation. As was Mokta tradition in formal ceremonies like these, everyone in the crowd had been given small pieces of sweet flatbread called kelara. As she kissed her new mate, the guests threw the kelara over the happy couple in celebration and symbolism.

"May your hut be filled with the laughter of children!" Jordan added, putting her hand on Zeetra's shoulder.

"Chieftess, what?" Zeetra fluttered, her cheeks becoming warm as she blushed.

"I happen to know that your people and the Mokta are very . . . compatible." Jordan winked.

"We are very grateful for your kindness and support, Chieftess," Jaidos interjected. He put his arm around Zeetra and pulled her close. It was fairly clear to her that the Chieftess' idea appealed to him.

"I—I had not thought of having any children," Zeetra admitted, looking at Jaidos but speaking to Jordan.

"Well, now you have something new to think about." Jordan grinned.

"I suppose so!" Zeetra replied, blushing once more.

———————

Not wanting to make the newlywed couple any more uncomfortable, Jordan walked away from them, spotting Zoska and Lynsha nearby. Zoska was holding Jordan's daughter, Jasta, who was wrapped in a silky green blanket. Zoska looked uncharacteristically tired while Lynsha looked amused.

"For a moment, I thought I was listening to Zoska, Chieftess," Lynsha laughed. "You practically told Zeetra to follow Hosp's example of creating a large brood!"

"I did not!" Jordan insisted, somewhat defensively.

"Do not misunderstand. I also hope they are happy together and can have children, if that is what they want," Lynsha replied. "I just wondered if it was part of some larger strategy of yours."

Jordan looked towards the happy couple then back at Lynsha.

"No. My reasons are simple," Jordan continued. "Zeetra is the last of her kind. Because her people were the Qui Tol, she suffered in many ways. It was not easy for her to adjust to life with the Mokta. So, if she and Jaidos have offspring, she will not only have love, but will no longer be alone in this world."

"Did Kitranor give you that idea?" Zoska wondered aloud.

"She may have mentioned it in passing," Jordan considered. "And I thought it was a wonderful idea! I knew Jaidos had taken an interest in Zeetra. It did not take much to make sure they spent time together."

"You still think like a zala beast—er, Chieftess," Zoska joked, correcting herself to remain properly respectful to Jordan in public. "Now here, take your daughter. Her desire for attention is as great as yours."

Zoska handed the little girl to Jordan, who immediately pulled her close and cuddled her, kissing her softly. The baby shrieked with joy to be with her mother again.

"I know that you needed time to prepare and perform the mating ceremony," Zoska added. "But between this child's needs and those of my own offspring, I have not slept since yesterday. I intend to fix that problem now."

"Zoska, your daughter can spend time with me," Lynsha responded. "And Mootsa has agreed to watch your twins. That way, you can get your rest."

Jordan chuckled. "When did you become Zoska's personal caretaker, Lynsha?"

"Someone has to help her," Lynsha insisted. "With three young children, a mate like Reiban—"

"Wait a moment—" Zoska interjected.

"—and always taking in your children when tribal business consumes you—" Lynsha added.

"Now hold on—" Jordan rebuked.

"My point is, I have watched during these cycles as you have depended on Zoska, Chieftess," Lynsha explained, now sounding more respectful. "And I have decided to help her when I see that she has pushed herself too much."

"That is very kind of you, Lynsha," Jordan replied.

"I am grateful." Zoska smiled.

With that, Zoska and Lynsha departed. Jordan looked over at Zeetra once more.

"It is very important to not feel like you are completely alone," Jordan said quietly to herself.

Jordan spotted a slender young female scout entering the Mountain Mokta village, her face alarmed. She frantically searched for and located Miitas. After she reported to the village's military authority, Miitas appeared to thank the young woman. Now looking troubled, Miitas immediately walked over to Jordan.

"Chieftess!" she shouted. "I have just received urgent news from the Kastadi lands!"

Jordan, still holding her daughter, was not used to her title being expressed in such a dire way. It made her a little unsettled, so she took a breath and comported her features.

"What is this news, Miitas?" Jordan asked.

"They burn, Chieftess. The Gulstaa have left and set fire to the territories they conquered."

Jordan gasped. "How—why would they do such a thing? What good does that do them?"

"With respect, Chieftess, I believe it is a military tactic," Miitas explained. "Perhaps the Gulstaa want to see if you will send our forces to assist the Kastadi or if you will let them burn to protect the Mokta first."

Jordan closed her eyes, trying to contain her anger. Her jaw tightened. When she opened her eyes again, she called to Bopol and handed Jasta to him. Then she turned again to Miitas.

"We are not limited to two options," Jordan suggested. "There is another way."

"Chieftess, I do not understand?" Miitas replied.

"Do not be concerned. I will let you know my decision shortly."

"Yes, Chieftess."

Without looking back, Jordan walked with a brisk pace, already regretting what she was about to do. And yet, she felt there was no alternative. It took only a minute before she located Zeetra, who was dancing with Jaidos. One look at the Chieftess' stern expression and all festivities halted.

"Chieftess, what is it?" Zeetra asked.

"I need your help . . . right now. I wish I did not have to ask for it."

"Of course. I will help however I can."

Jaidos nodded his approval.

"The Gulstaa are burning the Kastadi lands. They think they can force us to commit forces to put out the fires or that we will stay here to save ourselves," Jordan continued. "But I know there is a third option. I just need to know what we can do. How can Onchei technology help us?"

Zeetra pondered the situation for a couple of minutes. Then she smiled unexpectedly.

"I think you are the answer to this situation, Chieftess," Zeetra responded. "And the technology can take you to where you need to be and back."

"Explain what you mean," Jordan inquired.

"I was thinking about the legend that the Deathwing shared with you. If SnowFire could give the Deathwings their fire, doesn't that mean she can take away fire as well?"

"Perhaps. But that was SnowFire. And that was over ten thousand cycles ago. How does that help us now?"

"You seem to have every power that she did. You can communicate with the Deathwings, summon great strength, perhaps you can make ice as well as fire."

Surprised, Jordan considered it for a moment. Then she walked over to a table. She imagined extremely cold winds and snow and projected those thoughts towards her right hand and touched the table.

She watched intently but nothing happened.

"Well, that was a nice idea," Jordan scowled, feeling more than slightly embarrassed. "Let us try something else?"

"What about me, Gemta—I mean, Chieftess?" Arrow interrupted, standing close by.

"What do you mean?" Jordan replied.

"Maybe I could turn that place into SnowFire gems, like I did the akasva?"

Jordan pulled her son close and hugged him.

"That is very kind of you to offer," Jordan replied in her most maternal tone. "But I do not think even you, as strong as you are, could turn a whole land into SnowFire gems. And I am not sure the Kastadi would be happy about how harmful those new gems would be to them."

"I just wanted to help," Arrow answered, looking up at his mother.

"I know," Jordan responded with a proud smile, putting her hands on his shoulders. "But we need to find another way."

Bopol cleared his throat to get the Chieftess' attention.

"What about the Deathwings?" Bopol asked. "Do you think they could put out the fires?"

"They might," Jordan mused. "But I do not trust the Gulstaa. They know about the Deathwings now and might try to target them. We should keep them in reserve for scouting and battle only."

"Yes, Chieftess," Bopol responded.

Kitranor walked over to Jordan, her expression thoughtful and well-considered.

"Your son was partly right," Kitranor added. "But we do not need to create new SnowFire gems. We need to use the ones we already have."

"From the Mountain itself?" Jordan asked.

"Yes. They will not harm anyone. But if they were thrown or dropped into the fire, the intense heat might cause the crystals to grow rapidly."

Jordan's eyes filled with wonder as she comprehended what Kitranor was suggesting.

"If that happened, the SnowFire gems could consume the fire's fuel while transforming the landscape into something benevolent!" Jordan exclaimed.

"And beautiful," Zeetra said under her breath.

Two hours later, the Deathwing Alpha took flight with the Fire Bringer atop him. She was carrying a fairly large bag of ancient SnowFire gems which she and her mate had collected from the Mokta Mountain. The Alpha had responded quickly to her mental call across the miles. Now she and the Alpha were approaching the wildfires that were tearing across the Kastadi lands.

The Alpha was confused by the Fire Bringer's mood. He could sense that she was deeply saddened by the devastation below but there was a small part of her that was contemplating something that bordered on amusement. He said nothing but listened carefully as she communicated with him.

This feels strange, Fire Bringer thought. *What we are doing reminds me of Santa Claus for some reason.*

'San-tah Kloss? What is that?'

It is a legend on the world I come from, a story told to children. It is about a happy, fat old man with a white beard who rode in a, um, cart pulled by . . . wild beasts. The cart was full of bags of gifts for children who had been good all year long. Santa would deliver the gifts to the children all over the world in one night every year. The next day, everyone would celebrate the holiday called Christmas.

'What is a hawl-eh-day?'

It is a day of . . . happiness and celebration.

'But there is something I do not understand. You are not old; you are quite young. And you are not a man, so you do not have a beard. You are not being pulled in a cart. And these gems are not gifts for children. So, how does what we are doing remind you of that story?'

Yet he says nothing about the fat part?

'Do you mean that by riding me and carrying a sack full of gems that alone is enough to remind you of a children's legend?' the Alpha thought, ignoring her sarcastic jab.

Fire Bringer sighed. *Yes, that alone is enough to remind me.*

'I . . . do not fully understand. But it is an interesting story and comparison.'

He could tell she was still slightly irritated. *See if you get invited over for holiday parties now, Rudolph.*

'What?'

She sighed. *Nevermind. I was trying to be funny, but our experiences and ways of life are so different. It . . . lost something in translation.*

'*I would like to understand. My kind enjoys humor as well.*'

The Alpha could sense a new realization from the Fire Bringer.

It is only fair that I explain that there is another, deeper meaning for Christmas.

'*Can you explain that meaning to me? I would like to know.*'

Sure. Many people celebrate on that day to observe the birth of the Son of God, whose name is Jesus.

'*Do* you *celebrate for that reason?*'

Fire Bringer seemed to be taken aback by his simple and sincere question. *I did not used to. I do not know if this will make sense or not, but I remember when I was a child, I would wake up early to run to a—a central room in our home where there was a Christmas tree. I would be very happy to receive gifts, supposedly left by Santa Claus. My mother would bake cookies and other treats while my father would prepare turkey or ham and other side dishes.*

'*I do not know the names of these things. but I understand they were foods. And that you enjoyed receiving gifts.*'

Fire Bringer became lost in memory. *My parents were never religious. I do not know if they even believed in God, but we never went to any church— a building where people worship God. We never attended any Christmas programs. But my brother and I learned to sing many Christmas carols— songs—including one about the birth of Jesus.*

'*Your words are hard to understand but I know your mother, she believes in one she calls Father of Spirits. My kind refers to such a being as He Who Made All. We sing to one another about many things but not about He Who Made All. And we have never been told of His offspring. What do you believe, Fire Bringer?*'

Fire Bringer exhaled slowly. *You do not ask easy questions, do you? Six cycles ago, I nearly died after being poisoned by the Mosdon. God—the Father of Spirits, He Who Made All—appeared to me and saved my life. I know He is real. And if He is real, then His Son must be real. That is what I believe. I may not have celebrated Christmas for that reason before . . . but I will now.*

The Alpha silently accepted her explanation. It was very interesting, even if parts of it were mysterious and incomprehensible.

We are almost in position to drop the SnowFire gems.

As they soared over the heart of the burning lands, the Alpha tilted downward and to the right, allowing Fire Bringer a good view of where she would be dropping the hundred or so gems of various sizes.

Here is hoping . . .

'Here is hoping what?' the Alpha responded.

Oh, I was wishing for success . . . with the gems.

'Ah, I see! I hope for their success, too.' Once the bag was emptied, the Alpha righted himself and flew in a circling pattern.

Now we will see if they really are gifts or just lumps of coal.

'What?'

It is part of the legend where—oh, just forget it. We will wait and see what happens, now that we have dropped the gems.

'Very well.'

For at least thirty seconds, all they could see was the sparkling reflections of the gems impacting into flaming trees, brush, or the ground. Then there were crick-crack sounds, similar to fissures forming in melting ice. The sound became louder and faster. Small areas began to take on a blueish-white look, similar to patches of ice or snow. And those areas grew and connected to one another. The effect began to climb the remnants of trees and consume boulders and ruined houses, even skeletal remains. Within ten minutes, the billowing black and gray smoke started to dwindle.

Fire Bringer and the Alpha beheld the crystallization spread with increasing speed. At this rate, the entire wildfire would be consumed by the SnowFire gems in a matter of hours.

"Merry Christmas," Fire Bringer wished aloud, sounding gratified.

20

CROSSING THE RUBICON

ILSKETH LET HER ROASTED ZALA beast leg fall back onto her plate and stood up, pushing her chair backwards with the movement of her legs. Her expression twisted into confusion mixed with astonishment.

"I must not have heard you correctly," she stated. "Say that again."

The broad-shouldered scout looked frightened. He was just inside the entrance to Ilsketh's private tent. The cold wind was blowing the flap about wildly and the skies threatened rain.

The scout's eyes were wide and unsure. He took a deep breath.

"The Kastadi fire has gone out, Heng Da."

"You mean a portion of the fire has burned itself out?"

"No, Heng Da. None of the fire remains. It is all gone."

"That . . . is not possible!" Ilsketh exclaimed. "A blaze like that could burn for many dayturns. How can it be out already?"

"The Kastadi lands that were burning, they have all turned to some kind of crystal that does not burn, Heng Da."

Ilsketh blinked several times. A new dryness settled in her mouth and stress pulled at her temples, threatening to become a headache.

"Thank you for this information," Ilsketh responded. "Go now and tell Himstras I need to see him."

"Yes, Heng Da! At once!"

Minutes later, Himstras entered Ilsketh's tent and saluted.

"Heng Da, how may I serve you?"

"I feel like I am fighting the pending storm outside or the twin stars themselves."

"Heng Da?"

"This Jorr-Don SnowFire . . . she is no normal Chieftess. She does not send soldiers, she sends fire-breathing beasts. She fights one hundred warriors by herself. And now, somehow, she turns the burning Kastadi lands into some kind of crystal forest!"

"Incredible!" Himstras responded.

"How do I fight what I do not understand?" Ilsketh erupted.

She picked up her full plate and hurled it across the tent. It careened against one of her mallets mounted on a weapons rack to her right, its contents thrashing against the walls and ground.

Himstras considered his response carefully for several seconds, which felt like an eternity to Ilsketh.

"You use what she has been using," he finally answered.

"What? I possess none of the abilities she seems to have," Ilsketh attested.

"Yes, you do. The most important one. You have the ability to surprise her."

She lifted her hand twice in successive motion, intending for him to continue.

"You have superior numbers, weaponry, training and strength of the soldiers, Heng Da. All you have to do is utilize our forces in a way she cannot anticipate."

"We could send out many small groups trained in stealth," Ilsketh suggested. "They must use the forests as cover and move only at night. Even if Jorr-Don has the Deathwings scouting for our troops, they will be less likely to spot the groups. If they took different routes to arrive at the Mokta Mountain village and if each group was not made aware of the other groups' routes, it might work."

Himstras nodded in agreement.

"Even if one or two groups were compromised, they could not give away the positions of the others," he added. "You could also keep the full strategy from being known by each group."

"Yes! I could tell each group to assist any other Gulstaa they see attacking. But they would not know the scale or scope of the assault."

"Yes, Heng Da."

Ilsketh stood to her full height, confident and determined.

"Prepare a strategy and choose who should be in each group," she continued. "I will join one of those groups."

"You, Heng Da? Is that wise?"

"It is necessary. I must lead my soldiers on the field."

"Yes, Heng Da."

————

Arrow hid himself carefully behind a thick tree trunk. He peered around cautiously to see if anyone might be approaching. But he saw only the birds in other trees and heard the chirping and buzzing of insects. The wind was growing colder and stronger. It seemed as if a storm might be building.

A girl's hand grabbed his left shoulder. Whirling around, he was shocked to see a satisfied-looking Maska and the new Ullvarr child, Pamela, a few feet behind her.

"How did you find me?" Arrow glared at Maska. "And why did you bring her?"

"I can sense you now, wherever you are," Maska declared proudly. "I think it is because we share blood. And I brought Pahmeela because she is my new friend."

"I guess we cannot play this game anymore then," Arrow huffed.

Maska crossed her arms and teased him with her eyes.

"Oh? So, the great Arrow, son of Chieftess Jorr-Don, does not think he can handle the challenge of this game anymore?"

"There are no challenges too great for me, Maska!" he insisted. "You know that."

"Then we will play this game again?"

Arrow sighed. "You have gotten better at manipulation."

"I just know you well, Arrow."

————

Pamela did not understand a single word they were saying but she was happy to be near them. They were amusing children a few years younger than she. She enjoyed the bold and familiar ways they spoke to one another, the way Maska teased him and how he responded to her. For ones so young, they clearly cared for one another.

And the boy was cute. He would be a handsome young man in a handful of cycles.

This Mokta village would be her new home with Kacheela and Asta and it would take some time to get used to the Mokta's ways and learn their language. But children were children, wherever they happened to be. Pamela was glad to be welcomed by this strange but compelling girl, Maska. She enjoyed how Maska had not been made sad by war and loss; she was full of joy and hope. And the boy named Arrow, the son of the Chieftess, who like Maska had some blue hair mixed with white and ice eyes like Kacheela's. Were the Chieftess and Kacheela actually sisters, as they claimed? They did not really look like sisters. But then again, Pamela never thought she looked much like her older brother, Binoz, either.

The sudden memory lashed at Pamela savagely and she lost her footing. She stumbled and fell to her knees. Before she could stop them, the tears began to wash her cheeks and she heaved in great sobs.

It had been months since the attack on the Ullvarr village, but she had not thought of her brother once. In a flurry of thoughts, she re-lived so many times she had played, talked, and even argued with Binoz. She had dearly loved and looked up to him. It hurt to think that she would never see his gentle face or hear his tender voice again.

And her First Asta, the muscular natural leader who was harsh and intimidating with everyone but First Kacheela and his children. How could he be dead? She remembered his stories of wrestling with wild beasts twice his size. Could anyone overcome his might? And yet . . . someone had.

Poor First Kacheela, who had been a distant woman most of her life. Pamela, when she had been Makazi, knew First Kacheela loved her and her brother. And she delighted in First Asta, listening to his grand plans while looking at him adoringly. Pamela could not clearly remember the last time she saw First Asta. And now Pamela's final memory of First Kacheela would be the look in her eyes as she was dying on the ground.

Maska reached out to Pamela, putting her arms around her and holding her. Pamela didn't need to know what her words meant, it mattered only that she was trying to comfort her.

———

Arrow crouched down. "What's wrong with her? Did she hurt herself?"

"No," Maska replied. "Gemta told me that the rest of her family was lost when her village was attacked."

"I thought Chieftess' sister, Eree-kah, was her gemta and the other Ullvarr man was her torkomm?"

"Does she look like Chieftess' sister, Eree-kah?"

"No."

Maska continued to look at Arrow.

"I was with Gemta when she spoke with Chieftess and Eree-kah. Pahmeela asked for Eree-kah to be her gemta and the Ullvarr man, Vah-Kar, to be her torkomm. They agreed and they are family now."

"But she misses her old family?" Arrow asked.

"Of course, she does! Who would not?" Maska replied.

Arrow looked on Pamela with a newfound sympathy. Pamela tried to relay gratitude through the way she returned his gaze.

"I understand," he added. "How can we help her?"

"We must be like family to her," Maska answered. "Even if she does not ask us to."

"Yes! Yes, we will."

———

With the suns beginning their descent in the distance, Erica walked slowly alongside Vakar through the village, ready to assist him if needed. He had almost fully recovered from his abdominal wound, but he had also suffered a serious concussion. As a result, his balance was tentative at best. Despite Healer Latas' efforts, she knew Vakar might have to bear this condition for some time. They were wearing thick cloaks given to them by one of Jordan's friends, a clothes-maker named Reiban. They were in the midst of the cold season and the winds were bitter and stinging as the temperatures were at their lowest.

The cloaks added weight, which complicated walking. Vakar's steps were carefully chosen and his concentration fully absorbed in this simple task. But Erica knew him well enough to be where he needed, when he needed it. He could lean into her and she would gently nudge him, just lightly enough that he felt it but no one else saw. It preserved his pride. But even though he hid it well, she sensed his silent gratitude.

The other Mokta villagers had been kind to them but they did not hide their moods, either. They did not know Erica, Vakar, or Pamela. He and Pamela were Ullvarr, an enemy of their people not so long ago. And Erica was a stranger who also resembled SnowFire, which created its own distance. And though Vakar spoke Mokta, he rarely said anything, while Erica and Pamela did not yet speak that language. It led to some hesitancy from the villagers and awkwardness between all of them. But Erica didn't mind. It was honest and understandable, better than she had ever received from most of the Ullvarr villagers. She knew her family would have to earn the Mokta's trust. And it was worth taking some time to do that.

Erica knew Vakar would prefer to walk the perimeter of the whole village until his strength and abilities were fully restored. But that would not happen this night, all he would do was exhaust himself. So, she had been subtly redirecting him back to their new hut. Presently, his steps were erratic, and he was heavily leaning on her. She felt some strain, but her own strength had been increasing as well. Opening the door to their hut, she led him to his chair at the dining table. She was glad to see Pamela there, ready to assist, too.

"Pamela, get some water for your asta," Erica directed, somewhat winded.

"Yes, Kacheela."

The girl seemed more withdrawn than usual. She decided she would talk with her once Vakar was asleep, which usually happened after he had taken his walk and eaten the evening meal.

She watched as Pamela served a large mug of water to her father. "Do you need anything else, Asta?" Pamela asked.

"The water is enough," Vakar answered. "My thanks."

She seemed satisfied and returned to the mat she had been sitting on before. Vakar motioned for Erica to join him at the table. That was surprising, since he often ate alone. She sat beside him and turned to look at him, her arms resting in her lap.

"I . . . would like it if you would continue to spend time with me, Ere-Kah."

"Oh?"

"I have been . . . harsh with you since we met," he continued. "At first, I did not trust or like you. You were different from anyone I had encountered before—in appearance, language, and custom."

Erica's only response was to nod in acknowledgment, curious where he was going with this.

"But you adapted. You became Ullvarr," he continued. "And after you learned the way you were . . . being treated, you still remained Ullvarr. Then the Gulstaa attacked and . . . nearly destroyed our people."

Even Vakar could not say those words without a small quiver of emotion in his voice. He took a few seconds to settle himself.

"When you remained Ullvarr after that, I knew that nothing could turn your heart."

"You honor me with your words, Vakar," Erica replied tenderly. "But what are you trying to say to me?"

He looked in Erica's eyes for a moment and then forced himself to stand once more, leaning on the table with one hand for support. Not sure what to expect, Erica stood as well and faced him. He seemed to inwardly struggle, looking downward, then at Erica again. He did this twice before he wrapped both arms around her waist and pulled her into a kiss. And not just any kiss, it lasted quite a while. She relaxed, enjoying this incredible yet wonderful surprise. When they finally separated, her heart was beating so loud and fast. She felt a rush in her head and had to steady herself against the table, too. But her eyes never abandoned Vakar's.

"That is what I was trying to say," Vakar said, looking slightly nervous.

Erica smiled. "I love you, too."

"We are mates already," he added.

"That was for the girl," Erica replied, looking playful. "You just gave me everything else."

"Hm, that is true."

Pamela walked over to the two of them, a look of amazement seemingly glued to her face.

"Asta, Kacheela, I am so happy!" she exclaimed. "I had hoped, even dreamed this—"

Brimming over with emotion, she put her arms around them both and squeezed as tightly as she could.

21

THE BACKUP PLAN

EVEN WITH THE COMFORTING PRESENCE of her daughter in her arms, Jordan looked restless and uneasy. She kept looking out the window of her hut and pacing the floor. It unnerved Bopol, who observed her while sitting in his favorite chair on the other side of the room.

"What is wrong?" Bopol asked.

"I don't know. It's—it's been too quiet, too many weeks since the Gulstaa did anything," Jordan replied, her nose wrinkling a little in frustration. "They do not give up, so they must be planning something. I just cannot figure out what!"

Bopol stood up, walked over to Jordan and put his arms around her gently. He knew better than to try and dissuade her from a premise once she was exploring it. Even so, she relaxed somewhat at his touch.

"What do you want to do?" he inquired.

"I think we need to implement my alternate plan as a precaution," she responded.

"You want to evacuate all the elders, pregnant women, and children? For how long?"

"Until I know it is safe. Somehow, I feel like it is too late for conventional travel. We need to use the Onchei machine to send them there right away."

That seemed precarious at best to Bopol. "Is that not also dangerous?"

"It would be a greater risk to leave them here or let them travel by foot, Bopol."

"You think the Gulstaa are on their way here?"

"They may be even closer than we realize."

She kissed their child's forehead, causing the baby to smile and look up at her mother with curiosity. Jordan looked determined but sad. Bopol knew it would dishearten his mate for her to be separated from her child once more. She handed the girl to him.

"Carry out the plan," she proclaimed, now acting as Chieftess. "And send Arrow to me."

"Yes, Chieftess."

———

Over the years, Zeetra had learned to identify Bopol's approach by the sound of his footsteps. They were always heavy, but if they were slow and relaxed, she knew he was probably with Jordan and their children. If they were at a medium pace, he was likely taking his son somewhere. But today, they were brisk and deliberate. She knew there was trouble before she turned and saw his somber expression as he filled the doorway of her hut.

"Zeetra, the Chieftess has need of you," he stated.

"What is the matter?"

"She has ordered me to begin the evacuation plan we discussed before. And she wants to use your Onchei travel machine for the people."

Zeetra stifled a gasp but mastered her expression quickly. "The enemy is that close?"

"The Chieftess believes so," Bopol replied. "Do you have the machine ready for this? Can you go along to operate it?"

Zeetra nodded resolutely. "Tell the Chieftess I will get the machine and meet the others where we agreed upon in the plan."

"Very well."

———————

Jordan appreciated Zoska's reassuring farewell hug as Reiban held Jasta. He was also keeping an eye on his own daughter and twin sons next to him.

"I could always stay behind and aid the archers." Zoska needled Jordan with a mischievous grin.

Zoska would never disobey her. But that didn't stop Zoska from being Zoska.

"Reiban could tell endless stories to this group and keep everyone satisfied," she continued. "Or put them to sleep!"

"What?" Reiban protested.

"I am teasing," Zoska whispered to him.

Jordan tried to smile. But the burden of her position prevented her from fully enjoying the moment. "I appreciate the offer, Zoska, but I need both you and your mate there to protect everyone," Jordan insisted. "I am sending some sentries with you but you two are in command. Decide together and act quickly."

"Yes, Chieftess!" Zoska and Reiban answered as one.

Satisfied, Jordan turned to look for her son. He was talking to Maska and she motioned for him to come to her.

"Gemta—Chieftess, do I really have to go?" he asked, looking up at her.

"I need to know you are safe, Arrow."

"I will be safe! I can take care of myself!"

"I do not doubt that. But honor your gemta and forgive my fears. Be safe."

"I will be safe, Gemta."

She leaned over, kissed his cheek and hugged him tightly. "Did you already say goodbye to your torkomm?"

"Yes, Chieftess."

"Good. Join the others then. They will be leaving in a moment."

Arrow did as his mother told him. He soon disappeared into the gathered group of elders, mothers, and children.

Jordan walked over to Zeetra, who was making final adjustments to a small Onchei device. It was two and a half inches wide and half an inch thick, made of some smoothly polished metal alloy. It was attached to a thin leather strap which could be worn by tying it to the wrist. It had a small black screen that covered half of it and a dozen small buttons below the screen. Zeetra pressed a few of those buttons and then turned to face her Chieftess.

"The original Onchei device is still in a safe place," Jordan began. "Does this new one you made work the same?"

"Yes, Chieftess. As you can see, it is smaller, but I assure you, it is just as powerful," Zeetra replied. "It will take all of us to the caves in Kinsa province, where the Eastern Mokta dwell. And it will bring us back when all is safe again. I will operate and maintain it."

"Good. It is also good that our fellow Mokta are willing to harbor you," Jordan said.

"You made sure of that with your forethought, Chieftess." Zeetra paused. "Sending Kitranor all those moonturns ago to make fresh contact and restore the bonds of ancestry, friendship, and alliance was wise."

Jordan had complete confidence in Kitranor. She knew there was no one else who could have accomplished that.

"I am just glad she was successful. I will feel much better knowing all of you are there. Your mate will help us with the other machines in the village. So, I want you to go now. I fear time is short."

Zeetra nodded. "Yes, Chieftess."

Content that she had said her goodbyes to her mate earlier, Zeetra strapped the teleportation device to her wrist and walked over to the group of evacuees. She made eye contact with Jordan one final time and then pressed two buttons at the same time. This opened a swirling portal of light that was eight feet tall by ten feet wide. All of the evacuees walked through the portal, followed by Zeetra. After she entered the portal, it closed behind her. And Jordan sighed with relief.

In Kinsa province, the group arrived safely. Zeetra, Reiban, and Zoska quickly did a head count to verify that everyone was present. Reiban went to scout the caves to determine if they were still secure for use and not occupied. Zeetra spotted Zoska and walked over to her. Zoska had a grim look on her face which troubled Zeetra.

"What is the matter, Zoska?"

"Of all the stupid—I should have expected this!" Zoska muttered. "And now, it is too late to go back."

"I have no idea what you are talking about, my friend."

Zoska clenched her fists. She looked angry at herself as she whispered a few choice curses. Then she sighed deeply and looked at Zeetra.

"Arrow is not with the group." Zoska paused. "He must have stayed behind."

22

JORDAN'S ARROW

ILSKETH COULD SEE THE MOUNTAIN Mokta village entrance in the distance. Her group was comprised of herself, Himstras, and eight of her best soldiers. Their mission was to contact at least two of the other strike teams and force their way into the village. It was nighttime and the moons were high. Himstras made a sound like one of the common birds, low-pitched and fluttering. It echoed out a signal known to the Gulstaa troops. A minute later, there was a response in like manner, then two more.

Making eye contact with the two archers in her group, she signaled them to stay close to her. They all moved closer to the village. Ilsketh pointed at each of the Mokta sentries posted at the north and west entrances. The archers took their positions and waited for her hand to drop in a slicing motion. The sentries were dead before they could alert anyone.

But then she heard a sound like someone imitating the screeching roar of a Sasstonn. When Ilsketh followed the noise, she spotted a young blue-and-white-haired boy who was clearly trying to alert the village. She slapped the arm of one of her archers and pointed in the direction of the child. The archer was good, but his arrow missed its target. The boy leapt forward and rolled out of harm's way. Then he ran out of range.

Jaidos looked at the ten warriors before him, male and female, ranging from late teens to late thirties. They were all strong, fast, and brave. And all had a special device strapped to their right wrist, compact with two small gems embedded to the side facing up.

"These machines will give you a slight advantage over your enemy but do not depend on them alone," Jaidos sternly instructed. "It will be your skills as fighters that will determine your success. Remember all your training and protect this village. The Gulstaa are here. Now we will stop them!"

The warriors ran towards the Gulstaa, who were advancing in groups of two and three. Spotting the Mokta, some of the archers tried to kill them with arrows. As Jaidos had taught them, the Mokta pressed a blue gem on their wrist machines and a rectangular shield of pure energy, as long as their arm and nearly two feet wide, was projected in front of their arms. The shields easily deflected the projectile weapons. Then the Mokta rushed forward to fight hand to hand. Getting closer, the Mokta pressed a yellow gem on their wrist machines and the shields vanished.

Jordan, Bopol, and Miitas were currently at the center of the village. Bopol and Miitas took up defensive postures in front of her.

"I do not understand why you have to be here, Chieftess," Bopol stated. "I strongly recommended that you leave with the others."

"You know why I stayed," Jordan answered calmly.

"With all respect, Chieftess, what you said still does not make sense to me." Bopol sighed in frustration.

"I am the only one who can negotiate with the Gulstaa."

"Also with respect, Chieftess, they are not here to negotiate," Miitas added in.

"And in that case, I am the only one who can finish this conflict, one way or the other," Jordan replied with sorrow.

Suddenly, a dagger sliced through the air. Miitas instinctively turned to avoid it but the blade still pierced her shoulder and she fell backwards. Jordan bent down and verified that Miitas still lived, though she was in considerable pain. Bopol stood in front of his Chieftess, a living shield.

"Is this the great Jorr-Don SnowFire I have heard so much about?" the Heng Da mocked, speaking in Gulstaa. "Showing such tender concern for a fallen soldier? Where is the woman who slew one hundred of my warriors?"

Jordan knew not to let herself be baited by her enemy. But the insults angered her. She had to combat the urge to rush at her in a rage.

'Your war is already over.'

The voice that spoke to Jordan in her mind belonged to the Deathwing Alpha.

What? she responded mentally.

'She does not know it yet, Fire Bringer, but it is over,' the Alpha thought to Jordan.

I do not understand. What do you mean?

'Tell the Gulstaa leader she no longer has anything to fight for,' the Alpha answered. 'While she and her small groups moved to attack you there, I led my people to all of her villages.'

Jordan felt a dreadful sinking sensation in her chest.

The Deathwings attacked the entire Gulstaa population? Men, women, children? You killed them all?

'Yes, Fire Bringer. We left nothing and no one. You are no longer threatened.'

Why? I did not tell you to do that!

'Did you not ask me and my kind to help stop your enemy? Did you not tell me 'Destroy any Gulstaa you see?' We have done exactly as you asked us!'

Jordan suddenly felt ill, and she became faint. That distress did not go unnoticed by the Gulstaa leader.

"What is wrong with you, Mokta Chieftess?" Heng Da taunted. "Lost your will to fight?"

"You have to stop this!" Jordan insisted. "Something terrible has happened."

"What?" Heng Da half-laughed.

Jordan took a deep breath and motioned for Bopol to stay where he was. She walked slowly and deliberately towards the Heng Da. Bopol had to obey his Chieftess, but she could see he only wanted to protect her.

As Jordan continued towards the Heng Da, she closed her eyes and her hair flickered like flames.

"You could attack me now, but I would heal from any wound," Jordan stated. "You cannot kill me. No weapon or skill you have could accomplish that."

Ilsketh was intrigued. Jorr-Don hadn't spoken with an arrogant voice, she wasn't bragging. Jorr-Don was speaking as if her words were facts. But that didn't mean she had to believe them.

The Gulstaa leader pulled a second dagger from her belt and started to raise it but when she looked in Jorr-Don's eyes, she stopped and slowly lowered her arm. The heartache emanating from the Chieftess wasn't for herself or the Mokta people. Ilsketh knew that sadness was for her alone. She just couldn't comprehend why.

"You need to go home. If any of your people survived, they will need you," Jorr-Don urged.

"'If any of my people . . . survived?'" Ilsketh recoiled. "What *madness* are you speaking?"

"The Deathwings . . . they decided to end our war."

Jorr-Don's words stabbed through Ilsketh's heart like an arrow made of ice. The Heng Da didn't want to believe these words but they still caused her pain.

"A handful of Deathwings would do . . . some damage, but my people could—"

"Not a handful, Heng Da. You do not understand. It was all of them," Jorr-Don interrupted. "All of the Deathwings in the world."

Ilsketh's mind reeled at the untold damage that an army of Deathwings could do. The potential loss of life would be beyond catastrophic.

"You're lying!" Ilsketh snapped. "Why would the Deathwings do such a thing?"

"Because they thought it is what I wanted," Jorr-Don admitted, her words filled with regret.

Ilsketh didn't want to believe the Mokta Chieftess but she could not sense any deception from her.

"Surrender now and I will guarantee your safety. I will take you back to your land in the space of a few heartbeats. We will confirm this together."

"It . . . it is not our way to surrender."

"You no longer have anything to fight for, Heng Da," Jorr-Don repeated the Alpha's words to her. "But you need to live."

———————

Jordan SnowFire gazed at the Heng Da and studied the woman's body language. During those moments, she understood something new about the Gulstaa leader.

"How many?" Jordan said.

"What?"

"How many children do you have?" Jordan asked.

Heng Da's mask of invulnerability fractured and she took in a sharp breath that bordered on a sob.

"Four."

"I understand," Jordan responded.

Jordan beheld the conflicted face of the Heng Da. It seemed like she was at war with herself now. Part of her clearly wanted to fight to the last soldier. But she could see the leader in her considering her people's needs. Heng Da made eye contact with one of her soldiers, an older bald, muscular man who was positioned nearby. Seeing his leader's desolate face, he ran to her side.

"Have the soldiers stop their fighting, Himstras," Heng Da said, her eyes still hollow and numb. "I must learn the truth of the Mokta Chieftess' words."

"Heng Da-?" Himstras started to say, but he corrected himself. "Yes, Heng Da. At once!"

Jordan watched Himstras take his sword and grab a discarded shield laying on the ground. He pounded them together in a stark but distinguished rhythm. And within less than a minute's time, all combat ceased.

Jordan made eye contact with Bopol.

"Tend to Miitas in the Healer's hut," Jordan commanded. "And tell one of the soldiers to bring Jaidos to me."

"Yes, Chieftess."

She watched him gently pick up his wounded sister and run in the direction of his father's workplace. Within a short time, a young female soldier approached Jordan with Jaidos.

"You sent for me, Chieftess?" he asked.

"Did Zeetra tell you how to change locations on the teleporting machine?"

"Yes, but . . . my mate has the teleporting machine," Jaidos responded.

"I have another one," Jordan countered. "Can you make it send us to the Gulstaa lands?"

"I can try. I will need some information about where the location will be."

Jordan nodded. "The Gulstaa leader will give us what information we need. The war is over and . . . "

Jordan felt her brow furrow and she had trouble completing the thought.

" . . . we have won." The words were bereft of any satisfaction.

"That is wonderful news! I will let our soldiers know—" Jaidos replied excitedly.

"No, Jaidos. That will have to wait," Jordan interrupted brusquely.

"I see. I will assist you however you need."

Jordan went to retrieve the original teleporting device. Several soldiers stood near the Heng Da and Himstras. They watched but did not harm them, at their Chieftess' request. The remaining Gulstaa soldiers were being likewise carefully guarded by the Mokta.

She returned a short time later with the Onchei device. Jaidos inspected the machine and once he felt confident in adjusting its settings, he asked the Heng Da several questions about the Gulstaa provinces. Jordan translated her words to him. Heng Da answered him with as much detail as she could muster, telling him they must go to Kemethla. She looked like she was combatting fear and anxiety. Soon, Jaidos handed the device to Jordan.

"It will take you to Kemethla and back with no difficulty," Jaidos confirmed. "With what the Heng Da told me, the machine should make you appear in the center of the city."

"I thank you, Jaidos."

Jordan ordered two soldiers to go with her and Ilsketh to the Gulstaa city. Himstras was at his Heng Da's side, prepared to defend her if necessary. One of the Mokta soldiers stood next to Jordan and the other next to Himstras. Jordan turned and spoke to Heng Da.

"This is always . . . troubling the first time."

"What are you talking about?" Heng Da replied.

Jordan pressed a yellow-orange symbol on the device and a white spinning portal appeared several feet in front of her and the others. Heng Da looked both impressed and frightened.

"We have to walk through that spinning light," Jordan instructed. "Do not worry, it is safe. I will go first."

And she did.

23

AFTERMATH

AFTER A SHORT PERIOD OF disorientation, Ilsketh, Jorr-Don, and the other three fellow travelers emerged from the other end of the portal at the heart of Kemethla in the Gulstaa Empire. Nothing could have prepared them for the level of destruction and devastation they witnessed. Not a single building was left unscathed and remnants of fires still burned throughout the area. But it was the sheer amount of freshly killed bodies, especially the youngest ones, that shocked them the most. The majority were victims of falling debris or scorching flames, but some had clearly been torn apart by the Deathwings.

In abject silence, the living walked among the dead. There was nothing they could do for anyone. There were no screams or moans or cries for help, only the crackling of distant blazes and the crunching of falling stones from crumbling structures. The entire area smelled of sulfur and smoke.

Ilsketh spotted the fortress where she and her family had resided for the last eight cycles and froze. It was heavily damaged, its roof gone, with many walls torn down, blackened by fire. But it was not a complete loss and that sparked faint hope in the Heng Da. Without a word, she bolted towards what remained of the residence, alarming Himstras and the others. He followed her immediately while Jorr-Don and the two soldiers were close behind.

The top floor was mostly gone but she knew Gothmarl would have taken the children to the safest place: a special room constructed beneath the ground floor, known only to them and their most trusted guards. She navigated around half-smashed walls, overturned furniture, and scorched skeletons. Ilsketh felt like she could lift boulders to reach her family.

Then she saw her children, Kintoth and Lithtar, on the floor. Her legs lost their strength and she barely felt her knees hit the ground. Her eyes were transfixed on the young bodies before her. A collapsed wall had pinned them from the chest down, crushing them. Their eyes were still open, wide in shock. Ilsketh took small comfort that it had been quick. There was no possibility that she could lift the wall to free them. And she had to find the rest of her loved ones, no matter their condition. Taking in a deep breath, Ilsketh forced her trembling legs to make her stand.

In the furthest room, she found Gothmarl face down on the floor. He had suffered burns on his back and head. Ilsketh gasped when she saw a child's arm stretched out from beneath his corpse. Desperately with all her strength, she lifted his body and pushed it to one side, revealing her eldest daughter, Anci.

"You tried to protect her with your own body, even though you were wounded," Ilsketh spoke softly, her heart further torn by the loss of her mate. "You were such a good father."

Anci moaned.

Ilsketh was stunned yet unimaginably happy. She began to cry, covering her mouth with her hands. Then she felt the child's cheeks. They were warm but not feverish. Ilsketh embraced her daughter and sobbed uncontrollably.

After a time, Ilsketh realized others were in the room and lifted her head to look at them, smiling with joy.

"Anci yet lives, Himstras!" she exclaimed through her tears. "Gothmarl saved her!"

She looked down at Gothmarl and her smile became bittersweet.

"Gothmarl saved her," she repeated.

Ilsketh coaxed her child awake, wanting to be the first thing Anci saw. The girl looked pleased to see her mother but was overwhelmed with sadness as well. Anci turned her head and she saw her father's body. She put her arms around Ilsketh's neck and clung tightly, not wanting to let go. Ilsketh picked her up and looked at Jordan, hatred pouring through her eyes.

"You have defeated us," Ilsketh said, her voice low and simmering. "Now, I must see to the survival of my people and all you have left me of my family."

Jorr-Don, Bopol, and the two Mokta soldiers turned to leave. The Mokta Chieftess held the teleportation device in her hand.

"Your name is now engraved in our history, Jorr-Don SnowFire!" Ilsketh shouted spitefully as they exited the room. "We will tell our children of your deeds, just as other tribes of this world told of the first SnowFire. And they will tell their descendants. We will describe what you looked like and that you were the Chieftess of the Mokta Mountain. We will share how you commanded Deathwings to slaughter our children!"

As intended, Jorr-Don was stung by Ilsketh's words. The Chieftess paused, turned, and gazed at Ilsketh and her daughter, her emotions in turmoil. Then Jorr-Don's eyes narrowed, and her expression hardened.

"I know what I am responsible for, Heng Da," Jorr-Don replied. "But how could you, the mother of four children, start a war that butchered thousands of Kastadi and almost all of the Ullvarr?"

"It was my duty as my people's leader. I was born with the Clansign," Ilsketh said, pointing at the birthmark on her cheek. "I was prepared for this my whole life. The Gulstaa are conquerors. We are not afraid of battle or its consequences. My only regret . . . is underestimating my enemy."

"We had no quarrel with you. Your only enemy is yourself," Jordan answered bitterly. "If you had heeded my warning, this would not have happened."

The truth in Jordan's words troubled Ilsketh and aggravated her pride and grief.

"Leave my lands, Chieftess," Ilsketh admonished, her words laced with threat. "Before I do something we'll both regret."

Jorr-Don looked like she had more to say but chose to remain silent. With merely a glance, the Mokta Chieftess commanded the guards to follow her out of the ruins. Opening the way back home with her machine, the Mokta left behind the surviving Gulstaa.

Ilsketh would not utter a word until the light of the portal faded. Then she screamed with all her might—for her family and people. But also, for her failure.

She wanted to die but the child in her arms and the remaining soldiers under her command needed her. She did not have the luxury of self-indulgence. She had never been permitted that.

———

At sunrise the next day, Jaidos stepped through the portal of light to where the rest of his tribe were taking refuge in the Kinsa province. He found Reiban, Zoska, and his mate, Zeetra, quickly but it took some time to assemble everyone else to bring them back to the Mountain Mokta Village. Jordan had given him this task, as she was still physically and emotionally exhausted from the events of the day before. Bopol had returned to her side once Healer Latas had treated Miitas, who would recover. Bopol had seen Jordan in many moods but nothing like this. He did what he could to ease her burdens but knew it would take time.

Jaidos stood proudly before the amassed Mokta. He was ready to open the gateway home but had a few words to convey first.

"The war with the Gulstaa is over! Our Chieftess has presided over a great and terrible victory!" he declared.

The people started to cheer but Jaidos silenced them by motioning with his arms and shouting "Hear me!" It took a few moments, but the crowd settled down again.

"We Mokta have fought many times to protect our mountain and people! Though not since the ancient days have we destroyed a people," Jaidos recalled somberly. "Today, only a handful of Gulstaa survive. We and our allies are safe. We can celebrate our continued wellbeing but not the complete devastation of our enemy."

"How did this happen, Jaidos?" Reiban asked, standing next to Zoska and their children. "How is the Chieftess?"

"We had a more powerful ally than we realized in the Deathwings. While we defended our village, they attacked the enemy's lands," Jaidos answered. "The Chieftess is well, physically, but the cost of this war weighs heavily on her. She did not order the Deathwing attack; they did it to protect us."

Reiban, Zoska, and Zeetra exchanged astonished glances. Jaidos understood. Knowing Jordan as he did, he could only imagine the strain of so many deaths on her conscience.

Jaidos answered several more questions from those gathered. Then he opened up a portal and led the villagers back home.

That night, Kitranor visited Jordan, who had not rested since her return from Kamethla. The children were already sleeping and Bopol served tea to his gemta. Kitranor was cautious with her words, seeing how stressed and anguished her daughter was.

"Not long after I became Chieftess, a tribe of nomads called the Rozma attempted to take our village by force," Kitranor recounted. "The number of our people and theirs was the same and they were even stronger than us. But they did not know the land or how fierce we are when provoked. I devised a plan to save our tribe and commanded our warriors and hunters to carry it out."

Kitranor gazed at the far wall as she recalled the memory. Then she sighed heavily with regret. "We lured them to the ravine on the southern end of the mountain, where there is an entrance but no exit."

"The ravine? No one is allowed to go there. We were told it is too dangerous," Jordan interjected.

Kitranor nodded sadly. "That . . . is not entirely true. No one is allowed to go there because of what happened, what I did."

"I do not understand?" Jordan asked.

"I ordered my warriors to begin a rockslide which not only trapped the Rozma in the ravine, it killed most of them. And those that did not immediately perish were too injured to escape. Their deaths were longer and more—" Kitranor could not complete the sentence. It was a moment before she could speak again. "The ravine is forbidden because it is a mass grave . . . and should not be disturbed."

Kitranor peered out the window into the night sky. Her grief and rueful pangs, even after such a long time, were still palpable. Was she looking away to remember or for some other reason?

"It is also my greatest shame, because I failed to find a peaceful way to end that conflict," Kitranor continued. "The Rozma were tired of having no place to call home. I did not know it then, but all of their people came together to seize the Mokta Mountain. We could have found another way; we could have made peace. Instead, there are no more Rozma because of me."

A look of understanding passed between the two women. For several long moments, nothing needed to be said.

"I have led many battles since then. But I learned from that experience," Kitranor added. "And I have always tried to find the solution that would spare the most lives. I know you will learn from this experience, my daughter, and you will be a better Chieftess for it."

Jordan looked at Kitranor, her eyes heavy with guilt. "How—how do you live with it?"

"There was no way to atone for what I did. I could only try to honor those lives by making better decisions during the rest of my time as Chieftess," Kitranor said, putting her hand to Jordan's cheek. "And in my training the next one."

"Know this, Jorr-Don. Your actions not only saved the Mokta but prevented more deaths in this region," Kitranor added.

"I think that is an exaggeration!"

"The Gulstaa have been conquerors for most of their history. There are legends that they once had an empire which covered half of Algoran."

"If that is true, what happened to it?"

"I was told that there was a great war, very long ago, that spread to most of the world. It was a time that nearly destroyed everything. But enough of our peoples' ancestors survived to begin again."

"I did not know that. That is not in any of the storytelling legends?"

"It is known only to the Chiefs and Chieftesses," Kitranor shared. "And you must keep this knowledge to yourself until you select the next leader of the Mountain Mokta."

"I . . . understand."

24

APEX

AS THE EVENING STRETCHED ON, Jordan still couldn't sleep, tossing and turning restlessly. Her mind was assailed by flashes of the ruined city. The eyes of the deceased stared accusations at her. Even when she didn't see the Deathwings in her thoughts, Jordan heard the rush of their wings flapping, their roar or the sound of flames erupting out of their throats. When she managed to clear that imagery, she saw and heard Ilsketh:

Your name is now engraved in our history, Jorr-Don SnowFire! We will tell our children of your deeds, just as other tribes of this world told of the first SnowFire. And they will tell their descendants. We will describe what you looked like and that you were the Chieftess of the Mokta Mountain. We will share how you commanded Deathwings to slaughter our children!

All of it threatened to overwhelm Jordan, lashing at her very sanity. Bopol had done his very best to comfort her, gently putting his arms around her, speaking softly, trying to reassure her. None of it helped. Solace was completely elusive, her heart more wounded now than at any point in her life.

Finally, she sat up. A cold sweat coated her brow and ran down the back of her neck. Bopol had finally succumbed to exhaustion and was softly snoring. Jordan put her hand to his cheek. The raging storm within her would not allow her to smile, only to envy his peace. She stood up and walked out of the hut, not bothering to grab additional furs, only wearing her night robe. Jordan's hair half-covered her face. Barefoot, she walked slowly and numbly through the village, barely aware of her surroundings.

As she approached the entrance to the village, one of the sentries ran over to her. The sentry was young, perhaps in her early twenties. She was muscular yet surprisingly quick. Her long hair was braided and ran behind her shoulders. She gasped when she saw the demeanor of the Chieftess.

"Chieftess, is something wrong?" the sentry asked.

Jordan took a moment to focus her eyes on the young woman. "You are Hosp's daughter, Lekkina?"

"Yes, Chieftess!" Lekkina replied quickly.

"I need to go up the Mountain. It is . . . important."

"Very well. I will go with you, Chiefte—"

"No! I must go alone!" Jordan snarled, interrupting the sentry.

The sentry looked frightened by Jordan but was committed to her duty. She controlled herself and spoke calmly.

"Chieftess, you made the rule that no one leaves the village at night. It is for everyone's safety."

The young woman's words assaulted Jordan's memories. But they faded next to her emotional onslaught. She did not feel worthy to be Chieftess. Jordan continued walking without any additional words. She noticed Lekkina reaching towards her but saw her fellow sentry hold her back.

———

Ascending the slope, Bopol and Reiban were trying desperately to close the distance between themselves and Jordan, who had a two-hour head start. Bopol had been alerted by the sentries and asked Reiban to accompany him. The winds were becoming savage and frigid and a storm was brewing. As the gales pounded near-relentlessly against them as they progressed slowly up the mountain, Bopol was forced to grab onto a tree, boulder, or even the ground itself with one hand and his friend with the other. Sleet was falling and pelting against them like tiny darts of ice.

"Bopol, this is no good!" Reiban shouted over the wind. "We may be Mokta, but we are not SnowFire-born. Jorr-Don can survive this, but—"

"Do not say it, Reiban! Look!" Bopol exclaimed, pointing further up the ridge. "There she is! We can catch her and bring her back."

A bolt of lightning struck a tree at its base several hundred feet in front of them. The severed timber, now partially ablaze, fell to the ground, blocking the safest path between them and Jordan. Bopol was speechless, his mouth open and arms stretched helplessly to his sides. He felt as if the sleet splashing against his skin was mocking him. Reiban clamped a firm grip on Bopol's shoulder.

"We have tried our best, my friend," Reiban assured. "We can do no more. Let us go while we still can."

Bopol could no longer see his mate, since the smoke and flames from the burning wood obscured his view up the mountain. He clenched his fists in frustration and helplessness.

"Jorr-Don!" Bopol screamed as loud as he could into the howling tempest. "Return to me! I love you!"

Reiban tugged at his shoulder and Bopol turned abruptly in defeat. They cautiously descended the terrain to head back to the safety of the Mokta village.

Jordan turned suddenly.

"Bopol?" she whispered.

She looked back the way she'd come but all she saw was smoke and flames billowing from a storm-downed tree. She squinted, trying to look further but it was not possible. Then she returned her focus to the peak.

It took longer to move smaller distances as Jordan went higher towards the precipice. Conditions worsened exponentially, with near-one hundred mile per hour wind gusts. The sleet became pellet-sized hail that was growing larger by the minute. There were rapid temperature drops and even the air was growing thinner. It would have been punishing—even fatal—to the most rugged animal. Yet Jordan trudged on.

She was obsessed now, fixated on the top of the mountain. She barely noticed that her eyes and the jewels on the palms of her hands were glowing. She felt her hair dancing with blue flames. The ambient temperature surrounding her body had risen by dozens of degrees, such that the snow melted beneath her feet as she walked.

When she was perhaps fifty feet from the summit, she dropped to her knees and her arms collapsed at her sides. She was crying and she lifted her head to the raging skies.

"GOD, I KNOW YOU ARE UP THERE! I NEED TO REACH YOU! I NEED YOU TO HEAR ME!"

There was a rolling thunderclap that reverberated in the distance. More sleet was falling.

Jordan lowered her head and leaned forward, falling onto her hands. The images of the dead kept flashing through her thoughts, both from Kamethla and the soldiers whose lives she had ended at the Kastadi village.

"Why? Why did you save my life just to let me become this? I was happy being Janice Lewis' daughter; I did not want to become SnowFire's child! I did not want to be Chieftess! And I never wanted to be a killer! But that is who I am now—I hate it! What do you want for my life?"

She screamed and beat the ground and shed tears until she was exhausted and lying flat on her stomach. For many long minutes, nothing changed around her. If anything, the storm intensified. Golf ball-sized hail struck her back and legs, but she didn't care; she was spent.

Then the winds completely ceased. Jordan opened her eyes, only to see that she was lying on an area of bright blue grass, no snow at all in her immediate field of vision. She lifted herself up with her hands and looked around. For fifty feet in every direction, there was lush plant life, including flowers. The temperature was Spring-like and all was calm.

She felt a bit lightheaded and strange. When she looked down, she saw that her hair was completely brown for the first time in six years. She looked at her palms and though the gems were still there, they did not pulse and had no power. Unsteadily, she stood up. She could see the rest of the mountain still gripped by the terrible storm, but she was protected from it. Jordan felt completely safe.

"Am—am I dreaming? Did I fall asleep finally?" No answer came to her spoken words.

She heard something moving behind her, turned, and saw what looked like a man but he was shining so brightly, she could not verify any of his features. She had to turn away to avoid being blinded but could still feel unparalleled power emanating from him. It frightened her on an instinctive level, and she couldn't move. It felt like the power was surrounding her and something besides her own physical strength kept her from collapsing.

The voice which spoke next was soft and low but somehow, Jordan knew it was not from the glowing man. She did not know who it was or what language was spoken but she could understand every word perfectly:

"Shadrach, Meshach, and Abednego, answered and said to the king, O Nebuchadnezzar, we are not careful to answer thee in this matter. If it be so, our God whom we serve is able to deliver us from the burning fiery furnace, and he will deliver us out of thine hand, O king. But if not, be it known unto thee, O king, that we will not serve thy gods, nor worship the golden image which thou hast set up.

"Then was Nebuchadnezzar full of fury, and the form of his visage was changed against Shadrach, Meshach, and Abednego: therefore he spake, and commanded that they should heat the furnace one seven times more than it was wont to be heated. And he commanded the most mighty men that were in his army to bind Shadrach, Meshach, and Abednego, and to cast them into the burning fiery furnace. Then these men were bound in their coats, their hosen, and their hats, and their other garments, and were cast into the midst of the burning fiery furnace.

"Therefore because the king's commandment was urgent, and the furnace exceeding hot, the flames of the fire slew those men that took up Shadrach, Meshach, and Abednego. And these three men, Shadrach, Meshach, and Abednego, fell down bound into the midst of the burning fiery furnace. Then Nebuchadnezzar the king was astonied, and rose up in haste, and spake, and said unto his counsellors, Did not we cast three men bound into the midst of the fire? They answered and said unto the king, True, O king.

"He answered and said, Lo, I see four men loose, walking in the midst of the fire, and they have no hurt; and the form of the fourth is like the Son of God. Then Nebuchadnezzar came near to the mouth of the burning fiery furnace, and spake, and said, Shadrach, Meshach, and Abednego, ye servants of the most high God, come forth, and come hither. Then Shadrach, Meshach, and Abednego, came forth of the midst of the fire."

Jordan felt fresh tears coating her cheeks, but she was no longer sad. She wasn't sure how she felt.

The vivid brightness faded, and Jordan stood alone in the blue field.

"That is—that was from the Bible, right?" Jordan asked, not sure anyone would hear.

"Yes," the voice answered. "One day, you will understand."

"Am I like those three men . . . the ones who were put into the furnace?"

"They refused their king's order to worship other gods. That is why he punished them. But the Holy One would not let them perish in the flames. He was with them and protected them."

Jordan withdrew sheepishly. "Is He here for me now? I have done terrible things. I am a terrible thing!"

"Are you? Look at yourself. Are you a child of SnowFire at this moment?"

Jordan looked at herself once more. She felt completely human.

"No," she replied, softly and with astonishment. "Thank you! Thank you! This is wonderful! Am I going to remain this way?"

"That is not for me to decide," the voice replied. "For I am only a servant of The Most Holy. But be encouraged, all will be as it is meant to be. Know this: you have a purpose in this life, Jordan. And you are loved. Acknowledge the Most Holy in all your ways and He will bless you . . . and your people."

With that, the voice spoke no more. The zone of calm around Jordan began to dissipate, allowing the storm back in. And Jordan could feel the SnowFire gems thrum to life again in her body. Startled, she saw that she was now at the foot of the mountain. She had no idea how she had gotten there.

Her robe was soaked, and her hair was wet with near-frozen ends. She swept her waterlogged bangs away from her face and then attempted to wring the liquid from it. Her stomach growled its hunger and her muscles were sore, forcing her to limp.

Jordan slowly returned to the village. Her bare feet, coated in cold mud, took heavy and labored steps. The wind howled but was no longer harsh and the rain was light, almost comforting. A few small creatures scurried through the grass to the trees or other cover. For a brief moment, Jordan had a doubting thought about her experience, but it was firmly dismissed.

God, I know You are here for me and You love me. You told me I have a purpose.

Jordan paused and looked skyward then at the village before her.

I cannot change what I have already done. But as Chieftess and Jordan SnowFire, I will recognize and acknowledge what God has done for me. I do want Him to bless me and the Mokta. I want to maintain peace, in my home, the village, and this region. I cannot do that on my own . . . but God can help me to do it.

ACT FIVE

EPILOGUE

INTERLUDE IV

IN THE WEEKS THAT FOLLOWED the defeat of the Gulstaa, Jordan set out to accomplish several goals to maintain peace in the region. The first thing she did was arrange a meeting with Kitranor, Latas, Bopol, and Miitas, who was still recovering but able to participate. It took place in the morning after the community meal and at the Chieftess' hut, not her personal residence.

Jordan was still encumbered by the war and its consequences. She was determined to make good come out of these horrific events and the lives that stained her conscience. She had left behind the young woman she had been and was in uncharted territory now. She attempted a smile as she began the discussion but let it go when she couldn't convince herself of its sincerity.

"I know you have all been worried about me," she acknowledged. "You have my thanks."

"Chieftess, I would like to ask what happened when you ascended the mountain," Kitranor interjected.

Jordan had been expecting this. In fact, she had spent days preparing for this very discussion.

"I will tell you. You all deserve to know. One thing I have learned in my time on Algoran is that, while there are beliefs about SnowFire, she is not what you call a celestial being or avatar. From what I have learned, the people of Algoran do not worship any such beings."

"What is this word wur-ship, Jorr-Don?" Kitranor said. "What does it mean?"

Jordan found it strange and mildly ironic that she, a woman who had rarely attended any church services in her short life, was being asked to explain what worship meant. She directed her memories to the night near the mountain's peak, the feeling of wonder and excitement mixed with a kind of reverent fear.

"It is the feeling you have when in the presence of God, His Son, or one of His angels," she explained. "God is the first and ultimate celestial being. He created everything."

"You were in the presence of such a being?" Bopol asked sincerely. "You did not mention this before."

"I did not have the words before. I barely do now," Jordan continued. "Maybe I should start at the beginning."

Jordan told them how her life had been spared by God when she had been scratched and poisoned by the Mosdon years earlier. Then she shared her encounter on the mountain in great detail. Everyone listened intently and when Jordan finished, there was a long silence. No one doubted her words, but they had no common point of reference. This was all new and very extraordinary.

"I do not know why God spared me, then or now," Jordan admitted. "I do not know why He allowed me to become SnowFire's daughter or Chieftess of this tribe. But I cannot deny His power . . . and love for me, for all of us. I can only do what I feel in my heart is right."

"And what is that, Chieftess?" Miitas asked finally speaking up. She looked like she was still in pain, but she was alert. There was new respect for Jordan in her countenance. "Please . . . tell us."

Jordan looked down for a moment, collecting her thoughts. It had been easier to tell them about her experiences than she had expected. When she returned her gaze toward them, she had a new confidence.

"I need to have a meeting with the Deathwing Alpha, we need a new understanding," Jordan declared. "They are a powerful ally, but I made some terrible mistakes when I communicated with him . . . and them. I need to fix that and set some new limits."

"What kind of limits, Chieftess?" Kitranor asked.

"Deathwings are very smart but they are still predators, animals. They take what we—what I say—literally. I allowed my anger and frustration to influence my words when speaking with the Alpha. I was furious at the Gulstaa and at that time, I wanted them dead. The Deathwings felt that. And when combined with my words, they interpreted my intent. I believe that is why they attacked and destroyed the Gulstaa."

Jordan sighed. She knew the pain of that mistake would haunt her for the rest of her life.

"That cannot happen again. I believe we should call on the Deathwings only when there is no alternative," she finally said. "And even then, whether myself or another Chief or Chieftess, our words to the Deathwings will have to be clear. We will have to set good boundaries. We cannot leave room for any more errors. If we fail in that, more people will die."

The others nodded in understanding.

"Next, I must go speak with Chief Teebor of the Kastadi," Jordan insisted. "I need to make sure he and I have a good understanding as well."

Jordan conveyed her plans. As she continued, Kitranor became pensive and looked somewhat worried. She waited for the Chieftess to finish speaking before addressing the matter. Jordan knew the woman well enough not to need prompting.

"Something troubles you, Kitranor?" Jordan asked.

"Yes. I know Teebor and the Kastadi well," Kitranor answered. "He will not agree to what you want."

"Why?"

"Too many Kastadi died. He will feel responsible for them. And he will want vengeance."

"You do not think this is hopeless, do you?"

"No, Chieftess. But to ensure Teebor's agreement, you must insist on it. He likes you but he needs to respect you." She paused. "Daughter, he must fear you."

Jordan began to shake her head. "No —you are not saying I should—"

"You are the daughter of SnowFire. Use that . . . as only you can."

Jordan did not like that suggestion at all. It didn't feel right. Still looking at Kitranor in disbelief, her shoulders slumped. She closed her eyes, leaned her head forward, and put it in her hand.

"There must be another way," Jordan whispered softly.

"Forgive, Chieftess, but there is not," Kitranor reaffirmed, her arms folded. "Make Teebor respect you or that part of your plan will fail."

Kitranor was Chieftess for many cycles. If she says this is the only way, I want to believe her. But I wish I didn't have to do this.

———————

One week later, as Jordan held her daughter close to her chest, she gasped while staring into the crystallized forest before her. Bopol, Arrow, and the four guards who accompanied them were equally amazed. Some of the trees stretched hundreds of feet skyward while others had obviously been damaged by the fire before being altered to become SnowFire gems.

Jordan froze when she saw the first glass-like body: a young woman, from the looks of her. She had fallen forward, probably fleeing from the Gulstaa. The scars left by some sharp weapon were jagged lines on her translucent blue form. The outlines of her tunic stretched to her sides like her arms, making her appear as a fallen statue. As the group progressed further into the forest, they found dozens more like her, an entire community.

Even though he remained silent the whole time, Jordan could see that Arrow was visibly upset. A frown turned his lips downward, a sympathetic sadness coloring his ice-blue eyes and adding a slight furrow to his brow. He lost his balance for a second and caught himself with both hands against the thick trunk of one of the trees. When his hands clasped it, there was a flash of blue and white light. He quickly let go. Jordan watched in amazement as a two-hundred-foot tree changed from gem to bark once more in mere seconds. Even its leaves at the highest levels returned to their previously moist light blue, as if time had not passed at all.

"I do not understand!" Arrow exclaimed, looking down at his hands. "I have never been able to do that before!"

Jordan continued to gaze at the restored tree. What her son had done should not have been possible. Yet she could not deny the evidence right in front of her.

SnowFire said she took away the ability of anyone to transform objects into gems. Instead of removing Arrow's power, did she merely reverse it? Or did she anticipate this at all? Could it be . . . an unintended side-effect?

"One thing is certain, my son," Jordan assured. "Until we understand what you can do with this . . . ability, you must not touch any more SnowFire gems."

"Yes, Gemta."

Jordan looked around slowly, taking in the sad and bleak beauty of the crystal forest.

If I told Chief Teebor we could change the forest back, would he want us to? Is it better off now?

Then she spotted a shiny skeleton out of the corner of her eye. The body had been burned in the inferno the Gulstaa had created. Jordan hoped that whoever he or she was, they had died before the fire broke out . . . but there was no way to know that. Each of the dead weighed on her.

Could I have prevented this somehow? Should I have sent more aid to the Kastadi earlier?

Jordan quelled such thoughts. Kitranor had taught her that second guessing one's self was meaningless and a waste of time. The past was the past, it could not be changed. She could look only to the present and the future.

At the very least, the Chief will probably want to collect the Kastadi dead.

———

Three days later, Jordan SnowFire stood humbly before Chief Teebor the Mighty, her shoulders relaxed, and head slightly lowered in respect. They were in the heart of his village, with everyone gathered around them awaiting their leader's words. Easily twice Jordan's height and almost three times her real age, Teebor's musculature was impressive. His stolid expression was unreadable for some time . . . until he smiled at Jordan.

"When we first met, you were a rash girl who I turned away for her own good," Teebor recalled with a fond gleam. "But you did not listen to me."

Jordan nodded silently, repressing a nostalgic grin.

"I knew you would be Chieftess of the Mokta one day," he continued.

His words surprised Jordan. She remained silent but her questions were evident.

"I could see it in your eyes." Teebor paused. "And you proved me correct when you and your hunting pack returned to help save this village. You even jumped on a Deathwing. My fiercest warriors would never consider such a feat, but you—a young huntress—did it without hesitation."

Jordan knew Teebor was complimenting her but the mention of Deathwings made her uncomfortable. She did her best to hide it, though she wasn't sure she was entirely successful. Jordan couldn't tell whether he detected her mild distress or not.

Teebor stepped forward, looking towards the crowd as he addressed his people.

"You have heard me tell how four Mokta once fought at our side to defend this village! And how one of them, a strange-looking young woman named Jorr-Don, rode a Deathwing to accomplish that task. This is that woman!" Teebor proclaimed loudly. "She and the Mokta defended our people then, and as Mokta Chieftess, she fought for the Kastadi now! Leading those same Deathwings, she destroyed the Gulstaa, our hated foe, the ones who slaughtered the innocent and helpless! Show the Mokta Chieftess your gratitude, my people!"

Thundering shouts and cheers of joy rang out, the giant Kastadi banging their fists against their chests and legs, as was their custom. The sheer volume of their voices was near-deafening. For appearance's sake, Jordan forced herself to smile in appreciation, to publicly acknowledge the goodwill of the Kastadi and their Chief. But inwardly, she felt nauseated and chilled. It did not feel right to be so vigorously praised for killing one's enemy. Nor did she want what seemed like vindication for the worst and most costly failure of her life and tenure as Chieftess.

Oblivious to Jordan's inner turmoil, Teebor approached Bopol and clasped him by the shoulders, leaning forward to meet his gaze. Bopol's expression was a mixture of appreciation and concern for his mate.

"It is good to see you again, Bopol of the Mokta! I am pleased you survived this war." Teebor looked at Bopol and his children. "You chose your mate well and have a fine family!"

"Thank you, Mighty One," Bopol replied with no small amount of pride. Teebor grinned and then returned his attention to Jordan.

"Your appearance has changed some since I last saw you. I was told that you encountered the legendary SnowFire?"

"Are you sure this is a good thing to discuss in front of your people?" Jordan had concern in her voice.

Teebor considered the matter for a few seconds. Then he smiled again.

"Whether here or at the feast we have prepared for you, we will be before the people. Whatever you have to say can be heard by all. They would know of this in time anyway."

Now it was Jordan's turn to contemplate briefly. "I did not *just* encounter SnowFire," Jordan said. "She shared her blood with me. I became her daughter."

Teebor's eyes widened momentarily but he wisely chose to not speak right away. When he did, it was with some caution. "What do you mean, you became her daughter?"

Jordan had attempted to prepare herself for this conversation, as she had for the discussion with the Mokta leadership. She knew what she had to say, but it was difficult. She took a breath and steeled herself.

"I do not just share her appearance. I have her strength now . . . and her temper," Jordan replied. "At the village of Meddika, after the Deathwings initially scattered their ranks, I attacked and killed them—almost one hundred soldiers—by myself. I had no blade of my own, no shield. I used their weapons. I allowed only one wounded Gulstaa soldier to survive to warn their Heng Da. But she ignored my offer . . . and now . . . "

Jordan's face had been expressionless as she began to speak. But by the time she finished, tears were streaming from both eyes. "The Deathwings call me Fire Bringer and SnowFirechild. They have pledged to aid me whenever I call upon them," Jordan declared in a hollow tone. "And you should know this: my mother no longer walks this world."

Then she raised her eyes and looked at Teebor. Her hair flickered with flames around her face. When she next spoke, it sounded like more than one voice.

"I am Snow and Fire."

She could see that her words cut through the Chief. She imagined he was not used to feeling fear, especially concerning this young woman whom he treated like a granddaughter. She radiated authority and, with that simple utterance, had demanded respect of everyone present. It was not a description. It was a command.

She knew that no one had expected her to do this. In one short sentence, she had hushed an entire village. They feared her.

It was not what she wanted but it was a regrettable necessity.

"Why are you here?" Teebor broke the silence.

"I want to solidify and formalize the Mokta's alliance with the Kastadi, make it public and permanent," Jordan replied.

"That is good. We can agree to that," the Chief answered, sounding relieved.

"Good. But there is one condition."

"What is this word, kunn-dish-un? What does it mean?"

"It means I want something in return," Jordan answered, her expression hardening. "And I will not take no for an answer."

That displeased Teebor. But he looked like he respected her honesty.

"What is it you want?" he inquired.

"It is a big world. I believe there are Gulstaa who had nothing to do with this war, living in other regions and countries. I am working to have others find them and tell them what happened, to encourage them to return to their home country and help them to recover in some small way."

"Why would you do that?" Teebor raged, towering over her. "They killed Mokta as well as Kastadi! You are the one who destroyed them! Why would you now aid them?"

"Because it is the right thing to do," Jordan replied sternly. "And you will let them cross your borders to go home."

Teebor appeared incensed. "If any Kastadi sees any Gulstaa, they will kill them on sight!"

Jordan had known this would likely be the Kastadi Chief's reaction. She was prepared for it.

"Agree to my terms and I will greatly reward your village, Mighty One. I know how to turn your village into the most important place in this region. People will come here from all over the world to buy all things Kastadi. You will have wealth and influence like a king!"

"What? How?" Teebor asked, disarmed by her intriguing proposition.

"I can tell you . . . but you must first agree to what I have asked of you," she replied.

She saw Teebor wrestle with his pride for a moment. What she was asking was no small thing, but neither was what she was offering in return.

"What if any of the traveling Gulstaa attack us?" Teebor retorted.

Jordan nodded. "If they are foolish enough to do that, deal with them as you see fit."

That satisfied Teebor. "Very well. I agree to your terms."

"Declare it openly then, so that everyone will know."

Teebor nodded. And over the next several minutes, he explained to his people what needed to happen regarding the Gulstaa.

Then he, Jordan, and her family sat down to a massive feast and to discuss trade and development.

———

Two cycles later, Ilsketh Jartaf stood atop a hill and peered towards something in the distance. She was exhausted. Keymor, her mate, put his hand to her shoulder and steadied her. He was taller than her and had a lean but strong build. His eyes appeared sharp and alert.

"It is another group of our people. Eight or ten, from what I can see."

"Your eyes are better than mine," Ilsketh said.

"You need rest. You gave birth to our son only recently. You should not be—"

One harsh look from Ilsketh silenced him. Despite all the Gulstaa had suffered, she was still Heng Da. The needs of her people came before her own. But inwardly, she appreciated his concern for her wellbeing.

"It will take a long time to restore our population to even a fraction of what it once was," Ilsketh responded. "But at least now we are seeing regular migrations of Gulstaa from other parts of the world."

They stood in silence, continuing to watch the approaching travelers.

"They all say the same thing, you know," Keymor said.

Ilsketh nodded. "Yes. The Mokta sought them out and told them to return home. And they would not have done that unless their Chieftess commanded them to."

"We would not have made as much progress as we have without their efforts."

She sighed. "I know that. She destroys us then helps us. I do not understand it."

"Perhaps she is seeking forgiveness."

Ilsketh could clearly see the travelers now. It was a whole family, four adults and six children, including an infant. They carried quite a few bags. Many of the traveling Gulstaa had brought relief supplies, food, and even building tools and materials. Some had reported that they had been given assistance by the Mokta.

"It will be a long time before I can forgive that woman," Ilsketh declared with a bittersweet smile. "But it is no longer an impossibility."

25

BITTERSWEET MELODY

BOPOL HAD WITNESSED FORTY CYCLES of peace and relative prosperity come to the region of Algoran occupied by the Mokta and the Kastadi. And the lives and cultures of those peoples blossomed as well. This day, the Mountain Mokta villagers were gathered together for a special birthday celebration.

"This is a wonderful day!" Chieftess Jordan SnowFire shouted with pride and joy. "My daughter's firstborn, her daughter Altisa, has reached The Dawning Time!"

Altisa was tall and athletic, with long, wavy hair that blended white with blue. Sporting the ice-colored eyes of her gemta and gemtabana, she comported herself with a quiet dignity, as though she knew exactly what she wanted to do. Her gemta Jasta stood at her side wearing her maternal robe. Altisa's torkomm Kabi had perished nine cycles ago as a sentry protecting the village from a large pack of zala beasts. Bopol knew how much Kabi would have wanted to attend this, as he had Altisa's fifth birthday.

Bopol stood by his granddaughter's side in Kabi's place. He had done all he could to guide Altisa and her younger sister, Kalta, through childhood into adolescence. Smiling as he witnessed her accomplishment, Bopol realized he had finally gotten over his aversion to ceremony. He was still in good health but now that he was in his seventh

268

decade of life, time and experience had etched lines and wrinkles onto his face and body. He was surprisingly strong, but his stamina was fading with each cycle and his eyesight had begun to grow poor.

At the same time, he admired Jordan, his mate of forty-six cycles. She was the same age as him, but she looked the same as a woman of thirty cycles. Her blue hair, which she now kept at shoulder-length, had lightened some with the cycles. And when he looked into her eyes, that was the best reflection of her true age. He could see their relationship, both the love and sadness, the gains and losses, every day and night. She was just as beautiful to him now as she had been the day they met. And her actions throughout their marriage had proven to him that she felt the same about him. Sometimes he felt insecure about the differences in their appearance, but she always reassured him with her love and devotion. She had even given him one more son sixteen cycles ago. They named him Teesbin, the Mokta word for honor. He stood at his gemta's side as she invoked the ancient words for the Dawning Time:

"We are born into our families, who love and nurture us. They protect us and raise us until we reach the Dawning Time," Jordan recited from memory. "But there comes a day when we are children no longer. We leave behind who we were and become who we were meant to be. We join the hunt and go out into this world. We start on the path towards choosing a mate and one day, having children of our own, that we love and nurture."

Then Jordan turned and looked right at Altisa. "For you, my beloved granddaughter, this is that day."

Altisa smiled briefly, maintaining eye contact. "Yes, Chieftess."

"Do you have anything you wish to declare?" Jordan added.

"Yes, Chieftess. I know I am still young," Altisa responded. She then pointed at a young man in the audience. "But I wish for Antam to be my mate this day!"

Bopol was not really surprised by this development. Jasta had told him and Jordan of Altisa's close friendship with the young man. It was unusual to take a mate at this age, but it was entirely acceptable within Mokta custom.

Bopol watched Jordan make eye contact with Antam, who was obviously nervous and fidgety.

"Antam, do you also wish to become Altisa's mate?"

The young man straightened up and lifted his chin. His eyes showed determination.

"Yes, Chieftess, I do!"

Jordan smiled, clearly pleased with his response. She made eye contact with Altisa once more, as if to ask "are you sure?" Bopol smiled as Altisa nodded eagerly.

"Very well. With that, let everyone gathered be your witnesses! Altisa SnowFire has asked Antam to be her mate and he has agreed," Jordan proclaimed. "Now all that remains is the joining of blood. Antam and Altisa, step forward."

The young couple stood before their Chieftess. Bopol beheld them side by side. Antam was slightly shorter than Altisa but that was normal. She was one-quarter human. And despite his current abashedness, Antam was known for his speed and cunning. He was also Hosp's great grandson. Bopol knew he would be a fine hunter and after that, an artisan.

The Chieftess pulled her personal dagger from her own robes and handed it to Antam. He took it and sliced across his palm before handing it to Altisa. She made a quick cut and returned the blade to Jordan.

Then she and Antam put their palms together and smiled. Bopol knew what would happen next.

"Antam and Altisa, you have followed in the tradition of our ancestors and joined through blood," Jordan declared lovingly. "May your days together be many!"

"And may your hut be filled with the laughter of children!" a somewhat hoarse voice interjected unexpectedly.

It was Lynsha, who had arrived late, accompanied by her only child, her son Bektaz. Cycles ago, Lynsha had become a clothes maker who worked with Zoska. Now in her sixth decade, she leaned on a thick walking stick to support her leg, which had become arthritic with time. She proceeded forward, watched cautiously by Bektaz.

She appeared to be in good spirits, however, and pleased to see this union take place. She obviously took some satisfaction at making a scene, too.

"Well, somebody had to say it!" she continued.

"Aunt Lynsha?" Altisa exclaimed, blushing.

"I am glad you have taken a mate at this age," Lynsha added. "No one should be like me and wait so long. Have your little ones when you are young and can care for them well. Enjoy every moment with your mate."

Lynsha lived thirty-seven cycles before taking an older mate, a widower named Kimtas. He had passed away from an illness when their son was only nine cycles old.

"I will, Aunt Lynsha," Altisa assured.

"Stop trying to act so noble, my friend," Jordan interrupted, deliberately lightening the mood. "I know you have come only for the sweet bread and pastries!"

Lynsha laughed. "You know me so well, Chieftess!"

"Well, you will have to beat me to it this time! I intend to indulge myself today!" Jordan quipped, patting her stomach. She looked around. "Everyone, please enjoy yourselves and congratulate my granddaughter and new grandson!"

———————

Jordan greeted several people, but she was looking for someone in particular. When she was about to give up hope of their attendance, Jordan spotted her.

"Zoska! I am so glad you made it!" Jordan beamed.

"I am sorry I missed the ceremony, Chieftess," Zoska replied, looking tired and embarrassed. "But I knew I had to come. I wanted to be here, for you and your family."

"Thank you. It means a lot to us."

Time had been kind to Zoska. She stood tall and moved easily for a woman of her cycles. Her lines and wrinkles were accents to her strongest features: her eyes, her brow, and her smiling lips. But there was a sadness in her gaze that never went away.

"Reiban could not make it?" Jordan asked.

"No, his fever returned this morning." Zoska frowned, fighting back tears. "Maska is with him now."

Jordan pulled her best friend into a gentle hug. It had been twenty-five cycles since Reiban contracted the Shilvaba. Like Jordan's mother, he had survived. But in addition to being blinded by the illness, his own health had never fully recovered. He would go for months, sometimes whole cycles without fever or convulsions. But now that he was an elder, his immune system could no longer protect him as it once had. He was dying and knew it. So did everyone who was close to him.

"Is there anything I can do?" Jordan asked. "Healer Rizok may have something—"

"With respect, Chieftess, my daughter knows all the remedies," Zoska interrupted. "If there is a way to soothe him, she will find it."

Jordan nodded wistfully.

"I fear for my girl, Jorr-Don. She has cared for her torkomm for so many cycles, sacrificed so much. What will she do when he is gone?"

"She will find her place, hoszab," Jordan suggested, using the Mokta word for sister.

"We all do, I suppose," Zoska replied. "I always thought she would become Arrow's mate. She dreamed about it as a child . . . but then, her torkomm's illness happened."

"And Pamela was like Altisa. She chose Arrow and went after him with all her heart," Jordan responded. "And she got him."

Zoska nodded slowly.

"I resented and admired her at the same time," Zoska admitted.

"I know. I felt some of that also. Erica made Pamela aware of their history, asked her to make certain of her decision."

"It was his decision as well. And my daughter did not fight for him. Now she must live with that."

Jordan looked around nervously, considering alternate topics.

"I saw your sons here with their families," she finally said.

"Yes, they are the bright spots in my life. And now my sons are both torkommtas—which makes me feel old. But the little ones make me not care!"

Jordan couldn't help but chuckle at that. "They do have that effect, do they not?" Jordan agreed.

Zoska flashed a genuine smile at Jordan. "I am grateful your family has grown so, Jorr-Don! When you first arrived here, you were so alone, even with your gemta present. But now, you will never be alone again."

"I suppose you are right."

Zoska took on an air of contentment for the moment.

"Then when my time comes, I will not worry about you," she confided.

"Your time? You will outlive Kitranor, who saw ninety-two cycles before she passed last year!"

"No, Chieftess, I will not," Zoska replied soberly. "When Reiban is gone, I will not remain long without his love. It sustains me even now, when he is at his weakest. I have always known this, so do not be saddened. It is the way of things for us."

"Zoska . . . I am selfish. I need you."

The older woman raised an eyebrow at Jordan's meek statement.

"Jorr-Don, Chieftess of the Mountain Mokta? The woman who survived an attack by Queen Amstar? The one who was chosen by SnowFire herself? The leader who brought peace to Algoran and maintains it to this day? No, you do not need this old woman," Zoska blustered with an impish grin. "But I am happy that you care about me so much."

"I will protect Maska," Jordan answered Zoska's unspoken request. "You have my word."

Zoska nodded, looking relieved.

———

Maska kept the fire burning inside the hut and put a fresh blanket over her shivering torkomm, tenderly wiping his brow. She had aged very slowly, like Arrow, Jordan, and Erica. For a woman who had seen forty-six cycles, she did not look a day over twenty. She was strong and agile from the exercise she made of regular chores and errands. And though she told no one, during the times when her father was better, she slipped out of the village regularly to be alone and work out her stress by climbing trees, running through fields, and defending herself against the zala and other beasts. It was when she was caring for her father that she had the most time to think. And usually, that worked against her. So she preferred to keep herself busy.

"Maska," Reiban called, his voice raspy from dehydration. "Why do you not find a mate . . . and have children like your brothers?"

She had expected this question. It arose ever so often, so she smiled and recited the answer she had given before.

"I will live a long time, Torkomm," she replied, stroking his balding hair. "I can have any mate I choose and bear young when the time is right."

She brought him a bowl of cool water and helped him drink it. Then he leaned back and spoke in the direction he heard his daughter.

"I had just . . . hoped to know them myself," Reiban responded. "Now . . . I do not think I will."

This brought a frown to Maska's face.

"Do not talk like that. I will see you back to health and you will know many more cycles, Torkomm."

He reached for and found Maska's hand. He then pulled it to the middle of his chest.

"I have been fortunate to have you as a daughter, Maska. No torkomm could ask for more love and devotion from his child than you have shared. But you have given up too much to keep me alive . . . and I cannot ask that of you any longer."

"Torkomm?"

"Forgive. These are . . . merely the ramblings of an old man."

"You are not old, Torkomm!"

Her father breathed in as best he could and exhaled. Then he smiled. And though his eyes did not see any longer, they still conveyed his rich personality. She could tell he was now determined to enjoy this time with her, his firstborn.

"Can you sing to me? I want to hear *The Twin Stars*."

"Of course!" Maska replied with glee.

She closed her eyes and recalled lyrics to the ancient Mokta melody. A few seconds later, she opened her mouth and released the words in her crystal-clear soprano voice.

"Above the mountains and the clouds
Over beautiful skies of green
Live the brothers of the night
The twin stars must be seen
Hylot and Ghorot once roamed the lands of Algoran so fair
They tamed and rode only the wildest Govon mares
They fought the giants in the East and drove them to the North
They turned the course of the Kuseej River and split it into four
When all their fame spread the world round
And no more adventure could be found
They took their steeds into the skies
And the brothers left this world behind
They light the night, they are the Twin Stars
They are always right, we need the Twin Stars

"They will never burn out

They will never grow cold

They are the Twin Stars!

They are the Twin Stars!"

Maska danced all around the floor, twirling her arms happily as she sang. Knowing her father loved this tune, she repeated it from the beginning. She projected all her heart into every movement, word, and sound. When she stopped, she was tired but satisfied.

Apparently, so was her father. He had closed his eyes and had a beautiful grin on his face, a look of complete peace.

But he was so still.

"Torkomm?" Maska whispered softly and fearfully.

She moved closer. His chest no longer rose and fell. His lips and nostrils were still. She rushed to his side and felt his forehead and neck. The fever had broken. She put her hand to his chest but could not feel his heartbeat.

"Torkomm . . . no," she whimpered. "I was going to make you better. I was—I was—"

She collapsed to the ground next to her father's bed. Her grief welled up within her until, needing release, she heaved great sobs and wailed.

And the whole village knew that Reiban had died.

26

RUMINATIONS

ZOSKA REACHED THE HUT FIRST. She had been visiting with a neighbor when she heard Maska's cry. Slowly, she crossed the floor and kneeled as best she could beside her daughter. And she looked at her mate's face. Though tears streamed from her eyes, his final smile was infectious. Whatever had occurred, he was at peace . . . then and now.

"What happened?" Zoska managed to say.

"Gemta, he asked me to sing 'The Twin Stars' for him, so I did. But when I was done, he—"

Zoska put her arm around her daughter to comfort her.

"You did well. That was his last request and you made him happy. I am proud of you, daughter."

"I wanted to make him well again."

"I know. But no one could do that. You did all that was possible. He knew you loved him."

Zoska's twin sons, Keelto and Pasil, arrived next, joined by their mates and members of their families. Other villagers had gathered outside but, out of respect, did not enter.

Lastly, Jordan and Bopol entered the hut. When she saw Reiban, the Chieftess put her hand over her mouth and began to cry. Zoska could see that Jordan wanted to comfort her. But the Chieftess made herself stand still and motioned Bopol to go ahead. Reiban had been best friends with Bopol for as long as she could remember.

Bopol moved forward unsteadily. His brave demeanor crumbled with every step and his tears welled up. He looked on Reiban's serene face and smiled, though Zoska could tell his heart was breaking.

"Do you remember, Zoska, when the three of us met as children?" he said.

Zoska chuckled mirthlessly. "How could I forget? Reiban talked me into playing a joke on you. I pretended like Reiban was missing and I needed you to help me find him before dinner. It distracted you while Reiban sneaked up and poured dark blue dye on your head."

Bopol shook his head. "My hair was that terrible color for nearly sixty moonturns! How old were we then?"

"Five or six, I think."

"I will miss your mate's wonderful sense of humor. And his counsel. He was a great friend and man. If there is anything I can do, let me know."

Zoska nodded, too choked up to speak. Bopol gently put his hand on her shoulder and then walked out of the hut. Jordan silently sat down beside Zoska on the ground next to the bed.

"Thank you for coming, Chieftess," Zoska remarked hoarsely.

"You do not have to call me Chieftess now. I am here as a friend."

Zoska nodded then returned her view to her mate. A pained smile crossed her lips.

"I am . . . glad that he is no longer suffering." She paused. "But I am no longer complete."

"Gemta . . . " Maska worried, embracing her mother.

Hours later, Zoska noted that everyone went back home except for Jordan and Bopol. Bopol kept Maska company while Jordan took her outside to talk. They sat on some rocks close to the trees and off the main village path. The moons were bright. It was bitter cold, but the breeze was mild.

"My sons have their children and grandchildren but my daughter needs me," Zoska shared. "If it is possible, she loves her father as much as I do. It will be hard for her to move on."

"He was an incredible father. I envy her closeness with him," Jordan replied. "I loved my father, but I did not see him often enough. And now I will never see him again, either."

Zoska sighed and looked up at the night sky.

"You chose to leave your father and mother," she continued. "Maska would never do that. We have to leave her, force her to grow up."

"Zoska, is that not . . . cruel?"

"I will get her through this, Jorr-Don. She is my daughter. But I know her better than anyone. I should have carried the burden of Reiban's care all these cycles. It was not Maska's place."

"How can you say that? As his eldest—"

Zoska angrily slapped her hand down on the rock she sat upon.

"Jorr-Don, stop. Has your vision grown so dim with time that you cannot see? Maska was afraid to become an adult. Her father's illness was an excuse to avoid larger responsibilities. She loved your son but could not ask him to be her mate. And when he chose another, she chose no one else. She is trapped now and does not know what to do."

Jordan's shoulders slumped in sad contemplation.

"I had not considered that, Zoska."

"I have had a long time to think about this, as did Reiban. I think this is was what he wanted."

Jordan sat up straight again, startled.

"What?" she exclaimed.

"You have been a parent almost as long as I have. Would you not do something if you saw your child not living their life, not moving forward?"

"Yes, I guess I would."

Zoska smiled.

"Of course, you would, because you love your children. So did Reiban. He has set in motion a chain of events that cannot be stopped. And Maska will have to adjust. She will have to live for herself now and make her own decisions."

Jordan leaned forward, wrapped her hands around her legs and stared at the ground.

"When did you get so wise, old friend?"

"I will have you know I have always been wise, bluehair!"

"Not so blue as when I was a girl," Jordan chuckled, gently pulling Zoska into a side-hug.

"You know, I may not get to see you grow old." Zoska smiled. "But I have lived to see you become a great-grandmother like me. And that is almost as good."

Jordan pulled back in confusion.

"What are you talking about?"

"Arrow's oldest, Meespa, just learned she is with child. I overheard her telling her sister while I visited Hosp this afternoon. I am sure she and Karfoz will tell her parents, and you, soon."

"Wow," Jordan said under her breath.

Zoska laughed. "I have not heard you use an Errrth word in many cycles! You must be surprised!"

"Be quiet, old woman!" Jordan joked.

"You are an old woman, too. You just do not look like it."

"You are right," Jordan said. "I may not look it . . . but sometimes, I do feel it."

Zoska playfully smacked Jordan on the head. It jolted her out of what could have become a melancholy mood and made her laugh.

"What was that for?" Jordan asked.

"That was for taking what I said too seriously. You still have a son at home, only just past The Dawning Time. How can you think you are old, no matter what I say?"

"It might have something to do with that great-grandmother part!"

Zoska sighed. "I guess my daughter is not the only one who needs me."

"What is that supposed to mean?"

Zoska looked up at the moons again, ruminating in the moment. She knew Jordan was looking at her.

"How do you stay so beautiful?" Jordan whispered. Perhaps she thought Zoska couldn't hear her. Zoska appreciated the compliment, especially now.

"I have fulfilled almost everything I ever wanted to do with my life. I became a huntress, found a mate, had children and became a clothes designer. I have seen three more generations born to my family. I know my own time is short but that is how it should be. Once my daughter can manage on her own, I can die peacefully . . . like my mate."

Zoska looked at Jordan and smiled, momentarily contented.

"Do you know what a precious gift was shared with you, Jorr-Don? You will see many more cycles than I, remaining young and beautiful for who knows how long. But your children and their descendants will change the Mokta in a way that has not happened since SnowFire had children with First Chief. Even now, your blood runs in the veins of three generations of Mokta. It will extend their lives and give them an appearance similar to yours. Your blood will run in the veins of all Mokta forever! You really are Jordan SnowFire, daughter of a legend. You have now become a legend, too."

Jordan took on a distant expression.

"I never wanted to be a legend," she admitted softly.

"I do not think anyone who becomes one ever planned to," Zoska replied. "It just happens."

Jordan let out a long exhale.

"I did not even think I was capable of choosing a mate." Jordan paused. "Do you remember?"

"Yes. You thought you would wait many cycles before having your first child."

"And you teased me about that for many moonturns, until I learned I was pregnant! Even then, you still were not satisfied until I grew heavy with my second child, my daughter. After that, you left me alone."

"That was just to return your teasing for when I carried Maska," Zoska recalled.

"Was I really that bad?"

"How many times did you ask me if I was having twins?"

"I thought I asked if you were having three, not two."

"You did! I had forgotten. You see?"

Still sitting on the neighboring rocks, they leaned against each other fondly.

"I went easy on you when you really were having twins," Jordan added.

"You were running around after Arrow. I think you were too tired to harass me."

Jordan smiled. "You are probably right."

They sat in silence for a few minutes.

"You should have more children with Bopol, Jorr-Don."

"What? Where did that come from?"

"Your body is still young enough . . . and it would honor your mate."

"I . . . will consider it."

With a wry grin, Zoska looked her normal self for a moment.

"Perhaps this time, you can have the twins!" Zoska laughed.

Jordan playfully smacked Zoska on the head. "Now you are teasing me again!"

"For my dear friend, always."

"I will love you forever, hoszab."

"And I will love you as well."

They bid each other a good night and returned to Zoska's hut. Zoska watched Bopol walk Jordan home.

27

TRAVELING COMPANIONS

ARROW WAS AWAKENED BY A sweet kiss from Pamela, his bride of twenty-nine cycles. They had taken a trip to the Kastadi lands to celebrate their mating anniversary. It also coincided with Pamela's fiftieth birthday. They had rented a room at an inn in the capitol city of Mekit in the Harkaz province.

In the Kastadi rebuilding renaissance that followed the Gulstaa War, Mekit had grown from a medium-sized village to a large metropolitan hub. During that time, the Kastadi also experienced a population explosion while increasing their trade with the Mokta and anyone else interested in the craftsmanship of their people. The Kastadi produced fine clothing, material resources such as agriculture, refined metals, oils, grains, and spices. They were well known for their authentic beverages, jewelry, sculptures, and weapons.

After twenty cycles, the Chief died and his daughter, Hakorth, attained the role of Chieftess. Like many still living in Mekit, she had survived the Deathwing attack of nearly half a century before. She was more than pleased to entertain the son of Jorr-Don, Deathwing Rider. She afforded Arrow and his mate special discounts during their visit with a written note bearing her seal.

Presently, Arrow kept his eyes on Pamela as she laid on her back at an angle next to him, staring at the ceiling while holding him warmly.

She laughed suddenly, which caused a slight crinkling at the corners of her eyes and accentuated the lines between her nose and mouth. She was tall and somewhat pear-shaped. She wore her deep green hair long and free like a woman half her age. Unlike other Ullvarr, she did not shore one side of her hair.

"This must be the tallest, most spacious room I have ever stayed in," Pamela observed.

Arrow grinned. "Well, it was made for Kastadi, not Mokta or Ullvarr."

"It is grand, but I do not understand why you wanted to come to this city after so long?"

"Because this is where we went when we first became mates. Gemta would call it our honeymoon."

"What is this word HUH-nee-myoon?"

"It is a word from Gemta's world, in her first language. It is a customary trip that mates make upon their joining through blood."

His gemta had actually described *honeymoon* entirely in Earth terms. But Arrow had not understood all of it and filled in the gaps in a way he thought his mate would comprehend.

"So, you wanted to honor that custom? How sweet of you." She smiled, kissing him once more. "I am honored."

"I am surprised your kacheela did not tell you of it. She is also from Errrth."

"Kacheela does not say much about her time on her first world. I think many bad things happened."

Arrow ran his finger softly along the side of Pamela's round cheek. Then he pulled her close and looked up at her lovingly.

"Then I am glad that she found joy in joining with your asta," Arrow responded. "Everyone deserves happiness."

"It is good that they loved one another as we do," she agreed. "When Kacheela had my sister and then my brother, that is when I knew I could become your mate."

"Um, what? Why?"

"If an Ullvarr could have children with someone from Errrth and your gemta was from Errrth, then I knew I could have your children someday."

"You knew you wanted that at such a young age?"

Pamela turned, sat up, and let her legs dangle from the bed. Arrow sat next to her and massaged her shoulders and back.

"Thank you, my dearest one," she said regarding his tender ministrations. "You should know, I fell in love with you almost as soon as I met you, when I was ten. I felt strongly that we could become mates."

"So we did," Arrow added. "And now, we have children."

"Five children," she replied, looking at him with a satisfied smile. "No small accomplishment, eh?"

"Did you plan to have so many?" he asked.

Pamela stood up and stretched, which straightened out the silky, deep blue night dress she was wearing. Facing away from her mate, she slightly pulled back one of the curtains to look at the morning bustle outside. Merchants were selling vegetables and meats in wooden carts and stands not far from the inn. Tourists and other travelers were abundant, many sampling and buying their goods.

"I would have more if I could, but I am too old now," she admitted sadly.

"Who is old? You?" he quipped. "I think not."

She let go of the curtain and watched it close. She returned to Arrow's side and put her arms around his neck. He loved the way she was flirting with just her eyes and smile. She ran her hands through his thick mane of blue and white hair.

"You are kind, my Heartpath," she continued. "But while you may look exactly the same as the day we joined, I most certainly do not."

"That is all right. I am completely content."

"Can it be that since you do not age, you do not see age, either?"

"I age, just very slowly, it seems. And I do see age as well. But to me, you have grown only more beautiful with the cycles."

"You could sell a zala beast its own spots with that flattering tongue, Arrow!" She giggled.

He looked at her, feigning offense, as if to say, "Who, me?"

Just then, there was a knock at their door. He assumed it was Jaidos and Zeetra. They had accompanied Arrow and Pamela on this trip, as they had wanted to take a vacation as well. They had said they were inspired by the other couple's choice of locale.

"Are you two zala beasts ever going to get out of bed?" Jaidos shouted in mock annoyance. "We had to give up the table we reserved for the four of us, you've been taking so long!"

Arrow took off his shirt from the previous day and grabbed a clean pullover to put on. Pamela searched the closet for something appropriate to wear.

"You know, you really did not have to wait for us, Jaidos," Arrow muttered through the locked door. "I am sure you know how to eat breakfast without us."

"I told him this," Zeetra interjected. "But my mate wanted us all to be together. What can I say?"

"Tell him he will have to wait a little longer. I am ready but Pamela —"

"With that hair? I do not think so!" Pamela derided.

Ten minutes later, Arrow and Pamela joined the other couple outside their room. Jaidos had entered his sixth decade of life. He was still slender and strong, though his hair had receded, and he wore special glasses which his mate had constructed to help his vision. Due to her Onchei heritage, Zeetra still looked like a woman in her twenties. However, she had grown heavy after having four children. Today, she wore her long white hair with a wide fishtail style braid on the right side.

They walked around the corner to a bakery which also contained a small restaurant. The establishment owner had the foresight to add several non-Kastadi tables for tourists such as them. After a short wait, the four of them sat down. Arrow asked Zeetra to interpret the written menu for them. She had been required to learn all the main languages used on Algoran during her youth. Properly informed of the eatery's cuisine choices, they placed their orders.

"What have you thought of the city so far?" Arrow asked Jaidos and Zeetra.

"It is wondrous, truly," Jaidos replied. "The stories we were told do not give a fair account. We were particularly impressed with the jewelry at the market."

Arrow noted that Zeetra said nothing but touched upon a golden necklace she was wearing and smiled. It had a sapphire-like stone in the center. Against her pale skin, it was quite striking.

"My mate is modest, but she is also wearing some kasteeni stone earrings," Jaidos added.

"Have you been to Mekit before?" Pamela asked Zeetra.

"I have not been inside the gates, but I passed it several times on missions when I first joined the Onchei Science Directive," Zeetra replied, clearly uncomfortable with the topic.

"Well, that was then. What do you think of it now?" Pamela inquired

"It is lovely. And the Kastadi are such a handsome people. I admire them and what they have accomplished, especially since the end of the war."

"Yes, they are impressive," Pamela agreed.

There were a few awkward moments where the travelers had trouble deciding on their next discussion topic. They sipped on their mugs of water and beheld their surroundings, remaining pleasant.

Finally, Arrow spoke up. "Today we celebrate Pamela's fiftieth cycle."

Pamela nearly spat out the water in her mouth. For half a second, she looked at him as if to say, "What is *wrong* with you?"

"Much happiness," Zeetra replied, attempting to deflect Arrow's unintended mistake. "I think it is wonderful!"

"Yes, much happiness!" Jaidos added, picking up on his mate's objective.

"Thank you," Pamela responded. "I am glad for my life and everyone in it. I . . . wish I were not concerned about my age."

"If it makes you feel better, I know how you must feel," Jaidos interrupted with a nervous smile.

Pamela nodded. "Thank you. But I think we four have something else to celebrate: our children are the continuations of our peoples, the Onchei and the Ullvarr."

"Agreed. Thoroughly blended, to be sure." Zeetra laughed. "But continuations just the same."

"Yes!" Arrow raised his mug. "It is wondrous!"

"You also have the blood of SnowFire, Arrow, as your gemta does," Zeetra added.

"As does my kacheela," Pamela interjected. "A shame I was adopted. Were I her blood child, I would be as immortal as my mate."

"I am hardly immortal," Arrow replied defensively. "I may live a long time, but I will eventually grow old. As will Zeetra."

Zeetra nodded in response.

"That does not help us right now," Jaidos joked. "If our tribe did not know us well, they would mistake me for Zeetra's grandfather."

Pamela chuckled. "I comfort myself with the understanding that Arrow will defend my honor to anyone who may question us, even if I do look like . . . his older sister!"

That brought mirth, cheers, and laughter to the whole table. And shortly, their server brought their food.

28

FRAGILE SCULPTURE

ERICA SNOWFIRE HAD TAKEN UP sculpting about twenty-five cycles ago, not long after the birth of her first biological child. She had tried to become a teacher to the Mokta children, as she had been to the Ullvarr. But since they had no written language, most of her work was storytelling. That was fine when her children were young. However, she decided that she wanted a hobby, something creative that would also help her relax.

The clay from Algoran was different from any on Earth; it was especially gritty, even when wet. Erica had learned that this was advantageous, though, as it allowed for more variety of textures. It had taken almost a decade to hone her skill to her satisfaction. And only in the last few cycles had she begun to sell some of her sculptures at the market.

Her current work was a large vase about a foot tall and two feet wide. She was shaping the opening at the top to be narrower than the rest of it, forming a gradual arch from the sides. Once it dried, she would paint and finish it.

Erica's daughter, Izikaa, walked up to the pathway that stretched through the middle of the Mountain Mokta village. Izikaa was accompanied by her eight-year old son, Shamol. Izikaa was short, thick and muscular, with a coarse head of blue and green hair pulled into a bushy long ponytail to keep it out of her way. Her skin was a very light pink. Shamol, in contrast, was tall for his age and slender with his blue, green, and white hair shorn close to his head. Since his father was Mokta, his flesh was basically hot pink in appearance but like his mother and grandmother, he had ice blue eyes.

"Azjama!" Shamol shouted excitedly, using the Ullvarr word for grandmother.

Erica immediately ceased working, turned, and opened her arms wide, signaling the boy to come hug her. He ran and leaped into her arms and she did a complete spin with him.

"It is so good to see you, Shamol!" Erica replied in Ullvarr, grinning.

"I am glad to see you again too, Azjama," he responded in Ullvarr.

"How was the fishing today?"

"Asta and Kacheela caught many fish, I just watched. But tomorrow, Asta said he will show me how to skin and clean the fish. And Kacheela is making a fish-catcher for me!"

"How exciting!" Erica added. "Soon, you will be catching more fish than your parents."

"Yes, Azjama!"

Izikaa pointed to the sculpture and cleared her throat to get her mother's attention. "Are you finished with this one, Kacheela?"

"Yes, it just needs to dry overnight."

"I love the design. You have not made one like this before."

"You like it?" Erica asked.

Izikaa nodded.

"Then it will be yours when I am done."

"Are you sure, Kacheela? It is beautiful."

"Yes, I am sure. What colors would you like it to be?"

"Hmm, let me think about that. Can I tell you tomorrow?"

"Yes, as long as you bring your son with you when you do."

"Gladly, Kacheela."

Erica looked at Shamol for a moment and her smile lessened.

"What is it, Kacheela?"

"He looks so much like him. I wish your Asta had lived to see his grandson."

"At least I was able to give him the news. And that made him very happy and proud," Izikaa recalled. "He missed his birth only by ninety moons."

"Healer Rizok did all he could but the cancer had run its course," Erica lamented.

Izikaa crossed her arms and sighed. "Kacheela, the Mourning Time has passed. You are still young. I think you should find a new mate among the Mokta."

"I do not know if I am ready, Izikaa. Your asta was my mate for thirty-four cycles. It is not so easy."

"It may not be easy, but I think it is important. My brother, sister, and I are grown, we have children of our own. You deserve to know love and companionship again."

"You think I do not still carry what Vakar and I shared? I will have that forever."

"Of course, you will, Kacheela. I meant no disrespect."

"I know, my daughter."

Izikaa gave her mother a hug. "When you are ready, I will help you."

Erica looked out across the village, still somewhat uneasy. Her eyes were becoming misty, but she was trying to be strong and smile. "Your asta was there for me, ever since I arrived on this world. Even when he did not like me, he was still my protector. No man ever made me feel as secure or as loved as him," Erica admitted. "How do I start over? I have lived seventy cycles. How will I relate to a younger mate? How can I open my heart to anyone else? I do not want to be lonely, but I am not sure what to do."

"That is why I will help you, Kacheela."

Erica heard someone else walking up. When she glanced over, she saw that it was Jordan.

"And I will help you, too, my sister," Jordan added in Ullvarr.

"Chieftess, this is a surprise!" Izikaa exclaimed nervously.

"Why is it a surprise for me to check on my sister? Or to visit with my niece and great nephew?"

"Chieftess, I did not know you spoke Ullvarr," Shamol said.

Jordan held up her palms so they faced the boy. "These help me understand and speak other languages."

"Is it sorcery?"

"I do not think so. The gems are a part of me, like they are on your azjama. It is more like the muscles in your arms or legs. If you tell them to move, they move. If these stones hear another language, they make it so I can understand it. And if I speak, it will take my Mokta words and make them heard as the other language. Do you understand?"

"Yes, Chieftess! That is a great gift!" Shamol nodded.

"They do not do that for *me*," Erica responded flippantly.

"I have tried to teach you this skill for forty cycles, Erica," Jordan teased. "You just do not want to learn."

"I am content with what I have," Erica replied. "It is bad enough that I am so long-lived."

"You are complaining about that?"

They'd had this discussion more than a few times. It had become almost a running joke between them.

"You can call me old-fashioned, but I think grandmothers should look, you know, like grandmothers!"

"You mean we should look and feel old?" Jordan replied. "Well, we do not. Take that up with SnowFire."

"Like I could do that, even if I wanted to . . . "

Jordan rolled her eyes. Then she shook her head. The joke had finally gotten stale.

"I take it back," Jordan insisted.

"Take what back?" Erica asked.

"Do not look for a mate. Spend all your free time by yourself or with your grandchildren," Jordan quipped. "You may as well go ahead and dye your hair gray or white, too, and paint some wrinkles on yourself. I'll even bring you a walking stick. Then no one will mistake you for a young woman!"

"Chieftess?" Izikaa interrupted, stepping forward in defense of her mother.

"Stay back, girl," Jordan warned. "I have known your kacheela since we were young ones. I have every right to speak to her this way!"

Erica glared at Jordan. She motioned for Jordan to walk with her. They went out a little ways into the woods to continue their conversation.

"Can't I just be tired, Jordan?" Erica shared glumly.

"Tired? Of what?"

"Change. My whole life has been one upheaval after another," Erica replied. "What happened to my parents, what happened to you and Janice, my fiancé, coming here, becoming SnowFire's daughter, being drugged by the Ullvarr, watching the Ullvarr get slaughtered . . . the whole Gulstaa war. My only moments of peace and joy were in finding you, becoming Vakar's mate, and becoming a parent and grandparent. But even in that, my mate died. I don't know how to move on!"

Jordan walked up to Erica and grabbed her by the shoulders, looking in her eyes sincerely.

"Moving on is not something you learn how to do," Jordan related. "You just do it . . . and do not look back. If help is offered and you need it, take it."

Erica could no longer fight her tears. Jordan helped her remain standing and let her cry on her shoulder.

After a few moments, Erica looked up at Jordan. "I need help," she said softly.

"Then you will have it," Jordan answered.

29

OBJECT IN THE SKY

THE GENTLE MOTION OF THE waves on the small boat was soothing in the late morning light. Bopol sat with his daughter, Jasta, and they looked at the blooming spring flowers along the slate gray sloping lake shore near the mountain.

"This was an inspired idea, Torkomm," Jasta complimented. "It has been too long since I spent time alone with you like this."

"You have been busy raising your daughters," he replied.

"I could not have done that without you. The girls and I will forever honor you for that, as we honor Kabi."

"Kabi was a great man, the only one from the village worthy of you."

Jasta blushed then looked sad. "Yes, he was a great man. I will never love another."

Bopol nodded. "That is your choice and I will respect it."

"Thank you, Torkomm."

Bopol peered at the shore and then at his daughter. He smiled. "You have your gemta's eyes."

Jasta chuckled. "That is because of the SnowFire blood in my veins."

"No, not the color. I meant the shape of them and the way you share your deepest emotions through them."

"Oh," she responded, blushing once more and looking downward.

"She is preparing you to be Chieftess one day, you know."

"My brother is the firstborn. He should be Chief before me."

Bopol took on a serious air and looked on his daughter with a conviction born from experience. "I have always known that my eldest son would not be Chief, even as I did not become Chief. He is an adventurer, meant to do other things. But hear me: Arrow will write his own legend someday."

"I believe you."

"Your legend is beginning now, Jasta."

Her eyes widened at that.

"What do you mean? What legend?"

"I have known since you were a little child that you were a leader like your gemta and gemtabana," Bopol continued. "You do not have to try; it is just inside you. Chieftess knows this also."

"I do not feel like any kind of leader, Torkomm. All I can see for myself as Mokta is raising my daughters. I learn the things Gemta teaches me, but I feel neither worthy nor ready for them."

"It is not time yet anyway," Bopol said with a grin. "But even if it were, do you think your gemta felt ready to become Chieftess and go to war with the Gulstaa? You had only just been born. I assure you, she did not feel ready."

"I understand. But I have no desire to lead our people."

"Neither did your gemta. And yet, she is Chieftess."

Jasta looked at him curiously. "Why are you telling me all of this, Torkomm?"

"I thought it might help make the transition easier when the time eventually comes."

"You believe in me that much?"

"More than you can even imagine, my daughter."

She hugged Bopol. Then she startled at something and turned her gaze skyward. Bopol wasn't sure what was troubling her.

"Torkomm, do you see that?"

"See what?"

Jasta pointed high above the mountain, even above the clouds, to a twinkling in the emerald-hued sky. After squinting and allowing his vision to focus, Bopol saw it as well.

"It looks like one of the nightstars."

"Yes, but we normally do not see any stars in the dayshine," Jasta said.

"Perhaps it is a skylance." Bopol shrugged. "It is interesting but nothing to be concerned about."

"I suppose you are right, Torkomm."

Bopol and Jasta stared at the spectacle for a few more seconds. She was clearly trying to analyze it further. Abandoning that effort, she took one of the oars and began to steer the boat towards the shore.

———————

Arrow watched as the jewelry merchant held up a crystal bracelet that was see-through, glossy, and lavender-colored. The merchant, a woman named Keebara was short for a Kastadi, just over six feet tall, and middle-aged. She had bright eyes and a lovely smile. She wore a blue blouse and dark blue pants. Her dark red hair had white flourishes that made her even more fascinating to behold.

"It took me sixty moonturns to refine the crystal. That is its natural color," Keebara said. "Would it not look beautiful on your lady's wrist?"

Arrow looked to his bride and she nodded pleasantly.

"Very well. How much do you want for it?" Arrow asked.

"Forty kootyrs or equivalent," she declared. "I could get twice that amount, but you are a SnowFire child. Your gemta saved me and my children from the Deathwings when she first came here."

"You honor me and my family," Arrow replied with a humble half-bow.

He reached into the knapsack he was carrying. He pulled out a handful of the silver-colored metallic currency and handed it to the merchant.

The kootyrs had been developed as a regional method of payment that was rapidly replacing the old bartering methods. His gemta had developed the idea with Zeetra over thirty cycles ago. She'd proposed it to the leaders of the Kastadi and seven other tribes in a one-thousand-kilometer area. But it had taken decades for everyone involved to agree on values and terms. This fledgling trade authority then created businesses whose sole purpose was to take in bartered goods and exchange them for the currency. They also created secure storage facilities for each community. Only now were kootyrs being used regularly to buy goods and services.

"Fifty kootyrs," he offered. "Because you do good work."

"Back then, I was a healer," Keebara recalled, nodding at the compliment. "I tended your gemta's wounds after she rode the Deathwing. Like you, she was kind and generous with her praise. I am glad she taught it to her offspring."

"And I am glad you kept her alive." Arrow winked. "Or I would not be here today!"

"It was not easy," the merchant replied with a wry side-glance. "She was a very brash young woman, leaping and flailing like one insane. But she and her pack were brave and fierce. They worked alongside our warriors and saved the village."

"And then Chief Teebor saved her," Arrow added.

Keebara nodded. "He was a great Chief! And his daughter is on her way to being one—"

Just then, there was a muffled *boom* that shot through the sky, grabbing everyone's attention. Arrow looked for any signs of an explosion, either on the ground or in the air, but there was none. However, when he looked towards the clouds in the direction of the twin stars, he did see a small silhouette. It was too far away to make out the shape.

"Arrow, could that be a Deathwing?" Pamela asked, putting her hand on his arm.

"No. Even from here, I can tell there is no flapping," he replied. "I do not think that is alive, whatever it is."

"We should find Zeetra and Jaidos."

"Agreed. I think they said they were going to a clothing merchant on the west end of the city."

It took almost ten minutes for Arrow and Pamela to move through the crowds and find their friends. Arrow gained Jaidos' attention while Pamela went to locate Zeetra. They met outside the establishments to view the strange phenomenon in the skies.

It had come closer but was still shaded by the stars' light. Two things were certain to Arrow, though: it was huge, whatever it was, and it was no bird or dragon. It also appeared to be heading straight for Mekit.

"Is it a flying machine?" Jaidos wondered aloud.

When she heard those words, Zeetra took on a haunted look. Arrow thought she'd grown even more pale than usual.

"No . . . it could not be . . . " she said quietly. Then she looked at the flying object again. "Could it?"

As the flying mystery got closer, Arrow could hear a low-range hum emanating from it, almost a droning sound, and its shape became clear. The object was almost half the size of the city. It came to a stop and hovered over the heart of the metropolitan area. It had wide and round metallic shields at its front and rear. In between were six oval segments, each the size of a city block, connected by metal rods. And the oval segments were rotating slowly in a continuous motion.

Zeetra's mouth hung open in stunned silence. Her eyes on the verge of tears. Her arms hung loosely at her sides, but her hands trembled.

"Do you recognize this thing, Zeetra?" Jaidos questioned.

"Zeetra, what is wrong?" Arrow asked, concerned. "What is it? What does this thing mean to you?"

"Are we in danger?" Pamela said looking worried.

Pamela's question broke through Zeetra's astonishment and terror. She nodded slowly, put her hands over her mouth for a moment and let them slide down her chin. Her eyes never left the object in the sky.

"Yes. Yes, we are in danger," she answered. "Great danger."

"Why? What is that thing?" Jaidos inquired.

"It is a machine meant to travel between worlds," Zeetra replied.

"How do you know of it? Never has our world seen such large machines," Jaidos declared.

Zeetra turned and looked at them, her eyes still sad and fearful. Arrow had never seen her this upset.

"Not the rest of the world, no . . . but I have. That machine is Onchei," she revealed. "It has been so long, I had forgotten. But I saw this machine leave our world."

"When was that?" Jaidos questioned.

Zeetra looked terrified and amazed at the same time.

"I was only a small girl. I did not understand at the time, I just remember that it was important, and it was beautiful to watch," Zeetra explained. "When I first started working for the Onchei Science Directive, I asked about it. My instructor told me that it was a colony ship with an experimental drive system that was supposed to travel at faster than light speeds."

"Faster than light? That would be very fast!" Arrow exclaimed.

"Yes. But they needed it to be that fast because worlds are so far apart," Zeetra added. "At slower speeds, it could take most of an Onchei's lifespan just to reach a habitable world. That was definitely not practical."

Pamela stepped forward to speak with Zeetra.

"So, your people could be on that ship?"

"A lot of my people could be on that ship. It was designed to hold five thousand passengers, including the crew."

Jaidos looked confused. Arrow and Pamela did not know what to do. They looked to Zeetra for answers.

"Then why are we in danger, my love?" Jaidos asked. "Would they not be happy to find you again?"

Zeetra shook her head, her brow furrowing.

"Jaidos, my dearest, they will want to know why the rest of my people are gone and what happened to them," she replied, softly touching her mate's cheek. "And they will not be happy to learn that Arrow's gemtabana slew them all."

Arrow considered Zeetra's words and became grim.

"She is right about that," he agreed.

"With the weapons on that vessel, they could destroy the Mokta Mountain and everyone on it," Zeetra lamented. "So yes, we are in great danger."

"Well, you would be safe, right? Maybe you could talk to them and convince them not to attack?" Pamela suggested.

Zeetra shook her head once more and chuckled without humor. She sighed. "I have broken the highest law of the Onchei, Pamela. So, I am not safe, either."

"What law is that?" Pamela asked, surprised.

"I have mated with an outsider and had mixed-race children. To my people, that is treason. It is punishable by death."

Their group was silent, even as the other travelers and locals ran about in fear.

Arrow broke the silence. "What should we do? If we leave now—"

"There is nowhere on this world that they will not find me," Zeetra interjected. "Their machines have already located me. That is why they came here. But it is not too late for you."

Zeetra took something out of her bag. It was a portable teleport device she kept with her for emergencies. She handed the device to Arrow.

"Take this, go back home and tell Chieftess," Zeetra told him. "She needs to know about this. I will stall for time. I will not tell them what happened to the Onchei for as long as I can."

"I will stay with you!" Jaidos exclaimed. "You will not face this alone."

"If you love me, you will go, Jaidos! They will kill you as soon as they learn you are my mate."

Arrow grabbed Jaidos by the wrist and looked at him insistently. He shook his head at Jaidos. "You are more use to her with us, my friend.. And she will have joy knowing you are alive. Do not deny her that."

Jaidos was clearly torn. He looked at Arrow, then Pamela, who nodded at him. Then he looked back at Zeetra, whose eyes were pleading with him to go.

"Take care of our family, my love," she said. "I entrust them to you."

That settled his decision. But they all sympathized as they saw a tear roll down Jaidos' cheek.

"I will see you again," Jaidos told Zeetra.

"And I will hold that in my heart, Jaidos. Farewell."

Jaidos nodded sadly. Arrow yanked on Jaidos' wrist and pulled him into a run as Pamela closely followed them. Arrow activated the machine and they ran through the glowing portal of light.

———————

A minute later, another bright light flashed, signaling the creation of a new Onchei teleportal about twenty feet from Zeetra. Everyone else scattered but Zeetra took several deep breaths to calm her frantically beating heart. She was determined to face this with her dignity intact. A tall male Onchei in a protective suit of armor emerged. He looked at Zeetra for a long moment and then took off his helmet.

"You are Zeetra Ketranos of Southland Province?" he spoke in the Onchei language.

It was strange to Zeetra, hearing her maiden language after nearly half a century. She had not spoken it in nearly as long, but the words were never far from her. She lifted her head proudly as she responded.

"Yes, I am Zeetra."

"I am Canor Imbador, Commander of the Colony Ship *Kildee*."

"May I ask why you have returned?"

"We received your signals but could not communicate with you," Canor answered. "We returned to determine the cause. When we approached this world, yours was the only Onchei life sign we found, so we came here."

"What signals did you receive?"

"We lost contact with the homeworld nearly five zeens ago and all use of Onchei technology from there ceased. But we could not turn back as we approached the habitable colony world. We feared some disaster happened and wiped out our people or the world, so we developed the colony at an advanced rate.

"But two wiptas ago, we once again detected the use of Onchei technology on the homeworld," Canor continued. "Since our colony is forty light zohwas from the homeworld, we determined it took four zeens for the signals to reach us. It gave us hope that our people still lived."

Zeetra felt a pit open in her stomach as anxiety gripped her. But she kept her face solemn and stern.

I alerted them when I used our technology to evacuate the villagers and protect our warriors at the end of Gulstaa war. And when Jordan took the Gulstaa back to their lands. I brought my people here. This is my fault!

She balled her hands into fists and exhaled slowly. "And you were surprised to arrive and only find me," Zeetra declared flatly.

"Yes," Canor replied. "Where are our people?"

"Dead," she answered wistfully. "I am all that remains."

Canor was stunned by that. He stepped backwards.

"What happened to them?"

"I did not see it happen. I had gone to Earth to complete a mission," Zeetra replied. "When I returned, all were dead. I tended to their death rites."

"Do you know what killed them?"

"As I said, I did not see it happen."

Canor looked at Zeetra pensively. "I think you should come with me," he more than suggested. "Our people will want to know more. And you may have family on the colony."

"What?" Zeetra asked. *Is that possible?*

Canor activated a new portal. This close, it pulsed and hummed like a thing alive.

"This will take us to the ship. We can be at the colony in less than ten worldturns," Canor added.

Zeetra faked a smile and walked towards Canor. "Show me."

They disappeared into the portal, which closed behind them only seconds later.

30

WE ARE MOKTA

THE MOUNTAIN MOKTA VILLAGE

Near the center of the village, Jordan immediately recognized the hum of the teleport device. Knowing that no one would use such technology without urgent cause, she ran in the direction of the sound. Arrow, Pamela, and Jaidos ran out of the portal.

Moments later, Arrow told Jordan all that had happened.

Suddenly, there was another sonic boom in the air. All those gathered in the center of the village watched as the faraway silhouette of the Onchei spaceship ascended swiftly into orbit.

"My mate is on that vessel, Chieftess," Jaidos exclaimed. "I know it!"

"I am sure you are right," Jordan agreed. "She stopped an immediate attack. She is giving us the valuable time we need to prepare for them."

"They are leaving," Pamela noted. "What is there to prepare for?"

"This is their world as much as it ours," Jordan replied. "They will be back."

"What can we do, Chieftess?"

"I do not know yet," Jordan admitted.

Bopol and Jasta walked briskly towards them.

"Is it the Onchei? Where did they come from?" Bopol asked, clearly upset.

"Zeetra said something about that being a colony ship," Jaidos explained. "They must have established a presence on another world far away from here."

"You are familiar with their machines, Jaidos," Jasta interjected. "Can you make a defense for us or sabotage their machines?"

"I doubt anything I can make would match Zeetra's level of knowledge," Jaidos said. "Or be effective against a ship of that size. But I will do whatever I can to help."

"What about the Deathwings, Chieftess?" Bopol suggested. "They might be powerful enough."

"This is not an enemy we can use conventional methods against," Jordan countered. "That spaceship may not be the biggest weapon they have and there may be more of them. And they have had fifty cycles to improve their machines."

Jasta looked like she could not believe what she was hearing from her gemta.

"Are you saying that it is hopeless, Chieftess?" she cried in outrage. "That there is nothing we can do?"

Jordan looked at her daughter for a moment and then smiled. "No, I am not saying it is hopeless. We are Mokta. There is a way."

"Good!" Jasta replied, satisfied.

Jordan and Bopol walked back to their hut. He prepared two cups with irta juice, still Jordan's favorite fruit beverage. She lifted her cup and clinked it against his in a silent toast, a habit they had developed over the cycles. Then they began to sip their drinks.

"So, you told Jasta there is a way," Bopol stated, sitting down in his chair. "What is it?"

"I have no idea," Jordan confessed, sitting in Bopol's lap and leaning into him gently, subtly requesting his reassurance. "But I am open to suggestions."

"Your plans have always been better than mine," he responded.

"Why is it always up to me?" she complained.

They sat in each other's embrace for several long minutes. She looked up at him with a frown.

"It is a terrible burden, this responsibility. My actions may determine whether all Mokta on this world live or die, our family included."

Despite her concerns, gazing into his loving eyes always soothed her. "I do not know how we will do it, but we are going to defend this world," Jordan insisted. "And we are getting Zeetra back, alive!"

TO BE CONTINUED IN *JORDAN'S DELIVERANCE*

ACKNOWLEDGMENTS

I'd like to acknowledge and thank my God and His Son, Jesus Christ, for their presence and power in my life. They inspired me to continue this story with Jordan and the world of Algoran. I'd also like to thank my wife and children for their love and support. Many thanks to my editor, Daphne, and the entire Ambassador International family. Special mentions to Jeff VanMeter, Michael Bridges, Anjelina Hernandez, Allyssa Maldonado, Desda Ravanesi, Harry Hardcastle and the late Darlene Cates. Many thanks to all my family and friends who encouraged me in writing this novel.

ABOUT THE AUTHOR

Allen Steadham created comic books and webcomics before he started writing novels. He has been married to his wife, Angel, since 1995 and they have two sons and a daughter. When not writing stories or drawing comics, Allen and his wife are singers, songwriters, and musicians. They have been in a Christian band together since 1997. They live in Central Texas.

ENJOY THIS
SNEAK PEEK OF
JORDAN'S DELIVERANCE

COMING SOON
FROM AMBASSADOR
INTERNATIONAL!

PROLOGUE

Kazil Mikenajolis ran as fast as she could towards the glowing light in front of her carrying a metal box of incalculable importance. An Onchei who had lived eight hundred zohwas, she was in upper middle-age, nearly an elder. She had been a well-respected community member in the city of Rofizda in the Southlands. She had married relatively young and held a supervisor position in the Technology Division of the new Onchei Science Directorate.

And yet, Kazil had been tasked with a responsibility by her father, the same one he had been given by his grandmother, which she had received from her mother to generations before: preserving the ancient metal box, keeping it hidden from the public until it could be sent far away from Algoran.

Kazil had informed her mate but sworn him to secrecy. Their offspring had no knowledge of this. Only her immediate superiors knew of her special purpose, which made achieving her goal possible. Everyone else believed they were merely seeking exploration of other worlds for its own sake.

The receptacle in her grasp was fairly small, about one ebiin long by eleven doralns wide and six doralns deep. The metallic alloy was hollowed out and not very heavy. Its lid contained an engraving with one of the symbols of their people. Neither Kazil nor her ancestors knew what lay within. The container had been sealed in such a way that no one knew how to open it. However, they had been instructed that it needed to be permanently delivered to another world.

It had been within the last zohwa that the Onchei Science Directorate had created stable portal technology for study and ultimately, transportation. Until finally, the Onchei made contact with a habitable world. They discretely observed its people, determining that world's technological level of advancement. They also deciphered some of the dominant languages. From this, they learned this world was called "Earth" by its people. The Onchei believed this planet and its inhabitants were worth further study.

Kazil had extensive knowledge of the new teleportation machines, since she had been a part of the team that completed and tested them. Presently, she had verified the destination coordinates and steeled herself for the journey she was about to embark on. It saddened her that she would never see her family again; she would spend her remaining zohwas safeguarding the metal container. Kazil tried to comfort herself with the understanding that she had lived hundreds of zohwas with her dearest ones, and that they would go on without her. She had committed herself and there was no turning back.

She prepared a bag of tools and technology from Algoran to help her survive on Earth. Once she had jumped through the portal, it would shut behind her and no one would follow her for a long time. This would make it virtually impossible for her—and more importantly, what she took with her—to be found. But perhaps this mission would save her world, as her ancestors had said. That would make this worthwhile, even honorable. Taking a deep breath in that final moment, she pierced the shining light and became the first Onchei to traverse the pathway between her world and any other.

She arrived during the night in the northern hemisphere of Earth, just outside the bustling community of a place called Minsk, Russia. Kazil hid herself and her treasure in the forest. Covertly, over the next couple of wiptas, she renovated a small cottage that had been abandoned and was in disrepair, its frame still intact. And with a solar-powered cutting tool, she was able to cut and smooth down wood to make a ladder and replace a small part of the roof. She used a scanner to determine what local plants would make for a good sealant against the elements. Finding some knitting needles left by the former occupants, Kazil did her best to mend the old and tattered curtains.

Kazil was able to drink the water from a nearby river and quickly verified which plants and small animals she could safely consume. The studies her people had performed had been thorough and accurate. She would survive to carry out her mission.

All the while, she observed the townspeople from her cottage using surveillance technology. She continued to learn all she could about them. She had mastered their native tongue while still on Algoran, after determining where she would arrive on Earth. The Onchei were naturally good at picking up other languages. From her research into this new country and culture, Kazil created a new identity for herself and began using their terminologies.

She took the name "Jadwiga Bogdana" and became known as the eccentric old woman who lived in the forest. Before going into town, she would clothe herself in the style she saw most of the older women wearing. She donned a simple, long double-layered dress with wrist-length sleeves and a long scarf to cover her hair. Determining that the average human lifespan was approximately forty-five years at that time, Kazil more or less looked like a human woman in her early sixties. She used a dye she mixed from local plants to present a pale version of the human's skin color. When in public, Jadwiga kept her eyes closed and mimicked blindness. She knew her black scleras and lavender-colored irises would alarm anyone who saw them.

Using her machines to scan for precious stones and metals, Jadwiga would later sell or barter with them, taking care not to do this often. What she did sell gave her enough to provide for her initial needs yet was not enough to draw undue attention to herself. She used some of this money to buy crafting tools and furniture. As a profession, Kazil bought clay or gathered mud to create pottery to sell to the townspeople.

She became accustomed to being alone most of the time. Occasionally, some curious young children or teens would venture into the forest and try to mock her or cause trouble outside her home. Often, using a simple invisible energy field around her house would be enough to spook them if they bumped into it. But for the foolish and undeterred ones, she had another response. She would open the door and approach them with eyes wide open, showing her true appearance while projecting a fierce or angry expression at them. That always sent them running in terror.

A few times, concerned parents came to her door, relaying their children's frenzied stories about magic and a "demon witch" that lived in the woods. But when they saw how friendly and benign "Blind Old Jadwiga" seemed to be, combined with how discernible and spartan her home was, they chalked up the stories to children's overactive imaginations. Kazil would give them fresh fruit as a gift and the parents would apologize for troubling her.

Knowing that she would outlive the humans, Jadwiga would move to a new town or city once every twenty or thirty years. But she always resided away from those communities, preferring the forests. For two hundred years, she maintained that lifestyle, traveling all throughout Russia. She took some amusement that children and their parents had created folk stories about the strange old woman in the woods. Some of the more insistent children who had seen her face even believed her to be the legendary "Baba Yaga."

Eventually, Jadwiga returned to Minsk. Now stricken with age, she feared her time was short. She knew she had to find someone, a human, to carry on the tradition of guarding the metal box she still kept with her.

Jadwiga had developed a friendship with a baker named Ioann Markov and his wife, Agafya. They had three young sons and lived in a house near the center of town. Jadwiga had a bad back now and used a walking stick to keep her balance. She'd lost much of her strength and stamina. But she retained enough to make some pottery and plates for the family in exchange for bread, pastries, and conversation.

"What would you say if I told you I have a box of wonders?" Jadwiga asked with an air of mystery and intrigue. Her voice had become husky with the years but there was no mistaking her warmth and love for this family.

She sat in a wooden chair inside their home, next to the blazing fire. Ioann sat in a chair across the room while his sons sat on a wool rug laid across their wooden floor. Agafya was preparing bowls of hot vegetable stew for them. It smelled surprisingly good to Jadwiga, but perhaps she was just hungry.

"A 'box of wonders?!'" answered Kir, Ioann's oldest son. "Where?"

Kir was nine years old, stout with curly brown hair and piercing blue eyes.

The old woman smiled. "I keep it in my house in the forest."

"What wonders does it do? Can it make children fly? Make it rain or stop raining?" asked Lev, Kir's middle brother.

Lev was six, and slender and quick. He had blond hair and brown eyes which reflected his growing intellect. His younger brother, Matvey, was three years old, with short and wavy brown hair. His smoky gray eyes were riveted on Jadwiga but he said nothing.

"Mostly, it protects the contents within the box, which has been in my family for eight generations," Jadwiga replied. "But it can do much more, probably even some of the things you said. I have guarded it my whole life. But I am old and have no children to pass this onto. When I die, I fear men will find the box and open it to sell what lies within. I do not wish for this to happen."

She hoped that indulging the children's' imaginations might endear them to the idea of helping her. It didn't take long to see if it worked.

"Could we help?" Kir wondered, consulting no one.

"I do not wish to impose on your gracious family," Jadwiga insisted. "Forgive my foolish ramblings."

Ioann stared at Jadwiga from his chair with a mixture of curiosity and suspicion. He was a fat man in his late thirties with bushy brown hair and beard.

"Come with me, Jadwiga. I wish to speak with you outside."

He motioned for the children to remain quiet as he gently led her by the arm. They walked out of the house, his wife following. He was very patient with Jadwiga's frail condition and slow pace. Once outside, he waited a moment to say what was on his mind.

"What is actually in the box, Jadwiga?" he asked. "It is clear you want us to take this box. I want to know why."

"I was married long ago. My husband was an artist and he made me some small, intricate carvings from metal, wood, and ivory. We stored them in this box. It is locked and I long ago lost the key," she chose to say. "But it has sentimental value to me, so I could never throw it away. I would like your family to have it because I care for you so. Perhaps this is one way you could remember me."

Satisfied, Ioann nodded. "I see. Thank you for telling me."

"If you do not wish to have it, I will understand."

"No, it is alright. We will do this. You are a member of our family."

Jadwiga bowed humbly in the direction of the baker's voice. She kept her eyes closed as always. But as poor as her vision had become, she no longer had to feign blindness. Fortunately, she more or less knew every inch of this town.

"Thank you. I feel the same way," she replied.

They went back inside. Ioann viewed his children, who were all looking at him with begging eyes. Then he made eye contact with his wife, who looked at her sons then him. She nodded pleasantly. He nodded back at her before turning his attention back to Jadwiga.

"Jadwiga, bring your 'box of wonders' to us tomorrow," he declared. "We will protect it for you. You have my word."

Jadwiga had hoped they would agree but she hadn't been sure until a few minutes ago. Human behavior could be very hard to understand, much less anticipate.

She put her arms in front of her and slowly bowed numerous times where she was. It was worth the pain it caused her aching back, as she had secured her goal.

"Thank you! Thank you! I will be forever grateful. I can die in peace now."

The children had sounded excited at first to know they were helping her. But now, they quieted down.

"Do you have to go away someday, Jadwiga?" Lev asked, his voice trembling.

———————

FIFTEEN YEARS AGO ON EARTH

Kayla Lewis stood at the bottom of the stairs and looked up at her husband, Mark, with some concern. Descending toward her, he was carrying two stacked and very full moving boxes in his arms. And he was obviously straining.

"Mark, put one of those boxes down! You'll throw your back out again," Kayla warned.

"I'm using my legs, I'll be fine," he answered.

Neither impressed nor persuaded, she walked over and grabbed the top box. She angled her lips and blew a long strand of brown hair out of her face as she walked past him towards their minivan. The rest of her hair was pulled back into a long ponytail.

"You're not twenty anymore, Mark, and you don't have to impress me."

"I wasn't trying to impress you, honey. I just thought I could do it."

"My point is, you don't have to. I'm right here, I can help."

"Yes, ma'am," he replied with a hint of sarcasm. They'd had this conversation more than once before.

Kayla Lewis was forty-eight years old and her husband was a year older than her. They had been married for twenty-eight years and owned a graphic design company called "Markayla Designs." She was the artist while he managed the business. It had been profitable enough over the years, allowing them to buy a house, own two vehicles, pay the bills, and afford three daughters.

But maintaining and growing the business had been very stressful. Kayla had barely kept it together when Mark suffered a mild heart attack at the age of thirty-nine. Her own vision had suffered from her habit of working late into the night with less than ideal lighting. She ate when she remembered to, which usually was at irregular intervals. That had been fine when she was a teenager. But time and having children had altered her metabolism, causing her to steadily gain weight.

Still, Kayla was more concerned with her husband's well-being than her own.

The back hatch was already open, and their storage area was half-filled with boxes. The vehicle hovered a foot above the ground using magnetic propulsion technology which hummed quietly. Virtually all transportation had been clean, electric, and wheelless for over a decade. The van was more or less oval-shaped, large enough to accommodate up to six passengers with room to spare for hauling items.

Kayla put her box on top of one of the others. Mark put his next to hers, but it slipped from his grip. Falling to one side, its lid popped off and she heard him sigh in frustration.

"What's wrong?" She inquired, pushing her glasses back up her sweaty nose. She knew his sigh was about more than a moving box.

She was beside him now, one hand resting on his left arm while observing his wistful expression and furrowed brow.

"I just can't believe they're both gone," Mark lamented. "First Mom . . . now Dad. They lived together in this house ever since Mom . . . got back."

"I know," Kayla replied, nodding in understanding. "Your dad was a father to me a lot longer than my own. But they had a long life."

"At least they got back together," Mark added. "That was the best decision they ever made."

"And they got to know their grandkids," Kayla remarked with a sad smile.

Kayla decided to grab the moving box that had fallen to the side and lined it up with the others. Grabbing its lid, she glanced inside the box and something caught her eye: a gray, metallic shoebox-sized object which looked extremely old.

"What's this?"

"Hm?" Mark muttered, turning to look at her.

"This metal, um, container. I think I've seen it before?"

"Oh, that? It was Mom's. She kept it on the mantel above the fireplace with the family pictures."

"What's in it?"

"I don't know, I thought it was just an old jewelry box or something. I've never looked inside it."

"It looks sealed or something."

Mark nodded. "Yeah. Mom and Dad both tried to open it a few times over the years but never managed to. I think I even attempted it once. But there's such a long family history with it, we kept it."

Kayla picked up the old plated box and looked at it with fascination. She smiled.

"Seems a shame to put an old keepsake like this in storage. I doubt we could sell it if we don't know how to open it," Kayla noted, looking at Mark. "Do you think your mom would mind if I held onto it?"

Mark looked like he was thinking about it. He made a slight shrug.

"Knowing Mom, it would probably make her happy for you to have it," he replied. "Go ahead, keep it. Where do you want to put it?"

Kayla held the box close to her chest. "For a family heirloom like this? Your mom kept it on the fireplace, so I guess I'll do that, too!"

Mark smiled. "Sounds good. Now, let's go get those last few boxes and take all this to the self-storage facility."

"You go on up and get one of the boxes—and I mean *only* one!"

She put the family keepsake on the floorboard at the front of the vehicle. She put the family keepsake on the front passenger floorboard of the vehicle. As she exited the passenger front seat and stepped onto the driveway, she paused to watch her husband enter the house.

"I'm gonna call Jo and have her meet us to unload this stuff," Kayla stated.

"Won't she be studying for midterms?"

"This is our oldest daughter we're talking about. She'll either be gaming, eating pizza, or writing a new song."

"Right. Then she'll cram the night before and probably ace it."

"Exactly," Kayla answered with a proud chuckle.

Kayla pressed a button on her wristband as Mark went back inside. Her action caused a holographic interface to appear.

"Call Jo Lewis," Kayla told the device.

While the holo-interface on her wristband was attempting to contact her daughter, Kayla looked towards the front of the van. She was surprisingly captivated by the idea of that ancient artifact. Just then, the holo-screen flickered and displayed the words "Connection Established."

Kayla's daughter appeared in the waist-up holo-display. She was twenty-three years old and a junior in college, working on her Bachelor of Arts Degree in History. She was tall and average-sized, wearing a dark blue t-shirt. Her hair was shoulder-length, frizzy and half of it was covering her eyes. The apartment, which she shared with another female student, was lit only by the small amount of sunlight peeking through the blinds of one window.

"Oh, hey, Mom!" Jo smiled in recognition. "Sorry, I just got up."

"It's two in the afternoon," Kayla replied with measured patience.

"Izzit? Oh, wow. We went to see 'Eventually Watermelon' in concert last night. After we got home, we binge-watched a bunch of sci-fi."

Kayla pushed her glasses back up her nose again. This time, it was more to show her annoyance than to be functional.

"Your Dad and I have been packing up stuff from Grandma and Grandpa's house. We're about to take the boxes to storage. Can you help us unload? I don't want your Dad doing too much."

"Oh! Um, which storage place?"

"The one at Milea and Condor."

Jo looked unenthused, so Kayla gave an insistent stare. After a moment, her daughter gave a surrendering shrug.

"I can be there in twenty minutes. Is that okay?"

"Sure. Thanks, Jo! Love you."

"Love you, too, Mom."

Kayla pressed another button on her bracelet and the holo-interface dispersed. As she walked inside to see if her husband needed any more help, she couldn't help but reminisce for a moment. She thought about Mark's parents, memories with them in that house. And then suddenly, Mark's older sister came to mind. It had been over thirty years since she'd last seen Jordan Lewis. Sometimes, she still wondered how her sister-in-law was doing on that faraway world of Algoran.

For more information about
Allen Steadham
and
Jordan's Arrow
please visit:

www.allensteadham.com
allen@allensteadham.com
www.facebook.com/jaspecfiction
@Mindfirenovel
www.instagram.com/allensteadham

For more information about
AMBASSADOR INTERNATIONAL
please visit:

www.ambassador-international.com
@AmbassadorIntl
www.facebook.com/AmbassadorIntl

*If you enjoyed this book, please consider leaving us a review on
Amazon, Goodreads, or our website.*

www.ingramcontent.com/pod-product-compliance
Lightning Source LLC
Chambersburg PA
CBHW070540260626
47161CB00002B/459

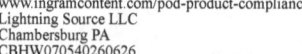